KATHERINE

THE MAW OF MAYHEM MC
BOOK 4

AK NEVERMORE

CONTENTS

Free Prequel — 1
Dedication — 3
A Heads Up on Content — 5
Before — 7
Chapter 1 — 14
Chapter 2 — 29
Chapter 3 — 42
Chapter 4 — 62
Chapter 5 — 80
Chapter 6 — 101
Chapter 7 — 123
Chapter 8 — 140
Chapter 9 — 155
Chapter 10 — 171
Chapter 11 — 191
Chapter 12 — 210
After — 219
Next in the Series — 223

Books by AK Nevermore — 237
About the Author — 239

FREE PREQUEL

CATS DON'T ALWAYS *LAND ON THEIR FEET...*

Grimdarke James has got problems. As Vice Prez of the Maw of Mayhem MC, he needs to keep his shit together, but between the constant threat of his inner cat going feral, and Nikki, one of the motorcycle club's mollys, blackmailing him, it's a fine line some days.

Then when an arms deal goes bad, everything goes to hell with it. All fingers point to an old club enemy, a man Grim has reason to both fear and loathe, but the facts don't add up, and everyone is a suspect... including Grim. Faced with the constant threat of Nikki revealing his past and his need to prove himself to the MC, the fragile peace he's made with his cat is threatened.

Out of options and running out of time, Grim sets a bold

plan into motion, and the consequences are far more dire than he could have imagined…

Download it at: bit.ly/readmayhem

AND FOR MORE SHORT stories from the world of the Maw of Mayhem MC, check out:

bit.ly/bitesofmayhem

DEDICATION

This one is for anyone out there who has put on their big girl panties and claimed their own power.

Especially if they were scared as hell and did it anyway.

CONTENT WARNING

Heads up & don't try this at home: This book explores themes which some readers may find uncomfortable or offensive. If violence, smut, various kinks, (i.e. breeding, spanking, and a host of other dirty, dirty stuff) salty language, drug / alcohol use, and generally unsavory behavior are triggers for you, please put this novella down and back away slowly.

And guys, it's not a cliffhanger. This series is all in novella form, and it's impossible to fit the whole story in one volume. So heads up number two, there's gonna be another one after this…

BEFORE

Kit gasped and slapped Grim's shoulder, leaning back as she straddled him. "You're such a frickin' liar, and don't for one minute think I really believe your mother named you Grimdarke." His fingers tensed around her hips and the playfulness drained from his face. Kit's stomach dropped. "Grim?"

What did I say?

—I dunno, but Darke's not talking either— Kat said, nervous.

Well, that was never good. Neither were Grim's lips pinching down and his pupils waffling. Why was he fighting with Darke?

Grim pulled Kit closer, nuzzling her neck. "Get on my dick, Kitten."

What? After that? No. They needed to talk about this. "I—"

He tongued that spot just beneath her ear and her brain skipped. She let out a low moan, tipping her chin away to give him better access, her fingers threading through his hair. "But..."

"This is me, asking," he rumbled against the column of her throat, slipping his fingers between her thighs to tease her.

Oh, sweet bliss, this man...but ugh, he was a jerk. Why did he never want to talk about anything? Kit threw her head back, scraping her nails across his scalp. A hotter than hell, entirely too digitally talented, jerk.

[SNICKERING]

— *You love it.* —

Shut up. "That's not asking."

"No? Then lemme try again." He nipped at her jaw, his thumb circling over her clit.

Kit's eyes rolled back as she gave up the fight, giving in to pleasure. Her core wept and a whimper eked from her lips.

"Do you need my cock in your pretty little pussy, Kitten?" His fingers hit a spot deep inside, and her hips chased after them as he dragged his hand away.

Oh God, if he tried to edge her right now… "Yes," she mewled.

Grim chuckled like he knew it, smug as hell. "Such a good girl, all wet and ready to take me."

He pulled away, and she cried out, relief flooding her as he gripped her hips and slid his swollen shaft against her core. She wrapped her arms around him, nails dimpling little moons into his broad shoulders, her breath coming fast. She raised up, eyes riveted by his broad, weeping tip disappearing and reappearing from between her swollen lips, slick with desire.

"Feed my cock into that juicy cunt," he murmured, sucking her nipple into his mouth. He groaned as it hardened, pulling it taut and shooting a line of carnal fire through her.

Her hand wrapped around the base of his dick, and she lowered herself onto him, stretching to accept his thick length, the slow slide of hardened flesh pressing deeper, bottoming out and rocking.

Grim moaned, one hand grabbing her ass and the other hand sliding up her back to fist her hair, drawing her closer. His mouth on hers, devouring and insistent. Tongues dueling, her nipples over-sensitized pebbles from the friction of his pecs. Oh, sweet baby Jesus, what this man did to her… She raised up, controlling their pace. Taking what she wanted. God, what she needed…

"You ride my cock so fucking good," he panted.

Kit purred, leaning down to nip at his jaw. "You get me so fucking hot."

"Yeah?" His eyes darkened with lust, and he thrust himself deep. Kit cried out as he flipped her onto her back and went still.

She opened her mouth again to protest, but the look on his face stopped her. This wasn't him edging her, this was… more.

The harshness of their breathing filled the room as Grim studied her face. He smoothed a lock of hair from her brow, raising up on his elbows above her. Her heels slid to hook around his thighs.

Slowly, he began to rock, his gaze trapping hers. "I'm gonna cream this pussy, and then I want you to lie there and keep it inside you." He dipped his head to kiss her. "Tell me you'll obey. That you want my baby."

Kit's breath caught. Oh, sweet baby Jesus, why the hell was that so fucking sexy?

—Hellooo…alpha…—

Yeah, he is, but don't you keep telling me I'm the damned queen?

—No, I keep telling you we're *the damned queen. Get it right, Katherine. Pronouns matter.—*

Right, and so do names. She licked her lips. "Tell me what your mother really named you."

Grim's pace faltered.

[LAUGHING]

—Girl, you are something else.—

Yeah, the queen.

—Well, it's about fuckin' time.—

His pupils waffled, and he grunted, getting his rhythm back. "My mother didn't name me anything," he muttered, abruptly working his hips like he was getting paid by the pump. "Doesn't fucking matter."

Kit gasped as Grim snapped his hips, driving himself into her over and over again.

—*Nice going, Katherine.*—

Oh, like you knew! God, she was an idiot. She gripped his shoulders tighter, taking her punishment. Wanting it for hurting him. Letting him exercise his demons while worshipping at her altar. She could be what he needed. Would be what he needed. Could let go and submit to his will and lose herself in the storm of his emotions, his passion, her cries a counterpoint to his groans, reveling in him using her body as an escape, her own desire cresting and breaking and swelling again.

Her pussy fluttered around him, and he gritted his teeth, feral.

"Tell me you want it," he growled.

She arched her back, her breasts slick against his chest. "I want it, oh God, I want it."

And she did. Wanted his baby, to obey—

[LAUGHING]

—him in the bedroom, to be his good girl... Kit's body clenched around his, her pussy throbbing and weeping, eyes rolling into the back of her head, cunt sucking at his dick, begging for his cum. He obliged, his cock swelling and the hot spurt of his seed filling her. He collapsed onto his forearms, panting, sweat dripping from his nose.

She made a face, and he laughed, wiping his face on a pillow. He kissed her softly, then rolled to the side, breathing heavy, one arm flung out in invitation. Kit pushed up under it, snuggling against his chest. He pulled her close and kissed the top of her head. She traced the roughly tattooed mourning band above Clay's.

Grim went still, then gave a deep sigh. "She called me Séan Micheal," he muttered.

Kit's finger froze on the tattoo, quickly making the connection. "The woman Grapple killed?"

"Yeah." Grim pulled the blankets up around them. "Now tell me you want my fucking kid and go to sleep."

She smiled against his chest. God, he was impossible. "I do want your kid."

He grunted and snagged his cell from the bedside table. She stretched out against him, one leg threaded between his and a hand resting on his chest, marveling at how well they fit together. He ran his fingers idly through her hair as he listened to messages and shot off some quick yes or no texts. Her eyes got heavier, drifting in and out of sleep as he fidgeted. Tried to settle. Then grabbed his phone again, the low squawk of Nikki melting coming from its speakers.

Kit nuzzled against Grim's chest, a smile stealing over her lips. That had been as rewarding as hell.

—*Putting uppity bitches in their places always is—* Kat murmured sleepily. —*I can't wait for you to scroll through those comments. Shit people write's always better than the post.—*

Grim lifted Kit's lax hand and pressed a kiss to her knuckles, breathing her in, then sighed. Her brow scrunched up as he moved from under her.

He gave her a quick kiss. "Bathroom," he murmured, turning away at her sigh of protest and pulling something out of his jacket on the way.

Kit's eyes popped open as he shut the door behind him. Wait a minute. Did he grab Claymore's will? The potential woke her right the hell up.

Kat groaned. —*So what if he did? Ain't nothin' in those pages we didn't see—*

Kit propped herself up on her elbow, not entirely sure about that. Claymore had always been so tricky. Maybe there was a turn of phrase in there that would mean something to Grim.

If he could read it.

A long sliver of light clicked on beneath the door. She didn't entirely understand what his brand of dyslexia entailed, but she got the impression it was at the upper end of the bell curve.

The toilet's lid clanged like he was sitting on it and there was a rustle of pages. Half a breath later he gave a snort of disgust.

Kit jumped at the slam of his hand, the toilet lid rattling. The water in the sink crashed on. Splashed. The towel bar squeaked. God, she hoped he was gonna hang it up properly.

—*Are you for real right now?*—

If I'm planning on having his damned baby, you better believe he better plan on playing house to my specifications. There's no way I'm dealing with nasty-ass, moldy towels.

—*God, you're anal*— Kat sighed. —*Whatever. You do you.*—

The crinkle of paper came from behind the door, and Kit's brow furrowed. Was she being cruel? Maybe she should just read it for him. She sighed and hooked her legs over the side of the bed as she sat, running a hand over her face. Why the hell did men have to be so damned needy?

Kit stood and tip-toed over to the door, not sure if she should just knock or go in—

A faint sniffle came from behind it and her heart broke.

She pushed the door open and wrapped her arms around his waist as he leaned against the vanity, arms rigid and head hanging. He turned, and she burrowed against his chest. "S'cold without you."

"I'm coming back now," he murmured, trying to play it off.

She looked up at him, his eyes moist and the tip of his nose pink. "You read it?"

He didn't even pretend not to know what she was talking about.

—*Baby steps*—

"I saw what I needed to."

"You can tell me about it in the morning." She took his hand and led him back to bed. "Come on, we're both dead on our feet."

Grim grunted, frowning as he nestled down beside her, then drew her against his chest. Kit sighed at the weight of his arms holding her tight. Totally at peace, and well aware that there was no way in hell that was gonna last.

CHAPTER ONE

GRIM'S phone wouldn't stop ringing.

He slapped it silent and groaned, pulling a pillow over his throbbing head. Jesus fuck, how was it light out already? Whatever, he didn't give a shit. Whoever was calling him could fuck off. At his side, Kit murmured, nestling closer. Her bent leg skated up the back of his thigh and hooked over his hip.

Mmm. He rolled to face her, and she snuggled against his chest with a sigh of contentment. Damn, she smelled good. He inhaled, drawing her scent into his lungs. Something about it eased his head. Woman just made him feel better all around. He traced his finger tips down her back to cup her juicy ass, morning wood going rigid as it brushed against her slick core.

"You dreamin' about me, baby?" he murmured, still groggy, running the length of his cock along her slit and notching himself at her entrance.

"Maybe." Her hands skimmed up his chest to lace around his neck. She tipped her hips, and Grim nudged into her, groaning as he sank home. Fuck, she was tight. Kit gave a soft cry, her nails rasping over his shoulders. "Maybe not."

His eyes flew open; a spike of jealousy shooting through him. He pinned her beneath him, growling, a hand rising to stroke her throat. "That right? You wanna clue me in to who the fuck you're thinkin' about while I'm dick deep inside your pussy?"

She shrugged, not intimidated in the least and so sinfully fucking sexy…

—*brat*— Darke muttered.

She is. Grim bared his teeth in anticipation. "You want that ass spanked, Kitten?" He twined his fingers with hers, raising her arms up over her head, slowly pistoning his hips between her spread thighs. " 'Cause sass like that? You're just asking to be punished."

"Am I?" Her lips parted at the snap of his hips, lust darkening her gaze. The scent of her heat thickened the air. Christ, the mating pheromones she was putting off were so ripe he could taste citrus and cinnamon.

"You are." He growled again, some deep, primal need waking. The urge to sate it, to fill her with his seed and make her *his*, thrummed through his being. He teased her lips, nipping at them. "You gonna be this sassy when my baby's in your belly?"

She bit back a smile. "Probably?"

Grim chuckled. Goddamn, he fucking loved—

A series of texts pinged on his phone. He shot a glare in its direction. Deuce? The fuck did he want? Kit's mouth traced Grim's jugular, nipping and diverting his attention. Mmm. His lips claimed hers, her scent Manna on his tongue, sheathing himself in the hot velvet of her cunt over and over again.

She panted, arching up, and he latched onto her breast, sucking its pebbled tip into his mouth. Christ, she was fucking perfect. He drove his cock into her wet heat, bottoming out and dragging back against that spot deep inside her. "Oh God, Grim! Please, I can't…" She gasped, crying out. Her eyelids fluttered, core convulsing, demanding…

He thrust into her again, tingles zinging the length of his

spine, balls drawing up, cock impossibly hard, spurting, emptying himself to fill her. He buried his face in the crook of her neck, groaning, pressing deep. "Goddamn, that's it. Fucking take it—"

BAM BAM BAM

He lifted his head. The hell?

BAM BAM. "Grim!"

Deuce was at the door. Shit, didn't he just try to call?

"Sec!" Grim yelled over his shoulder, then turned back to look down at Kit. She watched him with hooded eyes, her lips bee-stung and a sheen of sweat glossing her skin. Goddamn, she was fucking beautiful. He trailed his knuckles down her throat, just wanting to—

BAM BAM BAM. "Dude! Seriously, we got problems."

When didn't they? Grim sighed, all that banging racketing through his temples. He gave Kit a quick kiss. "Don't fucking move. I'm not done with you."

"Yes, sir." She smirked, folding her arms behind her head. His eyes dropped to her tits. Mmm—

BAM BAM BAM!

"Fuuuuck!" He flipped the covers off and rolled to sit at the side of the bed, wiping off his dick. "I swear to fucking Christ, a fucking meteor better be about to hit." He swept his jeans up off the floor, jamming his legs into them as he crossed the room and threw open the door. "What?!"

Deuce stood there, all keyed up. He recoiled, putting a hand to his face. Man's knuckles had blood on them, and fresh spatters decorated his cut. "Damn, that's fucking dank…" He sniffed, pinching the scent from his nose. "Look, sorry to interrupt, but it's almost noon and shit's hitting the fan. You need to come down to the playroom, pronto."

"Are you fucking kidding me?" How was it almost noon? Whatever, rest of that statement was more important. "Somebody spill?" Grim asked, riffling his hair.

"Yeah, and it's *Exxon Valdez* level what the fuck. And FYI, so is Hellspawn pulling up behind the feds camped out at our gates about fifteen minutes ago."

"Don't Asorav and Chanté have a handle on that?" Grim asked, rubbing his temple and grimacing. The migraine he'd been dancing with the past few days was abruptly insistent about punching his card. Pretty soon it wasn't gonna take no for an answer. Christ, he didn't have time for this.

"Dude, that's so far above and beyond the rest of this fuckery, I'm not even gonna hit you with it yet." Deuce's brow knit. "You take your meds?"

"No, Mom." Grim scowled. "I didn't take my fucking meds."

"They don't work right if you don't—"

"Yeah, I'm aware, so let's speed this up. Just tell Asorav and Chanté to let Hellspawn in. Where are they?"

"At the bar having brunch." Deuce frowned, glancing over Grim's shoulder into his room. "And I did, but neither one of them will do anything without Kit's say so."

"Without *Kit's* say so? This is my fucking club! And since when do we have brunch?"

"Since about ten am, and it's scheduled to run until two," Deuce deadpanned.

Kit laughed and the sound of her getting out of bed came from behind him. Goddamn it. "Guess I should go take care of that then. I do love a good brunch." She slipped around Grim wrapped in the bedsheet...

Like hell she was. He grabbed her around the waist. "Where the fuck do you think you're going like that?" he growled into her ear, glaring at Deuce. Dude was doing his best not to look at her, but the way he was jamming his hands into his pockets, he'd gotten an eyeful and liked what he saw.

Kit pulled the sheet higher up. "Umm..."

"Yeah, think again," Grim growled. "With what you're putting out for pheromones, every brother down there is gonna wanna fuck you. They see you in just a sheet and guaranteed I'm gonna have to put a bullet in somebody." Woman was beyond sexy, and if any one of those assholes tried to get handsy…

She laughed again, an arm raising to hook behind his neck as she tipped back her head. "Is that right, Pussycat?"

"Yeah, that's fucking right." His lips found the side of her throat, hands sliding up to cup her breasts, pulling her back into his room…

"Then it's a good thing I was going to get changed first," she said, wriggling away and darting off down the hall trailing sheet.

—chase!—

A wide smile split Grim's face. *Hell yeah, we're gonna—*

Deuce's arm clotheslined Grim's chest. "Dude. Tag it later. We got shit to do, Prez."

[ANNOYANCE]

Agreed, but the asshole's right. "Yeah, fine. Gimme a sec." Prez. Grim scowled, adjusting his semi. Clay's door clicked shut behind Kit. "You better lock that!" he called down the hall after her. Her muffled laughter followed him back into their room. He grabbed a shirt and his cut, then stomped into his boots and ran a toothbrush around his mouth, pent up as hell, despite the fact he'd just blown his load. Goddamn, she got him hot.

At some point, she'd fixed the hand towel. He smirked, balling it up and shoving it behind the rod again, hoping it would piss her off.

—stupid game— Darke muttered.

The fuck is up your ass this morning? Grim asked. *You still pissed we left that porcupine in the trunk? Look, we'll grab it as soon as this shit's settled, okay?*

—ruined—

Dude, it's not fucking ruined.

Darke chuffed like he didn't believe him, one hundred percent still pissed about that stupid spiky rat.

Whatever, Grim wasn't in the mood to deal with his cat's shitty attitude on top of everything else. He shrugged into his holster and jammed a piece into it, dead serious about poppin' caps into people, including a certain witch and vamp. The fuck were they thinking overruling the club's chain of command? If they were serious about staying, that shit wasn't gonna fly. Grim frowned, snagging his phone and going to the window. He pulled down a stack of mini-blind ribs with a finger…

The hell? The parking lot was full of people setting up tables beneath big white tents and workmen busy were unloading crates from a line of box trucks. And beyond it?

Jesus fuck.

Whatever Chanté and Asorav had done had transformed the woods into something straight outta a cheesy Dracula flick. Despite the midday sun, light wasn't penetrating past the mist-shrouded trees. Damn. Shit seriously looked like *Nosferatu* part two, complete with emaciated forms loping between their trunks. The scar on Grim's forearm burned cold and one of the creatures stopped, its head snapping to the side. Dead white eyes met Grim's across the milling expanse of the club's parking lot.

Not one of the workers missed a beat. Jesus, they all had to be in the vamp's thrall.

[HISSING]

Grim's proverbial fur stood on end, totally in agreement with Darke, but that shit was the lesser of two evils. That thing staring at him? That was a wight, and there was more than one of them. Jesus fucking Christ, on what planet was filling the woods with those things a good idea?

—not good. taste bad—

Grim snorted. Nothing about wights was good, taste or otherwise. He took a step back, releasing the blinds and running a heavy hand down his face, temples throbbing. Well, he supposed wights justified the mist. Nasty-ass things decomposed in sunlight, which was why they hung out underground. But it sure as hell didn't explain what all those thralls were doing, or how they'd been able to get past the clubhouse gates. Wights took exception to anything with a heartbeat and a fork to anything recently deprived of one.

Shit was nuts. Grim shook his head and thumbed through his phone. But, on the bright side, guess he didn't have to worry about the feds finding any overlooked corpses out there. Of course, they'd all become corpses if Asorav and Chanté couldn't keep a leash on the fucking monsters.

Grim winced, listening to his voicemail, his headache progressively getting worse. Lars, Hellspawn's prez, had left at least a dozen messages and easily that many texts. Him and his crew were fucking pissed they were stuck out there with the feds.

Great. Just what Grim needed, an entire contingent of redneck shifters ready to tear him a new one. He hit the Call Back button, the nerve behind his right eye twitching. His gaze landed on his bedside table drawer, wishing he could just take a pill and be done, but the damned things always knocked him out for the count. Deuce was right about them not working the way they should, but they made him logy as fuck when he took them regularly. He'd rather be KO'ed for half a day than live in a damned fog.

Of course, that logic wasn't currently working out so hot.

The call connected. "It's about fucking time, Mayhem," Lars barked out on the other end of the line. In the background, a woman's irate southern twang carried over the murmur of a crowd and the squawks and sirens of a police presence. Lars grunted at something she said. "How long you expect us to wait around this shithole? Ain't exactly keepin' the best company out here."

"Yeah, sorry about that," Grim muttered, pacing. "Situation went sideways after we last talked."

"No shit, we saw the reel"—Lars snorted—"and unless

you want it to go belly up, you got an hour to make these fucking pigs disappear and hand over whatever's left of that dirty cunt. You feel me?"

"Yeah."

"Good. Make it fucking happen." The line went dead.

Grim sighed, counting to twenty in time with the thudding in his head. An hour. He could make it another hour, then take one of those damned pills. Black the fuck out. Deuce and the crew could hold shit together.

Probably.

Christ! He pinched a hand across his temples. Pretty soon it wasn't gonna matter one way or the other. Migraine was gonna take him out regardless. He grabbed his cut and pocketed the aspirin from the bathroom, chewing a couple dry and praying for a miracle, then blew out a breath and headed downstairs. Deuce fell into step beside him. Clay's door was still shut and the water pipes running the length of the hall ticked. Kit must be taking a shower. Grim clomped down the steps, biting back the groan that visual induced.

The aroma of French toast and bacon threaded through the lingering tendrils of her heat. Grim's stomach growled, abruptly starving. Who the hell was cooking? Hannah, Miser's ol' lady, usually ran the kitchen, but the two of them hadn't made it back to the clubhouse last night. Still, given the prevalence of clinking silverware, someone was at the helm, and it smelled way better than what any of the mollys could come up with.

Grim's boots hit the entryway's flagstones and Deuce grabbed his elbow. "Trust me, you're not gonna want anything in your stomach before this."

Shit. Brick must be really going at it. Grim riffled his hair and they took a hard left, descending a second stairway to the laundry room in the basement. "Mouse still alive?"

"Yeah, but he sure as hell wishes he wasn't." Deuce snorted. "Kid cannot hold his liquor. Last I saw him, he was wrapped around the commode trying to outdo Brick's performance after he ate the fish special at the Cat House."

Grim snickered, eyeing the door to the tech nerd's lair and feeling sorry for him. The results of the fish special had been bad, but it'd served Brick right for eating anything from a strip club buffet. Pizza maybe, but stuffed cod with cream sauce? No fucking thank you. The brother who'd used to be in charge of the place'd had some bizarre ideas, that was for sure.

Double crossing the club and running a prostitution ring out of one of their businesses wasn't one of his better ones either, but he'd have plenty of time to lament that particular decision doing fifteen to twenty in the pen.

Asshole.

Deuce hit a code on one of the room's large security panels and a section of wall clicked open behind an industrial drier. The distinct smell of pot wafted from the gap of a hidden door. It opened to another hallway running the length of the clubhouse with several rooms branching off.

Logistically, the subterranean space spanned the area between the clubhouse and the garage, thanks again to Rockwell's misadventures in civil construction. Apparently a twenty-foot deep, smoking pit was not conducive to the creation of septic fields, but it was for a bunker. Clay had converted the gaping pit into an underground triage, a shit ton of storage, and a handful of holding cells outside of Brick's playroom at the end of the hall.

Chris and Eddie, the two prospects Grim'd told to watch Nikki, were sitting on the concrete floor, passing a joint between them. Chris swore and stubbed it out, the two of them scrambling to their feet and looking guilty as fuck.

—dumb asses—

You're just a fucking delight this morning, you know that?

—magic. hate how it feels— Darke muttered.

Yeah? Well, we're surrounded by the stuff for the foreseeable future, so buck the fuck up. "Chill out. As long as Nikki's still in there, you can smoke whatever the fuck you want," Grim said to the two prospects, sliding the panel on the steel door's viewing port aside. He pulled back and swore, blinking away the glare from the bright halogens. "She *is* still in there, right?"

Chris and Eddie looked at each other. Eddie shrugged. "Uh, yeah?"

Grim turned back to the port at that ringing endorsement. She was, seething in the far corner. Goo the color of chewed tobacco pooled beneath her and a nasty, filth-smeared sheet wrapped around her decaying flesh. Her eyes snapped to the *snick* of the panel moving aside, nothing but hate in those baby blues. Was about the only recognizable thing about her. Whatever Kit had done had turned her outsides as ugly as her insides. Shit was monstrous, but Grim couldn't help snickering at the faint strains of *Baby Shark* on repeat coming through the soundproofing. Goddamn, Brick was a twisted motherfucker.

Whelp, though Grim couldn't say he was glad to see her, it was good to know she was still breathing. For now, at least. He didn't need to piss Lars off any more than he already was.

Her, on the other hand... Grim grinned and blew her a kiss.

[LAUGHING]

She let out a screech and chucked something...

Holy fuck, was that one of the saline bags from her tits?

It splatted against the door and Grim didn't know whether to be amused or disgusted. He snicked the port shut, feeling both in equal measures. Christ, he wasn't gonna miss anything about her.

"Camp out for another hour, then she's someone else's problem," he said to the two prospects. Sighing, he turned to the door at the end of the hall. Right now, he had his own to deal with.

KIT STEPPED out of the shower and wrapped a towel around herself. Clay's bathroom was definitely nicer than the one in Grim's room. Or it had the potential to be, once all the filth from Nikki's infestation was expunged. Woman was a pig. Kit frowned at the drifts of body glitter, smears of self-tanner, and spattered toothpaste around the sink. She rubbed at it with the corner of her towel. Maybe that's what she would do today. A dedicated session of rage cleaning sounded pretty damned good...after she sorted things out with Mr. Asorav and Chanté.

—*Ain't nothin' to sort—* Kat chuffed. —*They got our back as queen. It's the rest of them that are gonna have to fall in line.—*

Um, no, just because we're queen doesn't mean they get to disrespect Grim.

—*How is answering to the queen disrespecting him? They're not a part of Mayhem.—*

Kit toweled off her hair, teeth dimpling her lip. *No, but he's right. This is his MC, and they're his guests. While they're here, they have to follow his rules.*

—*So where does that leave us?—*

I dunno yet, and I don't think he does, either. Kit was pretty sure that her being with him meant she was the alpha female for the club and in charge of the ol' ladies and the mollys. But since Clay had never officially taken Kit's mother as a mate, Kit hadn't actually seen what that looked like. She vaguely remembered a woman with shoulder-length hair that seemed like she was in charge of the kitchen, but Kit had been so young when they moved out of the clubhouse...

She shook her hair out and scrubbed at it with the towel. *Do you remember?*

—*No. I wasn't awake then.—*

Right. And it'd been so long since there had been a shifter queen, no one knew what that looked like, either. Well, Mr.

Asorav probably did, but Kit was pretty sure she shouldn't take everything he said as gospel. Not after the last shifter queen had partially succeeded in turning the current vampire queen into a fox. Aryanna had killed her for it, but she was still rocking whiskers. Their sects weren't on great terms.

Kit sighed. God, how was she going to do this?

Whatever. Clothes would help. Dress for the job you want, right? Except she didn't. Not really. Well, to be Grim's queen, yeah, but the rest of it?

—Girl, you'll see. Once they accept that we're it, the rest is gonna be gravy.—

If you say so, but what about until then?

Kat paused like she wasn't sure either. *—Um, until then—*

Ahem.

Kit froze at the decidedly masculine interruption in her brain. Her mouth went dry. *M-Mr. Asorav?*

Yes, my dear. Pardon me for the intrusion, but I couldn't help but note your angst and feel compelled to relieve you of it. After Ms. Yewling's reel of your confrontation last night and the resulting transformation of Ms. Hale, there is little doubt that you are the true shifter queen and the sects are responding in accordance. Mr. James's motorcycle club has accepted you as such and is thoroughly apprised of your status as his, ah, old lady.

Oh. Um, thank you?

My pleasure. I look forward to seeing you at brunch. Do come down as you are able.

Kit stood in the bathroom gripping her towel and listening to the silence in her head, afraid to think. *Is he gone?* she thought-whispered.

—Son of a bitch had better be.— Kat spat, her proverbial tail thrashing. *—Vamp is creepy as fuck.—*

Shh! What if he's listening?

—Then he can listen to this! YOU'RE CREEPY AS FUCK!—

Oh my God, you need to stop.

—No, only thing I need to stop is him from climbing into our head.—

Good luck with that. Kit sighed, going back into the bedroom. It looked like Nikki had just opened all of Kit's suitcases and shaken them out into one big pile before strewing things around the room. She stepped around the slick of nasty still coating the floor in front of the vanity to the largest pile of clothes, her anxiety ticking up. The bar downstairs sounded packed with brothers, and as soon as she walked into that room, all eyes were gonna be on her.

What the heck did a queen wear?

—Aside from being banned from bedsheets, whatever the hell she wants to— Kat murmured distractedly. *—What if I—*

Something twanged in Kit's head. She winced, but the static that'd been buzzing in the back of her brain since she'd changed abruptly cut off. A weird visual of Kat in coveralls messing around in her psyche with a wrench flitted through Kit's mind's eye. Great, just what she needed; a mind mechanic.

—Take that, motherfucker.—

You do it?

[SHRUGGING]

—I dunno, but it did something.—

You are not helpful.

—Oh please, like you need help. Bring your A game and all of 'em will be eating out the palm of your hand, including that man of yours. Remember Timmons, in Acquisitions? Absolute prick on the phone, tongue dragging in person. Once you get all dolled up and walk into the room, ain't nobody gonna remember who was waiting on whose say-so about what.—

Kit tapped her teeth. As much as she hated skating by on her looks, that would definitely make things easier. *My A game, huh?* Her A game was what Chanté referred to as boardroom boudoir. A smile tipped up Kit's lips as she knelt, sorting through the mess of clothes.

—Good. Now we gotta talk about this queen thing. Like, okay, I'm feelin' the MC baby-momma vibe, but not for nothin', we're made for more than hangin' around here, barefoot and pregnant.—

Kit snorted. *First off, have you seen the floors? There's not a frickin' chance I'm going barefoot anywhere around here.* She held up a gabardine pencil skirt, head cocked. *And the second I agree with, but Grim's not gonna let us do jack shit until he kills Reaper.*

—I hate that skirt. Find the black one with the zipper up the back— Kat said, distracted again. *—Why does Grim have to be the one to kill him?—*

Why does... Kit dropped the skirt to her lap. *Do you want to kill him?*

—I'm not opposed.—

She set aside a halter top. *You were also not doing a fucking thing except cowering under Grim's bed the last time we saw Daddy Dearest.*

—That was before we melted Nikki. If we could do the same to Reaper—

Before or after he takes control of our powers? No. It's too dangerous.

—Unless we're pregnant.—

Yeah... that. Kit ran a hand over her abdomen. It all sounded crazy. That she was going along with it was crazy, but when she was with Grim... Kit laughed. Yeah, whatever that was, it was crazy, too.

—And you fucking love it.—

I love him. Kit sighed, rubbing a thumb over a self-tanner stain on the underwire of one of her balconette bras. Man, that was so frickin' gross.

Kit tossed it to the side, starting another pile to send to the dry cleaner. Damn. Did they even have one in Flatts? *After everything Reaper put Grim through, he needs to be the one to put that prick down.*

—Maybe in a perfect world. All I'm sayin' is if I got the chance,

I'm taking it and your boy can go to therapy to get closure like everyone else.—

Noted. Ah! She pulled out the pencil skirt with the zipper up the back. Kat was right, it was exactly the one she wanted, and with that halter she'd set aside, Grim was gonna lose his mind. Now, which shoes…

—Don't even play. Wear the knock-off D&G lace and leather ankle booties.—

Oooh. Yes! Kit crawled over to the corner where it looked like the majority of her footwear had been dumped. Ugh. If she hadn't wanted to kill Nikki before, she sure did now. *However us being here shakes out, I'm pretty sure Grim having the final say on stuff's a given, at least in public. Hopefully Mr. Asorav and Chanté didn't made a big deal about getting my permission in front of the club.* She wasn't sure what Grim was gonna do if they had, but Kit couldn't imagine it being received well by either of them.

—Oh, I can imagine exactly what will happen.— Kat snorted. *—Your boy'll swing that massive dick of his around, Asorav'll do something sneaky as fuck, and Chanté will try to bitch-slap them both.—*

And Kit would end up having to take someone's side. She frowned, pulling one of the booties from the pile, sick at the thought of having to choose between Chanté and Grim.

—So don't. We're gonna take that cat by the whiskers instead. You just worry about dressing the part and let me handle the rest.—

Kit snagged her other shoe and stood, sighing. Kat handling the rest was exactly what she was afraid of.

CHAPTER TWO

GRIM PUNCHED his code into the playroom's door, each high-pitched beep a dagger in his skull. The reinforced steel slab thunked open to Brick whistling the Camp Granada theme song. Christ, that wasn't any better. And judging by the amount of gore splashed around the drain in the center of the room, he was definitely hitting his stride. Jesus fuck, was that a kidney on the floor?

Grim shook his head and stepped inside, Deuce closing the door behind them. The playroom was the largest of the cells, the floor pitching to the aforementioned drain and every surface epoxied in gray resin. A stainless-steel workbench covered with everything from surgical tools to kitchen implements and a pink feathered boa ran the length of one wall, and a high-pressure water hose coiled on another. A track of meat hooks hung from the I-beams above.

So did three men.

Well, what was left of them. Fucking place stank like slaughterhouse barbecue and hot asphalt.

Two of them had dark sacks over their heads, but the third...damn. Grim was pretty sure that'd been Riff, and Deuce hadn't been kidding about waiting to eat.

A frenetic trail of Brick's footprints danced crimson around the dangling men to where he stood at the workbench in his boxer-briefs. Spattered and stippled red, gore streaked up his forearms and over his chest and thighs. He tapped one foot, off-beat to what he was whistling, stirring something bubbling away over a hotplate and eyeing the assortment of tools like they were dessert samples.

Apparently satisfied with whatever he was cooking, he grinned, sweeping up a new acetylene tank, and swapped it for the one in the torch by his side. He turned to Deuce and Grim as they came in. "Hey there, Grimmers. You here to go a couple rounds like Deucey?"

Grim raised an eyebrow at his VP, and the man shrugged, kicking a handful of severed digits out of his way to amble over to the lump of dangling meat on the right. Damn. Looked like Riff's fingers had been snipped off knuckle by knuckle. The remaining stumps on his hands were bloodied and blackened, thin tendrils of smoke still rising.

Deuce turned his head and spat to the side. "Rat fuck asshole got what was comin' to him for disrespecting Triss."

Because Deuce was a perfect fucking gentleman. Grim snorted. Whatever; he wasn't about to tackle that squirrel's cage of logic.

Riff had definitely seen better days. Aside from the loss of his fingers, his face'd been beaten to an unrecognizable pulp and bubbles of red snot and gore slicked down his chest. What was left of his hands were shackled; the chain looped through a hook above his head, suspending him with his toes barely brushing the floor. They left faint circles in the spattered gore and drifts of rock salt beneath him as he swayed. The rise and fall of his chest was negligible, which, until Kit had started healing shifters, would've been pretty impressive considering the strips of flayed skin littering the floor. What was left of his back had been charred into blackened, weeping sores. Grim's stomach churned, and it had nothing to do with his throbbing head.

Whelp, that was one way to remove Mayhem's tat.

"Why isn't he healing?" he asked, pulling his piece and

dropping the magazine. Should've checked it before he left his room, but this damned headache…six bullets.

"Cuffs are silver." Brick clicked on the acetylene torch, leaning back against the workbench and adjusting the flame. He motioned at Riff's wrists. "Argents to be exact. Tried regular cuffs, but they just slow the healing process down. Spikes on the inside of those stop that shit cold."

[REVULSION]

Yeah, no shit. Just—just go the fuck to sleep and let me handle this, okay? Grim was having enough trouble keeping his own shit together with a pair of those cuffs in the room. Both him and Darke were well acquainted with what argents did, and he didn't need his fucking cat wigging out and complicating things.

Brick snagged a cigar from the table and lit it with the torch. Man, that had to taste like shit. He exhaled a stream of smoke, unfazed if it did, and inspected its cherry. "Deucey and I did some experimenting while he worked Riff over. Long story short, watching a kidney grow back is fucking surreal, and he didn't have shit to say aside from how sorry he was. Pretty positive he was just lickin' Satan's Vengeance's ass and passin' on our club business thinkin' he'd get a bigger slice of pie with them. You want, I can take the argents off and he can tell you himself. Should be blubbering and begging for you to end him in under five once I do."

"How many times did it take you to figure that out?" Grim asked.

"Not enough," Deuce muttered.

"Deucey, Deucey, Deucey," Brick tsked, coming over to sling an arm around his shoulders. The enforcer sucked in a deep inhale against his face, then growled and gave Deuce a sloppy kiss on the cheek. "Damn, you're fucking sexy with your vengeance on."

Deuce batted him away scowling. "Get off me, you fucking nut. At least I've got something on."

"Makes clean up easier." Brick shrugged, scratching his junk through his briefs.

"Before or after you jerk off?"

"Now that'd be telling." He grinned, waggling his eyebrows then psh'ing at Deuce's scowl. "Such a sourpuss. Just because Riff had his fingers in Triss's—"

"Don't fucking say it," Deuce growled.

Brick leaned forward enunciating, "*Tight. Little. Cunt.*"

Deuce threw a punch at the enforcer, and Brick ducked, laughing.

"Goddamn it, you're a fucking asshole!" Deuce yelled, turning and driving his fist into Riff's gut. Gore sprayed from his mouth, spattering the VP. "Fuck! Fuck, fuck, fuck!"

Brick chortled like a lunatic, a manic smile splitting his face as he turned to Grim. "Have I told you how much I love my job?"

"Technically, it's not to piss people off, but yeah, repeatedly." Grim pinched the bridge of his nose. "I'm assuming Riff's not the source of this *Valdez*-sized spill Deuce hauled my ass down here for?"

"Nah, he's just fun," Brick said, motioning to the man dangling on the right with his cigar. "For that, we gotta go to candidate number two."

"Then we don't need Riff anymore," Grim said, racking his piece and putting a bullet through the rat's temple before he thought better of it. The *crack* of the 9mm was like a sledgehammer through his skull. Fuuuck... He grimaced, trying not to puke. "There's wights in the woods. Have a couple prospects pitch what's left of him in and be done with it. Unless you want the honors?" Grim winced, glancing at Deuce and trying to blink away the halo from the light behind him.

"Yeah, actually. I think I would... You gonna make it?" Deuce's brow knit.

Grim pulled his hand away from his temple, scowling. "I'm fine."

Brick snatched off the hood the remaining member of SV's crew. The balding biker whimpered, blinking. The hell was his name…Weasel. He'd been the only one that'd offered to narc. With a name like that, go fucking figure.

"Liar," Brick said, eyeing Grim. "You're fucking with your meds again."

"No, he's not taking his meds again."

"Dude, they don't work right if—"

"Jesus Christ, yeah, I know. Now get off my dick about it!" Grim snapped, riffling his hair. Fuck, this was fucking painful enough without being nagged to death by Mama D and Auntie Brick.

The enforcer stepped back with his hands in the air, and Deuce snorted, dropping Riff's corpse from the hook. It thudded onto the floor with the heavy finality that only dead bodies made. "Keys?"

Brick snagged a ring of them from his workbench and tossed them over to Deuce. "S'one of those." He turned back to Weasel, pulling a pair of headphones off the narc's balding head, the dulcet tones of death metal screeching from them. He'd been stripped down and trussed up like the rest, and his knees looked like they'd repeatedly made the acquaintance of a baseball bat. But, aside from that and some strategic cuts designed to bleed more than anything else, it didn't look like Brick had fucked with him too much.

Rat must've been cooperative. Good thing he wasn't the only one the enforcer had to play with. Brick got peckish when they spilled shit too quick.

"This one," he said, moving behind Weasel and tugging on his scraggly ponytail. "This one says he can finger Reaper for putting the hit on Cantone's nephew." Brick waved the torch over the man's hair, and it ignited like a fuse.

Weasel screamed, words spilling from his lips faster and

faster. "I can! I can! He hired the Nifftides to do the job. Brought them up from Lake Ontario special so SV wouldn't get fingered. Contact was a man named Sly. Ah! Stop, please! I'll tell you whatever you want!"

Christ, Grim knew exactly who Weasel was talking about. Sly headed up a gang of fish shifters. Dude was a legit shark. Grim grunted and Brick snuffed Weasel's head. Damn, that was rank. "Nifftides… I didn't think they were big enough to pull off a hit like that. They still operating out of Toronto Bay?"

Weasel nodded, sobbing. "Yeah, but they've been expanding, patching in jacobs specifically for shit like that. They handled the land side of things; shifters stick to the water."

"Jacobs." Brick snickered at the slur.

Grim glanced at him askance. Shifter wannabes were about as funny as the vamp version, and edwards weren't funny at all. "Keep talking."

"Nifftides waited until Cantone's crew was on the bridge to take them out. Had special orders to make sure the kid got snuffed. Reaper was real specific about that."

"You know why he wanted the kid dead?"

Weasel shook his head, sweat pouring down his face. "No, man. He didn't say, just wanted it done. You know how he is. Could be a real reason, could be God showed up in his cornflakes."

Grim snorted. Wasn't that the truth. "Put him in a cell. Cantone's gonna want to hear what he's gotta say, and I'm sure he'll have follow-up questions."

"Well, that's no fun," Brick said, puffing a mouthful of smoke into Weasel's face. He grinned as the man choked on the fumes. "But cell number two is, and you'll be right at home with the rest of the rats."

Weasel's throat bobbed. "Rats?"

"Big ones." Brick grinned, unhooking him. The man

screamed as he collapsed onto his busted kneecaps. Brick dragged his abruptly unconscious form to the door. He wet his lips, pointing a finger at the last man hanging. "I'll be right back. Do not start that party without me."

Grim gave him a thumbs up and the enforcer grunted.

"You believe him?" Deuce asked as the door shut behind them.

Grim winced at the *clunk*, pulling out his bottle of aspirin. "About the rats?"

"No, I've seen those. I meant what Weasel said about the Nifftides."

"It's definitely possible." Grim shrugged, throwing back another two and chewing. "What I'm more leery about is Reaper leaving Weasel and the rest of his crew behind. Shit was sloppy. Reaper might be batshit crazy, but he's usually meticulous."

Deuce frowned at the bottle as Grim put it away. "Yeah, but last night had to've fucked with his head, hardcore. I mean, Grapple's dead, and from what you said, Shiv had to have been all messed up. There's no way Reaper could've expected you to trounce the two of them."

[ANNOYANCE]

—not you, me—

Whatever. He's still got a point. But there was a reason Reaper had managed to head up Satan's Vengeance for the past thirty-three years, despite being behind bars for half of that. The majority of his club thought he was some kind of fucking prophet the way he could anticipate how things would play out, and the rest didn't want to test the theory. Man always had a fallback plan for every eventuality.

Though granted, the decapitation and maiming of his eldest and youngest sons respectively probably weren't very high on the list. Especially given Grim's track record with his littermates. They usually beat the fuck out of him, then hauled him in for whatever delight Reaper had planned. If it wasn't for that damned porcupine—

—ruined—

It's not ruined, it's still in the trunk.

[HUFFING]

Grim rubbed his temples. *Dude, I told you, we'll get it after this.*

"Think he's got any insight?" Deuce asked, jerking his head at MK's dangling form.

"I dunno." But as soon as Brick got back, Grim planned on finding out.

———

KIT PAUSED at the top of the stairs, patting her hair and then running a hand down her abdomen, her anxiety on overdrive.

—Girl, you got this,— Kat said, totally downplaying Kit's nerves.

She fiddled with the dick scarf wrapped around her wrist. *Lies. Aren't you the one who's always telling me not to bullshit someone who lives in my head?*

—All right, fine, but seriously, who the hell cares what any of them think?—

If I'm gonna be queen, especially Grim's queen, I need to care. That's his MC down there. Kit's stomach roiled. *Shit. I'm overdressed. They're gonna think I'm all uppity, and then what if they hate me?*

Kat chuffed.*— Then they can fucking leave. You're Grim's mate. It's a package deal, and girl, you're not overdressed, you're hella fierce. And, if Nikki was any indication, this club could use some class. The only bitches gonna be hatin' on you are the skanky ones jealous as fuck.—*

Well, that was probably true and damn if it didn't feel good to be back in her own clothes. Her ankle booties gave her four-foot-eleven frame another five inches. The knee-length black pencil skirt paired with a cobalt halter top was sexy without being slutty, and Grim was gonna lose his mind when he saw it. She smirked, patting her updo again. She'd paired the look with a smokey cat eye and a bold red lip.

Sounds drifted up from below along with the scent of maple syrup. Kit's stomach rumbled, starving.

—*So what are you waiting for? Go get something to eat!*—

Kit tongued the corner of her mouth, then pressed her lips together. Right. What *was* she waiting for? An engraved invitation? Fat chance of getting one of those here. She took a deep breath and started down the steps.

In her mind, the flight was longer. The entryway with its muddy flagstones, wider. She paused, one hand on the newel post, the sounds of breakfast in full swing just past the entrance to the bar. Getting lost in the past. A Sunday when her mother'd made cinnamon toast, and Claymore had let her eat it at his desk…

Tears pricked her eyes. *I can't do this.*

—*Do what? Have waffles or whatever they're eating in there?*—

No… I… God, the last time she'd been in that room—

—*The last time you were in that room, your boy just about bent you over the bar.*—

Kit barked out a laugh then slapped a hand over her mouth. Kat had a point…

—*Of course I have a point, and you heard Deuce. Chanté and Asorav are in there having brunch. Ugh, you also heard Mr. Creepy-as-fuck himself, and he's expecting you. Now hike up your big girl panties, walk in there like you own the damned place, and get something to eat, Queen Katherine!*—

Right. Yes. Okay. Kit straightened her spine, and strutted through the…

What in the hell?

Maybe she did need an engraved invitation. The dingy room looked like a wedding planner had thrown up on it and then bikers had invaded. She laughed, and everyone stopped what they were doing and turned to look at her.

Twelve—no fourteen round tables, swathed in white and peach linens and topped with massive sprays of coordinating flowers, were filled shoulder to shoulder by burly, grungy bikers shoveling down a catered meal on fine china. They, and one table of extremely hostile mollys plus Triss, stared at her.

Kit took a step backward. *Run away, Kit, run away—*

—Don't you fucking dare.— Kat growled.

Triss sprang up, her squeal breaking the tense silence. Brothers turned back to their plates and conversations, more than one of them eyeing the petite blonde as she clapped her hands over her mouth and hopped up and down.

—Girl needs to invest in a real bra.—

Kit bit back a laugh, watching Triss weave through the crowded tables. Brothers she was passing certainly didn't seem to mind, and it would serve Deuce right to see all of them ogling her. Maybe it would help him to pull his head out of his ass.

—Doubtful.—

You're probably right. Kit sighed. Man was so good looking it was criminal, but she couldn't say she'd been impressed with his brains.

—Well, not everyone is as blessed as us, Katherine.— Kat preened.

Kit laughed again, and at the very end of the bar, Mr. Asorav rose from his stool. He straightened his suit jacket's lapels and gave Kit a curt bow. Beside him, Chanté gave a drunken salute with a flute of something, downed it, then grabbed another from a passing waiter's tray.

Oh, sweet baby Jesus. Were they serving Bellinis? It would match the peach theme, and the way her bestie was cozying up to Mr. Asorav? Red flags were definitely waving. Kit's brow knit—

"You're awake!" Triss squealed, throwing her arms

around her. "Oh my God, I feel like you've been asleep *forever!*"

Kit stumbled back. What? She'd seen Triss just last night.

—Aww, she's like a puppy. Look at her wiggle!—

Be nice, Kit chided, but Kat wasn't wrong, and Triss was vibrating with more excitement than usual. "Yeah…what is all this?"

Triss shook her head, miming locking her lips and throwing the key away. "Squee! Nope. Not telling! You want a Bellini? Lemme get you a Bellini." She looped her arm through Kit's dragging her toward the bar.

Oh, hell no. "Um. Sure." Kit's gaze locked on Chanté's half-finished glass. Lord knew peach anything was Chanté's kryptonite, and add alcohol to the mix? *Psh.* And nobody here would have the good sense to cut her off before she went off the deep end.

Yeah, it didn't matter when Kit had been in the room last, or what any of them thought of her. Fuck them. Especially the mollys. Chanté's self-destruct sequence had begun. Kit got her feet under her and gave the room a wide smile—

Her steps faltered as they passed the big picture window. What the hell were they setting up outside? Out in the parking lot, big open tents with tables were strung with fairy lights and in the center of them, men were laying out…was that a dance floor?

Kit's hands closed around the back of a ribbon-bedecked chair, steadying herself. The balloons attached to it swayed, and she pulled back, batting them away. *She Said Yes.* Kit did a double take at the script on the largest of them.

What in the fresh hell… She turned to Triss. The younger girl bit down on her lips, like she was about to explode.

"Katherine." Mr. Asorav greeted her with open arms and a kiss on each cheek. He steered her away from Triss to the end of the bar where Chanté was all fabulous and smug in a pinstripe sheath. No way it coordinating with the vamp's suit was an accident. "I've missed your internal dialog for the past half hour or so."

Oh good. That must mean whatever Kat had done worked.

—Darn. Then he won't be able to hear me calling him a CREEPY FUCKING VAMP.—

Did you seriously have to yell that? Kit grimaced, brushing an errant lock from her brow. "Mr. Asorav," she said, reaching past him to pluck the flute from Chanté's hand. Her bestie scowled at her, and Kit raised an eyebrow, taking a sip. Oh, thank God, they were weak as hell. Not that it mattered if Chanté had already guzzled a dozen of the damned things. "She's officially cut off," Kit informed a passing waiter, "and could use some coffee."

Mr. Asorav pulled out a barstool and Kit sat, glaring at her bestie. She frickin' knew better. Triss took the seat next to Kit, looking between her and Chanté expectantly. Damn. Whatever was going on had better hurry up and happen before the girl stroked out.

Chanté sighed with a little shrug, then swallowed a hiccup. "Listen—"

"Don't," Kit snapped back, huffing as a plate of French toast with peach compote and bacon was set on the bar in front of her. Damn, that looked good. She pulled a fork from the linen-wrapped bundle that'd been delivered with it and stabbed the tines at Chanté. "You and I both know where that was gonna go." Kit's eyes flicked from the empty flute to the vamp.

As in downhill, fast. She thought hard at Mr. Asorav. *Do NOT let her have Bellinis unless you plan on holding her hair back later. Girl has zero self-regulation where peach anything is involved.*

The vampire's brow rose. *Duly noted, and I must say I'm impressed at your quick grasp of telepathy. Had you not reached out, I'd have no way of sensing you. Well done.*

"Oh, I surely do know where things are going, but do

you?" Chanté asked, too coy, cutting off Kit's reply to Mr. Asorav. Her bestie batted her lashes. "I bet you don't," she said singsong, twirling a long, tawny finger at her, smug as hell.

Triss giggled and Kit's eyes narrowed.

"How do you figure?" she asked, digging into her meal and then trying not to moan around the maple-pecan-loaded deliciousness she'd just put in her mouth. She swallowed the bite of heaven and paused before scooping up another, suddenly very, very wary. Her eyes flicked around the room. "What is all of this?"

"You're getting married!" Triss burst out, then slapped a hand over her mouth. "Oh. My. God. I am *so* sorry. But I still get to be a bridesmaid, right? Please, tell me I get to be a bridesmaid!" She turned to Kit, her eyes huge. "I do, right?"

"Girl, we're good." Chanté grinned, waving Triss's concern away. "I just wanted to make sure I got to see Kit's face when she found out."

"Yay!" Triss squealed, hands clasped beneath her chin as she bounced in her seat. "Oh, my God, I can't wait for you to see the dresses!"

"The dresses? Are you for…" The words died on Kit's lips looking around. Holy shit. The orange and peach theme. Bellinis and her favorite kind of French toast. This… this was bad break-up, gallon of ice-cream on the couch, chillin' with a movie and your bestie, if wishes were horses dreaming right here. Kit's eyes got hot, and she dropped her fork onto her plate to waft a hand at her face. "This is you," she whispered huskily at Chanté.

Her bestie toasted her with her coffee. "The vision yes, but Mikhail made it happen."

Kit's eyebrow quirked. "Mikhail?"

"Mikhail," Chanté smirked around her mug with a sly glance at Mr. Asorav.

Oh, Sweet baby Jesus, she *did* have him in her sights.

CHAPTER THREE

GRIM POCKETED his phone as the door to the playroom slammed open. He winced, leaning back against the wall and letting the cool surface of the underground room bleed into him. Whelp, he'd been right about Cantone wanting to talk to Weasel, but he hadn't expected the crime lord to drop everything to do it. Man's helicopter would be landing on the club's back forty in under two hours.

Because Grim didn't have enough shit on his plate to deal with.

But as much as he wanted to go find a dark hole to crawl into, there wasn't a doubt in his mind that MK was the reason Clay was dead. Grim glowered at the last dangling figure, fully planning on returning the favor.

After he pumped the rat dry of intel about Reaper.

"Damn. You know, nothing says job well done quite like a grown man crying. I love that shit," Brick announced, closing the door behind him. He thumped a fist against his chest and took a deep breath. "Gets me right in the feels, ya know?"

"This asshole's way past well done," Deuce muttered, toeing what was left of Riff. "And you can keep your feels to yourself, you psychopath. You put your lips on me again, and you're gonna eat a bullet."

"Promises, promises. And I keep telling you, that's been clinically disproven," Brick said, snatching the hood off MK.

Fucker blinked, trying to scrape his headphones off. Too bad they were taped to his head. His nostrils flared above the ball gag jammed into his mouth.

"From what you've said about the VA hospital, forgive me if I call shenanigans on that whomping load of horseshit," Deuce said, rolling his eyes. "Tell me those headphones are streaming Rush."

"Of course they're streaming Rush." Brick slapped their ex-road captain on the back, sending him swinging. "I distinctly remember ol' Mud Knuckle here once saying he'd 'rather be tarred and feathered than listen to that shit,' so what d'ya say we see if that's true?"

"Aww yeah." Deuce slow clapped. "Look at you makin' dreams happen."

Brick took a bow.

Ah. So that explained the pink boa and the bubbling pot of asphalt on the hotplate. Grim shook his head. Deuce was right. The enforcer was a fucking psychopath.

MK glared at the three of them, his face purpling as the enforcer ripped the industrial tape off his head along with chunks of greasy gray hair and patches of skin. Brick tossed the headphones onto his workbench, the synthesized strains of *Tom Sawyer* blaring from them. He reached for the ball gag's clasp.

"Y'all ready for this?" At Grim's nod, Brick grinned, clapping his hands together and shaking his hips, whistling the damned 90s techno track—poorly. Dude was out of control.

Ball gag removed, MK hung there, glaring at them, his chest heaving like he'd run a mile. "Well? Ya gonna get on with it, or you just gonna eye fuck me to death?" the piece of shit growled.

"Yeah, I wanna get on with it. How about you kick things off by telling us why the fuck you turned coat," Grim spat, crossing the room to stand nose to nose with the man, his rage visceral. "Clay was your Goddamned alpha—Christ, he thought you were his friend! You started this fucking club with him. What the fuck possessed you to offer him up for slaughter?"

"I got nothin' t'say about that." MK glowered.

"Yesss." Brick fist pumped behind him.

"You got nothing to say about that." Grim laughed. He stepped away, then hauled back and slammed his fist into MK's jaw, snapping his head back with an uppercut. "Bull fucking shit." Grim landed another blow to the traitorous fuck's gut, and MK retched.

Brick held out a blade and Grim grabbed it, swiping it along MK's throat. A hot, sticky trickle slicked over Grim's knuckles as he teased the wickedly honed edge into the soft flesh below MK's jawline, waiting for that glimmer of fear to spark in his eyes.

It didn't.

Grim swore, flicking the blade up and shearing off the prick's ear. MK howled, thrashing like a fish on a line. "You got something to say now, motherfucker?" Grim growled, stepping back and putting a hand to his throbbing head, his vision pulsing with his temper.

MK just looked at him.

No fear, but there was a trace of pity.

Grim laughed again and spat. Was that right? Fine. Fuck this shit. He wanted an answer. Whelp, he knew how to get one regardless of the prick's desire to cooperate. "Tell me why you turned rat," he growled, the dual resonance of the alpha command building through his chest, tearing from his—

White light exploded across the back of his eyes.

Grim staggered, gripping his head. Fuuuck! What the—

"Holy shit! What the fuck is wrong with him?" Deuce yelled.

"I dunno, drop the hook!"

The hook? The hell were they talking about? Grim winced,

falling to one knee and knuckling against his eyes. The inside of his head felt like something'd just ruptured—

[CRINGING]

—bad game— Darke mewled, his voice small and tight.

The fuck was that?

—dunno. hurt—

Yeah, it did. Done. He was done. Brick and Deuce could figure this shit out. Grim raked a hand through his hair, staggering as he straightened up—nope. wasn't happening...

MK was sprawled face-up on the floor, and Brick was giving him CPR. He grunted in disgust and rolled back onto his heels. "Goddamn it. He's seriously fucking dead."

"What d'you mean he's dead?" Grim gritted out, bewildered. He swiped a hand beneath his nose and his fingers came away bloody. What the hell had just happened?

The two of them glanced over at him and paled.

"Holy shit, dude, you don't look much better," Deuce said, rushing over and helping him stand. "Soon as you issued that command, MK started foaming at the mouth. Fucker convulsed, and that was it. Dead."

Fuck. Grim blinked away the spots dancing across his vision as he stood. *You okay?* he asked Darke.

—want Kat— he grumbled, sending Grim a visual of the two big cats curled up beside a disemboweled porcupine.

Christ, that sounded good right about now. He staggered over to the hose, dousing his head. *You know where she is?*

—no—

What do you mean no?

—head hurts. can't hear good—

Grim grunted, sluicing blood out of his beard. He'd check the bar first and then their room. She couldn't have gone far. Damn. His fucking nose wouldn't stop bleeding. Why the hell that wasn't healing... "Toss me a rag, would ya?"

Brick sucked his teeth as he stood and threw one over from his workbench. "I'll bet you fifty Reaper issued a command for MK to keep quiet and you countermanding it triggered some shit." The enforcer put his hands on his hips, looking over the corpses. "That wheelbarrow and the coal shovel still in the garage?"

"Yeah, but be warned, Wrench's set up shop out there." Deuce frowned, crossing his arms over his chest. "If Grim triggered a command, then Reaper planned on us figuring out MK was a rat."

"Seems likely," Brick said, kicking bits of finger into a pile. "Begs the question, if he'd planned for that possibility, why the fuck was Weasel able to spill?"

Christ. Grim dabbed at a nostril, tentatively sniffing. After that weird, blinding burst of pain, the migraine that'd been stalking him had dwindled, but this shit was inviting it right the hell back. He was not up for the mental gymnastics required to figure out Reaper's logic, but Jesus fuck, had calling Cantone been a mistake? Goddamn it. It was too late now, and the last thing he needed was the crime boss pissed at—

"Fuck." Grim groaned. "Hellspawn's still waiting outside."

"Sounds like a job for whoever's prez," Brick quipped, relighting his cigar.

"Yeah," Deuce muttered, scrubbing his face. "Shit's above my pay grade, but you're gonna need a spotter. Brick's got this. Let's go deal with that."

Grim glared at the two of them, but the fuckers were right. Chanté and Asorav needed to be put in their place. Queen or not, Grim was in charge of this MC, not Kit. He frowned, leaving Brick to it and heading back upstairs with Deuce, hoping like hell Kit was gonna understand.

They passed Chris and Eddie, still in the hallway and stoned out of their minds. Must be fucking nice. Grim sighed, the stench of tar, blood, and charred flesh fading beneath a cloud of reefer and then cut off sharply as he exited the bunker. It was replaced with the aroma of bacon and maple syrup. The scent of Kit's heat hit him like a wall as soon as he put a boot on the stairs leading up from the laundry room. Beside him, Deuce gave a pained grunt. Yeah, she'd definitely made it downstairs.

Grim took the steps two at a time up to the entryway and into the—

Deuce ran into him as Grim stopped cold in the doorway. The fuck?

Round tables with white cloths and massive bouquets of orange and pink flowers were set up throughout the room, the couches and pool table noticeably absent. Brothers in grungy jeans and cuts packed around them, sitting on too-small folding chairs bedecked with bows and balloons. Asorav's human thralls wove throughout the crowd, dressed in crisp white shirts with coordinating pinky-orange bowties, black slacks, and long white aprons. They bussed tables or carried trays stacked with powdered French toast, bacon, and slim glasses of some foofy drink.

This had to be what Deuce was talking about. Fucking vamp was out of his Goddamned mind. Grim pinched across his temples, the throbbing back.

"All this was here when I came up from the playroom earlier," Deuce muttered. "Some shit about a queen needing 'a certain standard to be met,' whatever the fuck that means. No fucking clue how he made it happen."

A muscle in Grim's jaw ticked at the insinuation he couldn't take care of Kit the way she deserved. Vamp sure as fuck wasn't winning any brownie points this morning. Grim started across the room. "Then let's find out."

Despite the society Sunday brunch flare, it was tense as hell. Brothers muttered around their meals, casting dark looks at the little group sitting at the far end of the bar.

Namely, at Asorav. Grim caught the Darkling's name whispered more than once with a mixture of reverence and loathing. The vamp's reputation had definitely preceded him, and the fact that he was sitting in a sunlit room wasn't doing anything to dispel it. That, and his reasons for being here, were gonna have to be addressed, fast.

Not that the fucker seemed the least bit concerned by any of it.

He sat at the far end of the bar with Chanté, Kit, and Triss, not giving a fuck that everyone else was tense as hell. Chanté didn't seem to care either. The witch and vamp's heads were close together, laughing like they were on a date or some shit. Good. Maybe the prick would take his heart back from Kit and fuck off to wherever he kept getting those suits. Vamp was in a navy blue three-piece this morning, and Grim would bet money that the coordinating Jackie O ensemble Chanté was dolled up in was his doing too.

Fucking vamps. Not that witches were any less pretentious, but for Kit's sake, Grim supposed he'd give Chanté the benefit of the doubt. He wasn't giving Asorav anything aside from a good long look at his middle finger.

Grim glanced at the half-dozen mollys huddled together at a table by the window as he and Deuce passed. They wouldn't meet his eye, their conversation abruptly dropping off. Grim snorted. He didn't know if they'd heard about what Kit had done to Kelsey, but he was positive they'd seen what she'd done to Nikki on Triss's Insta, and that'd been savage. Between the reel and Kit's pheromones pervading the clubhouse, he wasn't surprised they were so on edge.

That, and they were right in front of the big picture window facing those creepy-ass woods...

Shit.

That wight was still right where Grim had last seen it, and a bunch of his buddies had joined him. The way they were just standing there staring at the clubhouse didn't give Grim the warm fuzzies. He ran a hand over the scar on his arm, its cold burn standing the small hairs at his nape on end.

A brother went by, giving him a nod and slapping his shoulder. "Congrats, my man!"

"Yeah, thanks." Grim grunted, the contact helping to shake off his dread. He blew out a breath and waded across the rest of the room, brothers coming up to him every few steps to offer their congrats. If all this was to celebrate him taking prez, the vamp needed to seriously rethink his aesthetic. Beers around a bonfire would've been a hell of a lot more appropriate.

Kit glanced up as Grim drew nearer, her cheeks pinking when her eyes met his. She pressed her bright red lips together like she was biting back a smile and spun to say something to…

Grim's hand smacked down on a seated brother's shoulder, trying to absorb the gut punch of what Kit's bare back was doing to him. Goddamn. The sides of her top were barely held together by a slim gold chain across her lower back.

He had the abrupt urge to snap it.

The brother looked up at him, then followed Grim's gaze. "Jesus fuck, you're a lucky son of a bitch," he muttered around a mouthful of bacon. "That piece's seriously your ol' lady?"

"Yeah." Grim grinned, running a hand over his mouth as Kit slid off her stool to saunter over to him, the press in the room parting for her like the Red Sea.

No fucking question, she was beyond beautiful. Sky-high heels, a skirt that hugged every sinful curve, and her top… The front of it dripped from around her neck to cover her tits like an afterthought, and that scent…her heat, it thickened the air, melting over his tongue. Citrus and cinnamon and holy Jesus fuck.

She stopped in front of him, hands on her hips, the top of her head just even with his collarbones. "Nothing to say, Pussycat?"

"I'll see you at the bar," Deuce said, clapping him on the shoulder and leaving them. Grim hardly registered it.

—WANT—

Yes, we do… "I got plenty to say," he rumbled, his hands caging her hips and pulling her close. "I told you I wasn't done with you."

Kit pursed her lips around a smile and all Grim could think about was a ring of that lipstick around his dick. She shrugged. "I had things to do."

"That makes two of us, and your sassy mouth just added something else to my list," he murmured close to her ear. "You need me to pull you over my knee in front of all these people?"

Her pupils blew out, and her breath hitched, eyes darting to the rapt crowd. A flush crept up her throat to bloom over her cheeks. "Y-you wouldn't."

—would—

"Try me. I got no issues with an audience. Then there won't be any question that you're mine." His lips dropped to hers, hand raising to fondle her breast. The room erupted in catcalls, and she groaned into his mouth, her nipple hardening against his palm. He tugged on it, the scent of her heat thickening. "You wanna ride my dick in front of Mayhem, Kitten?" he murmured.

She pulled back with a sharp intake of breath, her pupils waffling. "I…" Her tongue darted out to wet her lips and then she stomped her foot, huffing. "Grimdarke James, this was not how this conversation was supposed to go!"

"What?" He laughed.

"Just, ugh. Come on." She took his hand and pulled him back toward where she'd been sitting. Shit, the hell was this about? Was she mad he'd felt her up in front of the club? No way. Woman got off on people watching. He bet her panties were soaked clean through.

If she was wearing panties. She sure as fuck wasn't

wearing a bra. Grim followed where she led, his eyes skating down her bare back to the oversized zipper of her skirt running up the center of her luscious ass. No panty lines. Grim adjusted the bulge in his jeans, wondering what she'd do if he went all caveman and threw her over his—

"Mr. James," Asorav said, standing with his hand extended to shake.

[ANNOYANCE]

Ditto. Grim ignored the vamp, glancing at Deuce to see if he was ready for this. And that was gonna be a no. Man looked like Triss had just seriously pissed in his cornflakes. She, on the other hand, looked pleased as fucking punch. Grim frowned. Great. More drama he didn't need.

He turned back to Chanté and Asorav. "So which one of you wants to explain to me and my VP what the hell is going on?" Grim growled, widening his stance and crossing his arms over his chest. Kit rested her hand on his forearm, her fingers tense.

Chanté turned, laughing at something one of the thralls had said. "I'm sorry, what's this now?"

"I asked you a question. Now you answer it."

Chanté's eyebrow cocked, and she glanced at Kit before sitting back, her body language closing off to mirror Grim's. "Funny, I didn't hear a question. Did you hear a question, Mikhail?"

Asorav took a seat, ankle over his knee. Asshole's socks were paisley, and his patent leather loafers had stupid little tassels. "I'm not sure I did, my dear. Perhaps we should begin again. Good morning, Mr. James. Mr. Cransworth. Was there something we can assist you with?"

—hate him—

So Goddamned much. Grim exchanged a look with Deuce, the both of them fighting the urge to hit something. "Yeah," Grim gritted out, his headache redoubling. "How 'bout you tell me what all this shit's about, move on to how you're gonna fucking listen when my VP tells you to do something, and finish up by clearing the wights outta my woods."

"Ah, yes. The wights." Asorav tapped a long finger against his lips like it'd been a request for him to ponder or some shit. "I would advise against that."

"Ditto," Chanté said, spinning the stem of her cocktail. A growl rumbled through Grim's chest, and she rolled her eyes. "Look, Imma lay it out for you, Mr. Alpha-hole—"

Triss snickered and it didn't fucking improve Grim's mood.

"—nasty-ass people wanna get a hold of Kit and the way I see it," Chanté continued, "it's our job to prevent that. Those wights out there? Hello. Ain't nobody but my friend, Mikhail —yeah, you know, the Darkling? Um, yes, *that* Darkling—is controlling 'em, and they ain't leaving their dead-zone donut of mist. Compound's on the inside, trouble's on the outside, mission accomplished. And now if you'll excuse me, I need another cocktail." She drained her glass and held it up over her shoulder. A passing edward took it and handed her another like it was a choreographed routine.

Kit opened her mouth to protest, and her eyes flicked to Asorav's like the prick had said something.

—probably talking in their minds—
Is that fucking right?
[SHRUGGING]
—dunno. can't hear—

Grim's teeth gritted together. Well, if they were, that was just one more reason to hate the vamp, and Alpha-hole? Had Chanté seriously called him... Grim pinched the bridge of his nose, the pounding in his head fierce. He ran a finger beneath his nose, surprised it wasn't bleeding again, and pulled out more aspirin.

"Okay, look. I've got approximately five minutes to get rid of the feds so Hellspawn can collect Nikki, so how the fuck do we do that and get Lars in and out of your donut?"

Chanté snickered behind the rim of her flute. "Baby, anytime you boys wanna get into my donut, all you gotta do is ask."

Christ. How many of those fucking things had she had?

Asorav sucked in his cheeks, apparently not amused by the innuendo. Chanté caught it, her expression going thoughtful, like...wait. Was she... Oh no. Grim shook his head and looked away. Nope. He was not getting sucked into whatever the hell that was shaping up to be.

"The same way my thralls were able to access your compound, Mr. James," the vamp said. "The lovely Ms. Sue and I shall hold a path open, whilst several of my associates vet those seeking ingress, maintaining the security of the inner circle. I'm sure you'll agree, that's of the highest import."

Grim scrubbed his face. "You've got vamps manning my gate?"

"I do. Three of my children to be precise, and several more are around the perimeter dissuading those attempting to enter clandestinely. And as far as the federal agents are concerned, it's very difficult to apprehend that which you're unaware of." The vamp picked the side of a tooth with a too-long pinky nail, smug as hell.

Figures. Vamps were masters of the mind-fuck and got off on messing with humans. Assholes must be coming in their pants sneaking all this shit past the feds. Regardless, Grim frowned. "Well, they sure as hell noticed Hellspawn riding up on them, so how do you propose we play that hand?"

"We open the gate and invite everybody in." Chanté shrugged.

Oh, yeah, she was definitely drunk. "Why the fuck would I do that?"

"Because, my dear boy," Asorav said with a smirk, "today you're getting married."

KIT COULD EMPATHIZE with Grim's poleaxed expression, having worn the same look not too long ago. He pinched the bridge of his nose, wincing, and she turned to the vamp. "Mr. Asorav, all of this—"

"Is no more than a queen deserves, and provides both you and Mr. James with exactly the shiny new thing to distract the masses whilst the rest of us clean house."

"How do you figure?" Grim asked, rubbing his furrowed brow.

"Well, it seems to me that instead of chasing after your enemies, it makes eminently more sense to lure them to their doom. And who doesn't love a wedding? I can't imagine Mr. Ells will be able to resist the temptation to give his lovely daughter away."

Kit's stomach clenched. "You want Reaper to walk me down the aisle?"

"Yeah, and while he's doing that, I'll ask Shiv to be my best man." Grim's fingers tightened on her shoulder. "No fucking way. Not happening, and I don't want either of those psychos anywhere near Kit."

Asorav shrugged. "I suppose the guest list is entirely up to you, but I'd be remiss if I didn't point out that you're missing a golden opportunity to reunite your sect. Not only do you have the most eminent of the Southern shifters at your gate, Navarro's pack will be arriving shortly with that Kraelle fellow hot on their heels."

Grim's fingers clenched tighter. "Is that right?"

"It is." Asorav's eyes flicked to Kit. "And what better occasion will you have to present their queen than during an event in which *hospitium* applies."

She turned to ask Grim what that was, and he was pinching the bridge of his nose again.

—Earlier, Darke said his head hurts really bad today, and I

haven't been able to talk to my boy for the past few hours. It's like he's totally walled off,— Kat murmured, concerned. *—Grim needs to take his meds and sleep it off.—*

Kit bit her lip. Yeah, she didn't see that happening anytime soon. *Why can't we just auto heal Grim, like when Brick got shot?*

—I dunno, probably for the same reason Grim's still dyslexic, Brick still has PTSD, we didn't cure Deuce's IBS, and Wrench's OCD is full in effect. Maybe we can't do anything with people's brains.—

Kat might be on to something, but... *How is Deuce's IBS a brain thing?*

—After that last stunt he pulled with Triss? Man's are obviously for shit.—

Kit bit back a groan. *That was so not funny.*

—Oh, come on, yes it was, admit it.—

Okay, sure. I mean, if you're over forty and wear black socks with your Tevas.

—You are such a bitch.—

Kit rolled her eyes. *Like you can throw stones in that department.* She chewed her lip, looking around the room at all the burly bikers. "Since I'm their queen they're gonna want to protect me, right?" she asked Mr. Asorav.

"They better," Grim growled.

"They will," the vamp agreed, "and you'll also have the considerable talents of Ms. Sue and I, along with Mr. James and his, ah, crew."

Fur sprouted along Grim's nape at Mr. Asorav's dismissive tone, and Kit ran her fingers through it, annoyed. Was the vampire being a jerk on purpose? Grim leaned into Kit's touch and sighed, obviously not happy about any of it, then buzzed his lips and turned to Deuce.

"What d'you think?"

"I don't have a problem with Hellspawn coming in, but even if the wights clean up the woods, letting the feds in is dicey. I say no, especially if we got Cantone touching down." Deuce rapped his knuckles against the bar. "Pretty sure he's got an outstanding warrant stateside, and if I'm not mistaken, you've still got one too," he said, looking at Grim.

Kit frowned. She'd forgotten about that.

"Then we allow Hellspawn in and feed the federal agents a fever dream." A smile slide across the vamp's face she didn't much like.

"A fever dream? That won't hurt them, will it?" she asked.

Mr. Asorav pursed his lips. "The dream? No, of course not. It's actually quite enjoyable."

"Until something fucks with them while they're hallucinating about their heart's delight," Grim muttered, giving the vamp an icy glare. Nope. They definitely did not like each other.

"Is that true?" Kit narrowed her eyes, and Mr. Asorav spread his hands like there was nothing could do.

"Theoretically, but I've no issue with having one of my children play nursemaid if it would make you feel better, my dear."

Theoretically. Yeah, no, it didn't make her feel better, but at least if one of the feds got hurt, they'd know who to blame, and it wouldn't be Grim. Well, okay, realistically it probably would be Grim, but at least he'd have an alibi. "It would, thank you."

"Very well, the queen has spoken," Asorav said, standing. He snapped his lapels square and buttoned his suit jacket. "If you'd be so good as to pardon Ms. Sue and myself, I believe we have business to attend to."

"How long is letting them in gonna take?" Grim asked.

Chanté shrugged. "After I make a detour to the powder room, about as long as it'll take us to walk out there."

"That won't be necessary, my dear. I've a car awaiting our pleasure," Asorav said, adjusting a cufflink.

"You hear that? Mikhail's got a car awaiting our pleasure."

A smirk plumped Chanté's lips. "Figure your boy will be here in under twenty. You good with that, boo?"

"Yeah, but my name is Grim," he growled at her. "Use it."

She cocked a hip and looked him up and down. "Oh no, way you had my girl on the back foot earlier? You are definitely a boo."

—*Don't let her hear you call him Pussycat.*— Kat snickered.

Kit bit back a laugh. Yeah, no way that would go over well. Not that this was. She raised an eyebrow at her bestie. No lie, all those Bellinis had her feelin' frisky, but baiting Grim was not the play she wanted to make if she planned on staying on his good side.

Asorav cleared his throat. "Well then. I believe now would be the appropriate time for you to introduce your betrothed to the rest of, ah, Mayhem, would it not, Mr. James? We'll leave you to it." He offered his arm to Chanté, and she slipped off her stool, standing several inches taller than the vamp in her heels.

Kit shook her head, and Chanté grinned, smoothing the sleeve of Mr. Asorav's jacket like she already owned him. He beamed up at her. "Shall we, my dear?"

"We shall, Mikhail." She smirked at Kit again as the vamp led her out on his arm.

Kit grabbed another Bellini, wishing they were stronger.

Grim watched them go with a funny look on his face. "Do you think he knows…"

"If he doesn't, he will soon," Kit broke in before Grim could finish. "I haven't seen Chanté that into a man since Robert Paco." She downed half her drink, remembering how badly that mess had turned out. Dear Lord, please let Mr. Asorav be open-minded. The likelihood of that definitely called for a stronger drink. Kit flagged down the thrall behind the bar. "Tequila, stat."

"You gonna share a glass with me this time, baby?" Grim asked, nuzzling behind her ear.

Kit laughed, taking the bottle the thrall handed her. "Who says I'm using a glass?"

"Savage. You're gonna fit in here just fine." He tipped her chin up to meet her eyes. His were bloodshot. Her brow furrowed. Man was definitely not feeling his best, and she could tell he didn't want to talk about it. "You want this?" he asked.

"Every second of every day since I met you," she purred, rubbing up against him and trying to ignore the seed of anxiety that had taken root.

"Feelings mutual, and I'm not complaining"—he grinned, running his hands over her—"but that's not what I was asking."

Kit tsk'd. "And here I thought you didn't do that."

"Ask? I don't usually, but I need to be sure this is something you're willing to give." He raised her hand to his lips and kissed her knuckles. "You want to be my wife, Kitten?"

She took a sharp breath, blinking back tears. "I want to be your everything."

He pulled her close, his chest rumbling. "Oh, baby, you already are."

—Barf.—

Shut up, don't you have a porcupine to disembowel or something?

—If only— Kat grumbled.

Whatever. Kit threw her arms around Grim's neck. "Ugh! Stop saying all the right things, you're gonna mess up my makeup." She sniffled, wiping a finger under her eye.

"That a yes?"

"A yes to what?" she teased. "Oh, you mean marrying the man I'm crazy about and doing it with the wedding of my dreams?"

Grim shrugged. "I dunno, is it?"

"Well"—Kit tapped her lip—"I'll admit there's a lot more bikers here than I'd previously envisioned."

"Yeah, and a bunch more are coming." Grim turned to face the room. "That gonna be a problem?"

She took a pull off the bottle and hissed in air through her teeth. "I'm thinking it'll be more of a clusterfuck, but...six of one, half dozen of another...and regardless, it's definitely a yes."

"Good." Grim laughed. "'Cause it's definitely gonna be a clusterfuck. Hellspawn is...different. There's a reason they stay south." He pulled her close and sighed, kissing the top of her head. "You ready to get your intro out of the way?"

"Nope."

"Awesome." He turned to face the room, holding up a hand. "Hey! Listen up assholes!" The din in the room quieted as everyone gave Grim their attention. He stepped behind Kit, his arms wrapping around her waist, positioning her in front of him. "Apparently, I'm getting married today!"

The crowd sent up a whoop, less the table of mollys in the back. A couple of them clapped politely, but most of them just glared. Well, that was gonna be fun.

—Anyone gives you shit, and we'll melt their asses.—

Weren't you the one all fixated on setting a precedent? Like, we're not the evil queen, we just steal shoes?

—Nope. They stole ours first, and our fucking panties, which means this is war.—

Kit snorted, not worried about winning despite the shade the mollys were throwing in her direction. Grim was oblivious, completely focused on her. How frickin' adorable was that?

—Oh, totally adorable.—

What is your problem? Kit snapped.

—Nothing, I just—I'm really worried I can't hear Darke, okay? I'm worried about the both of them. It doesn't feel right, Kit.—

You think there's something going on with his migraines?

—I think he needs to take his meds.—

And I don't think that's gonna happen, not voluntarily at least. And nagging him wasn't gonna work either.

—Then we roofie his ass.—

Kit chewed her lip, trying to imagine what that would look like as she refocused on what Grim was saying.

"…told you about her, but this is Kit, my queen." His fingers brushed along her throat to trace the scar from his mating bite. "I've claimed her as my ol' lady, but I'm locking' her down any way I can."

A bunch of the brothers laughed, and someone whistled shrilly. Grim winced putting. hand to his temple…

"How can she be queen if she's a half-breed?" one of the mollys called out.

"Isn't she Reaper's kid?" another chimed in.

Fuck. Nikki had certainly spread her poison, now, hadn't she?

The room went still, all eyes on Kit. Behind her, Grim's breath was ragged, his eyes squeezed shut. Kit's hand gripped Grim's, anxiety churning—

—Oh, hell no. Outta my way. I got this. Our boys cannot look weak right now.—

Kat pushed forward, and Kit fell back, letting her inner cat take control, shifting into a sleek lioness and capturing the room's attention. She dropped to all fours, stalking between the tables to the brunette that'd felt the need to speak up. The scent of the molly's fear ripened the closer Kat got. She stopped in the center of the room.

—Half-breed. You say that like it's a bad thing.— She chuffed, broadcasting her thoughts to the entire room as she paused to lick a paw and run it over her ear. Chairs squeaked back, and murmurs filled the air, the club's disbelief apparent. Kat stretched out, flicking her tail and luxuriating in it.

—Spoiler, baby. Half-breed or not, anything you can do, I can do better. Regardless of my origins, I can assure you that I am entirely

a shifter…of the royal variety. And if Grimdarke doesn't end Reaper, you better fucking believe that I will, along with anyone else that needs to be put down. — She sauntered to the molly's side and fell back, thrusting Kit forward.

Kit caught herself on the molly's chair. "But thanks for asking," she breathed in her ear, smelling piss as the club whore's bladder let go. *Shit. I fucking hate it when you do that to me,* Kit grumbled, crossing back through the stunned crowd to Grim's side.

—Get over it. At least you're dressed this time. —

You and me are gonna have words when this shit is done.

—Bring it, baby. —

He wrapped an arm around her, recovered from whatever that'd been a moment ago. "Kit is Mayhem's alpha female, and she's not just *my* queen. She's *the* queen," Grim added. "You got a problem with that?" he asked, meeting the brunette's eye.

"No." She smiled at him and then Kit. "No problem at all."

Bullshit.

If Grim'd caught how fake that was, he didn't seem to care. "Good. Quick heads up. We got Hellspawn and Navarro's pack on the guest list." He held a hand up at the murmurs. "I'll remind you and them *hospitium* applies. Anyone caught inciting violence forfeits their own life and not even your queen or prez can save your ass. Got it? Good, then we're done here," Grim said, clapping his hands together and calling for a whiskey and round of real drinks for the rest of the bar.

Kit smiled back at the molly, calling bullshit. Done? They hadn't even fucking started.

CHAPTER FOUR

GRIM TIPPED BACK his glass of whiskey. He swished around a mouthful, resisting the urge to gargle it and drown out the pervasive taste of blood at the back of his throat. Whatever that'd been down in the playroom had fucked him up and the fact that he'd just been shanghai'd into enacting *hospitium…*

—stupid—

No, it makes sense, but I still don't fucking like it.

—won't play fair—

That's a given. But it would definitely get Reaper and Shiv to come out of the woodwork, if only to piss all over the mandatory peace while they expected everyone else to keep it. Clay would've, no matter who sat down at his table during it.

Grim's breath caught.

Shit. Clay would've…but he wasn't Clay. Grim chewed his lip, thinking back to all the shit that was going on when this started, before they knew Reaper was out of prison and Clay was still alive. Those fucking spies, they were exactly what he needed.

—?—

Don't worry about it. I think I just got a handle on something.

Darke chuffed. *—lies—*

Whatever, just…don't worry about it. Grim scrubbed at his

face. Christ, plotting, politics, and getting married were not what he wanted to spend his day doing.

It wasn't that he didn't want to marry Kit—of course he wanted to marry Kit—she was his mate. But for fuck's sake, that bullshit proposal he'd just made… He'd wanted to ask her properly. He didn't even have a real ring—

—porcupine—

What? No. I'm not proposing to her with a carcass.

[EYE ROLL]

—same—

Fucking cat. *Trust me, it's not.* Grim pinched the bridge of his nose, trying to focus on what Kit was saying.

"…keeps digging himself in deeper, doesn't he?" she murmured, looking past Grim's shoulder. Her eyebrow rose and he turned his head. Down at the other end of the bar, Deuce was saying something to Triss. Grim couldn't hear what it was about, but from Triss' body language…

She hauled back and decked him. Deuce fell back covering his eye and Grim snickered. Nice.

"Oooh!" Kit's hand flew to her mouth as the petite blonde hopped off her stool and stormed over. "Damn, girl, you got him good!"

Triss huffed, her glower turning to a wide smile as she flicked one of her curlicue pigtails back. "I did, didn't I?" She beamed. "Whatever. Forget him. I have," she said too loudly in Deuce's direction. "Come on, we've got wedding things to do."

"Wedding things?"

Triss rolled her eyes. "Duh, yeah, wedding things. Hair, makeup, and the Darkling had like a hundred dresses delivered."

"He—what?"

"Yes! And I wanna look at dresses. Don't you wanna look at dresses? Tell me you wanna look at dresses!" she begged, shaking Kit by the shoulders.

"Um, okay. I wanna look at dresses?" Kit laughed.

"Yesss!" Triss fist pumped with a little jump. She grabbed Kit's bottle of tequila and her hand. "And you," she said, pointing the bottle at Grim, "you are off limits until she walks down the aisle. It's bad luck otherwise."

He snorted over the rim of his glass. "So you're cockblocking me for how long?"

Triss rolled her eyes. "Like six or seven whole hours."

"Seems excessive," he said, taking a sip and running his eyes over Kit despite the throbbing between his temples. For whatever reason, the shit seemed bearable with her around.

A sly smile tipped up her lips, and she slipped a fingertip behind the button of his jeans, tugging. Her teeth dimpled her bottom lip. "I promise I'll make the wait worth it, Pussycat. In fact, maybe you should go rest up until the main event."

Grim's eyes narrowed. The way she was batting her lashes all innocent…had Deuce said something to her? Last thing he needed—okay, one of the last things he needed on his ever-growing list of un-needed shit—was her on his ass about his pills. "Not an option, Kitten. How about I give you a teaser instead?" he asked, slipping his hand around her throat and pulling her to him.

"Ugh, gag. You guys are so gross," Triss grumbled as he kissed Kit, throwing in some extra tongue just to irritate the petite blonde. She smacked his shoulder and he moaned, groping Kit's ass. She giggled, playing along. "Ew! Seriously, Grim! Save it for the honeymoon."

"There's a honeymoon?" Kit gasped, pulling away.

"Um. No?" Triss said, totally full of shit. Grim's hackles rose, his eyes narrowing again. What the fuck was Asorav up to laying out all this cash? Triss shrugged way too brightly. "Right, so, because there *definitely isn't a honeymoon*, we should look at dresses." She looped her arm through Kit's and pulled her away. "Come on, there's like a bajillion set up in the mollys' dorm, and I'm *dying* to know which one you're gonna pick!"

Kit shot a look of alarm back over her shoulder at Grim, and he shrugged. Triss was a force of nature, and when she got going, the best way to survive was to hunker down until she and her whirlwind blew somewhere else. He took another sip of his whiskey as they disappeared, and Deuce ambled over.

"I'm guessing you saw that."

"Saw what? Triss deck you?" Grim snorted. "Dude, everyone saw that."

"Yeah. I keep trying to explain..." Deuce sighed, jamming his hands into his pockets, his face screwed up like someone had killed his dog. He frowned at a couple of mollys making their way over.

Grim did the same. He'd seen them around but didn't remember their names. The rest of them had disappeared as soon as he'd called for drinks. Probably to pack. New queens weren't typically keen on mollys they hadn't approved of hanging around, and considering how Kit felt about them in general... Yeah. Brothers weren't gonna be real happy about that, especially with the pheromones Kit was putting out. The entire room was primed for action, and it was about to get a lot harder to find an outlet.

Christ. One more fucking thing he didn't want to deal with.

Deuce sighed, looking in the direction Triss had gone off in. "She's pissed at me."

"No...ya think?" Grim asked, tipping his glass. The redhead in a bikini top and itty-bitty cutoffs sidled up to Deuce, and he absently put his arm around her. Grim frowned. Kit was right. Man did keep digging himself in deeper. The blonde wet her lips expectantly at Grim. He sighed. Seriously? After what Kit had just done? How dumb was she? "Don't."

Her brow furrowed, but she didn't come any closer.

Deuce didn't register any of it, his thumb skating back and forth over the redhead's shoulder. "Hey, I meant to tell you, I called Zhu's office this morning to sic him on the feds."

"Good. He needs to earn that retainer Clay dropped on him." The amount had been excessive, and it wasn't like the club could afford it, even if the rabid little lawyer was worth every penny. "I'd feel a hell of a lot better about Zhu clearing out the feds than Asorav putting them into a fever dream. Shit's sketchy as fuck."

"Agreed, but I dunno if Zhu's gonna happen." Deuce rubbed the back of his neck at Grim's glower. "Apparently, he's at some kind of 'religious retreat' for the foreseeable future, and his kid's taking his cases."

"Religious—what, like a cult?" Deuce shrugged, and Grim threw back the rest of what was in his glass. Goddamned, this day just kept getting better and fucking better. "Who the hell is his kid?"

"I dunno, but I got a text about an hour ago that they'd be on site shortly. Name's Shen."

"Great. No, you know what? Fan-fucking-tastic." Grim motioned to the bartender to refill his glass. "Hey, who the hell do I talk to about the reception's seating arrangements? They're gonna need to add a plate for my lawyer."

The thrall just blinked at him. Fucking edwards. Give them a task and they'd do it to the exclusion of all else, but try to deviate them from it and what little was left of their brains skipped. Grim snagged his drink from the vamp-bedazzled idiot. Whatever.

Deuce frowned as Grim downed two more aspirin and swallowed them with half of what was in his glass. "You sure you should be doing that with your head all fucked?"

"Absolutely, Mom. That's me, medicating," Grim quipped. The redhead giggled, and Deuce shot her a dirty look. So did Grim. Shouldn't she be packing with the other club whores? "Where's Stitch and Bones?"

"I haven't seen Stitch, or Doc, for that matter, which means they're probably fucking like rabbits somewhere."

Christ. If the potential of walking in on that wasn't a reason to drink, Grim didn't know what was. The two of them were even more nauseating together than they were annoying as fuck apart. Hopefully they stayed holed up somewhere until Stitch did something to piss her off again.

The molly wrapped around Deuce, whispered something in his ear, and slid a hand down the front of his jeans. He took a deep breath, throat bobbing, and stepped away from her. "Nah honey, I'm good. Why don't you go make the rounds? One of the brothers is probably in need."

She stared at him slack-jawed, and Grim had to make a concerted effort to keep his own closed. Did Deuce seriously just turn down pussy? The fuck? That shit never happened. He caught Grim's look and scowled as the mollys drifted away. "I'm not feelin' it, okay?"

"Since when?" Brick asked, coming out of nowhere with a waffle-bacon-sandwich-thing dripping syrup everywhere. "You had a threesome on the pool table fifteen minutes after your grandma got hit by that bus."

"Dude! You gotta stop telling people that story. She wasn't really my grandma."

"Since Triss decked him." Grim snorted. "And yeah, she was."

Brick nodded as he chewed. "She totally was. Any woman that old that makes you cookies qualifies. Her oatmeal raisin was legit, too," he said around another sloppy bite. "And what the fuck? I always miss the good stuff. Think Triss'll hit him again?"

"Normally I'd say yes, but seeing him turn down that molly…" Grim shrugged. Maybe there was hope for the two of them yet.

"Whoa, there, Trigger…" Brick held a hand to his ear. "Are you guys hearing odds? 'Cause I'm hearing odds." He put his weird waffle sandwich on the bar and pulled a little spiral bound notebook and a pencil nub out of his back pocket.

"You're an asshole."

"Now Deucey, I believe the term you're looking for is opportunist." He tapped the pencil against his lip. "So what's the bet…under/over, how long is it gonna take her to slug him again? Meh. Boring, and the wedding's gonna up the ante. Women always get all needy during this shit and…" He smacked his forehead. "Hot damn! Fuck the under/over, we're betting on futures." He raised his voice over the din in the bar. "Hey! How many of you assholes are in for fifty if Triss bangs a brother other than Deuce tonight?"

A swarm of hands went up, and Deuce's face flared scarlet. "You stupid son of a bitch! Now they're all gonna try to fuck her to cash in!"

Brick shrugged, collecting bills and marking bets down in his notebook. "You wanna put fifty on yourself? Miracle happens, you'll make a killing with the odds. I'm figuring those are like a bazillion to one."

"Yeah, you win, and Brick'll have to mortgage his ass to settle up." Grim smirked.

The enforcer slapped his rear. "Lucky for me it's prime real estate. All the honeys want in on this, and now that a certain tweaky blonde is on the table…" His eyes lit up and he pursed his lips, rolling his hips. "Oh, baby! Imma see what she looks like without those pigtails. Mmm…Beatriss, Beatriss, Beatriss, let down your hair…"

Deuce seethed, clenching his fists. "You are such a fucking prick."

"A prick." Brick scoffed. "Please. I'm a businessman, and have I got an opportunity for you. Who's in for another five if she gets handsy with a chick?"

Grim slapped Deuce's shoulder, pulling him back from

Brick and the press of the encroaching crowd. "You know you brought this on yourself, right?"

"I'm gonna kill him."

"Someone's gonna sooner or later." Grim shrugged. "So, where did you say Bones was?"

Deuce raked a hand through his hair, frowning in the direction Triss and Kit had disappeared in. "He's in your office."

His office.

Grim's throat bobbed, the door behind him abruptly gaining a ridiculous amount of weight.

Wasn't his office, it was Clay's office.

Goddamn it. No, it wasn't. Clay was dead. Grim jammed his hands into his pockets. Office went with the job, and he was prez. Now he needed to man the fuck up about it.

Christ, he didn't fucking want to.

Didn't have a choice.

Grim sighed, heading for *his* office. He caught himself right before he knocked and pushed into the windowless room. It wasn't wide, but it was long. The table the MC's officers met at took up two-thirds of the space, and the last of it held a massive oak desk. He stood staring at the empty leather chair, pushed back at an angle. Christ, it was like Clay had just been sitting there…

"S'up man?" Bones asked from the table, typing away on a laptop with a stack of papers in front of him.

"Ah, Hellspawn's gonna be here in a few. You got a cousin that rides with them, right?"

"Nah, I got a cousin who rides *them*. Zoe's a molly, but last I knew, she was hookin' up with one of their main crew. Some dude named Eggs."

"Eggs? Do I wanna know?"

Bones shrugged. "She said his mama called him Benedict or something stupid like that."

Made sense. "You got time to come out and meet 'em with me?"

The MC's newly elected chaplain sat back in his chair, the whites of his eyes stark within the tattooed pits around them. "You're my prez. I got time for whatever you need me to do."

"Right." Grim knocked his knuckles against the table. "What you working on?" he asked, jerking his head at the stack of papers.

"Updating the roster to account for who got nixed past few days. Rats'll get shit, but some of the brothers that stayed true had families. I'm assuming you'll wanna do right by them."

Grim nodded. Yeah. Hopefully they could when all was said and done. Last he knew, Mayhem was broke as fuck. All the cash Asorav was throwing around for this bullshit wedding wasn't gonna look good when the MC couldn't pay an ol' lady's rent or for some kid's asthma meds. Grim frowned. Wasn't the best way to kick off his tenure as prez. Asshole was making him look bad on more than one front.

"Not for nothin'," Bones said, "but while all this shit with Reaper and Shiv is goin' down, might be a good idea to bring the table's families in-house and let brothers do the same. If I were those two pricks, I'd be looking to hit us where it hurts, especially after you eighty-sixed Grapple, and you know they got no bones putting hits on women and kids."

Damn. "You've got a point." Grim scratched his jaw. Shit was gonna be tight, and it was too fucking cold to camp on the club's back lawn, but if Asorav could whip up a fucking wedding, he could probably make some trailers appear. Grim didn't like the idea of the club being indebted to the vamp, but he liked the idea of women and kids getting snuffed less.

"Yeah, do it, and we'll figure something out. So that's who for table? Mouse's mom, your *abuela* and sister…Mama Roe's not happening." And thank fucking God for that. "Rockwell's probably out there with Hellspawn waiting for the damned donut to clear. Wrench's parents are out of the country—"

"And Deuce's sorry excuse for genetic donors should picket themselves outside the gate and beg for bullets."

Grim snorted. "I wasn't gonna say it, but…" He could not disagree. "There'll be plenty of free beds for them in the mollys' dorm. Looks like we had a mass exodus on that front, and whatever stuck around is on its way out after meeting Kit."

"Might not be over. A couple of days with my *abuela* and Ivie, and I'll be begging for a way out myself." Bones sighed, standing and snagging the keys to the MC's van from Clay's —shit, Grim's—desk. "Especially if she brings her *chancla*. She will bring her dog."

"Christ. Mouse is gonna lose his shit…the fuck is a *chancla*?"

Bones slapped Grim's shoulder. "Pray you never have to find out my friend, but Miss Pickle is non-negotiable."

—?!—

[DISGUST]

Dude, it's not an actual pickle, it's just a stupid name for a dog. Chill the fuck out.

—hate pickles. hate dogs—

Yeah, I know. "Take a couple of other brothers with you and Mouse. His hungover ass needs to convince his mom to hole up here until this shit is settled. I don't get the impression she's real cooperative."

Bones snorted. "That's an understatement. I helped the *cabrito* move out of her basement. His mom's fucking scary."

And this was coming from a dude whose entire body was tattooed in negative ink to look like a skeleton. "Great," Grim muttered, leaving the room. "Just fucking great."

KIT STUMBLED AFTER TRISS, her heels clicking across the entryway's flagstones. The door to the mollys' dorm loomed ahead of them.

"Hey, wait, give me a sec...my shoe," she said, the bullshit excuse letting her wiggle out of Triss's grasp and kneel to mess with a bootie that didn't need it. Her stomach was doing all kinds of weird things at the prospect of going into the mollys' territory.

—*Umm...we're alpha female. All this is* our *territory and those whores are here at* our *sufferance.*—

Yeah, I get that, but... It was hard to wrap her head around. That part of the club had been strictly off-limits when she was a kid, and Kit still felt like something horrible was waiting for her beyond the door. Her mother had sure as hell made it seem like there was.

—*The only bad things in there are life choices and attitudes, none of which belong to you.*—

You're right. I got this. She didn't, but how was that any different from the rest of her life? Kit stopped messing with the little zipper on her instep and stood.

"You set?" Triss asked.

"Yeah, just something rubbing weird." Like her being queen, but whatever.

—*Get over it.*—

Triss frowned at Kit's shoe then glanced back toward the bar. "Sucks. The pretty ones are always problematic," she said, heading for the door again. "Come on!"

—*She talking about footwear or Deuce?*—

Pretty sure it's both, Kit murmured, following. Deuce might be an idiot, but the man was GQ in a cut and familiarity was not diminishing his curb appeal. Physically, he was sexy as hell. But his personality? That was a different story. Fortunately for Triss, it read more like a "he needs to be smacked around until he sees the light," plotline rather than an "unredeemable pussy chaser" one.

—You sure about that?—

No, but a girl can dream.

Triss rapped her knuckles on the door before pushing into the room. A wave of molly wafted out. Kit's nose wrinkled at the weird combo of competing body products and girl's locker room. *Ugh. Please tell me whatever I'm wearing is not going to smell like this.*

—Even with time to air out, no promises. Somebody's certainly got a thing for freesia.—

That was apparent, and it wasn't particularly appealing mashed up with whoever was vibing on patchouli. Yuck.

And the space itself? That was a lot more utilitarian than Kit had envisioned.

—Um, no, it's fucking depressing. What is this, the Gulag?—

It wasn't far off. Painted a dingy tan, it was one big, windowless space lit by buzzing fluorescents. Another door across the room led to what she assumed was the bathroom. A dozen bunks lined the walls, and a makeshift shelving system vomiting skank-wear had been haphazardly installed between them. That was currently being picked clean by a couple of the mollys Kit had seen at the table in the other room. The one with thick dreads sniffled loudly and shoved something lacy into a duffle.

Another pair sat on one of the lower bunks with puffy red eyes. They glared at Kit from around two long, rolling racks of dresses. It looked like a card table and chairs had been in the center of the room before their arrival. Someone had carelessly shoved it to the side, scattering puzzle pieces across a ratty throw rug that'd been bunched up with it. The rack to its left held formal dresses all in peach tones, and the one to the right had gowns in ivories, whites, and a blush.

Kit's breath caught at the dress at the end. Sweet baby Jesus. Was that a Vera Wang from this season's collection? "He cannot be serious."

"I know, right?" Triss squealed, bouncing.

"No." Kit put a hand to her churning stomach, squirming under the hate the mollys were throwing her way. "This is too much…all of it…it's too much…"

"Well, if you don't want them, we do," a familiar voice said from behind the rack of peach dresses. A slim hand lifted one from the rest. "You know how much we could get for one of these on consignment?" The brunette from earlier sashayed into view and over to a full-length mirror, holding a ruffled high-low gown against herself.

—*Oh look, slut-bag Skipper changed her pants.*—

Kit bit back a laugh. Probably not the best way to continue this conversation. Not that making the molly piss herself earlier was.

The woman glared at Kit's reflection in the mirror. "This is a security deposit and a good chunk of first month's rent."

"It'd cover way more than that." Kit snorted. She knew to the dollar how much some of those designer gowns were going for, having drooled over that exact Alexander McQueen less than a week ago. It was trending right around thirty-seven hundred, wholesale. No way was anything in Flatts that expensive.

"Maybe an apartment here, but not one in Ottawa," the curly-haired brunette on the bunk muttered.

The molly bedside her burst into tears. "I d-don't w-wanna leave my Pawpa!"

"No one wants to leave, Pepper," the curly-haired girl beside her murmured, scowling at Kit. "You're such a bitch for kicking us out! The least you can do is let us take a couple dresses."

What? Kit's jaw went slack.

—*The fuck are they talking about?*—

I-I dunno. She took a step back, looking at Triss for help.

The petite blonde sighed with a little frown, then did a double-take at Kit's expression. Her eyes went wide. "Oh. My. God. You don't know? Guys! She didn't know!"

"Bullshit," the brunette with the dress said, turning with a hand on her hip.

"No, for real, she didn't grow up with shifters. Look, when an alpha claims his queen, she gets to clean house. That's why there's hardly any mollys here now. Nikki kicked most of them out, and none of the ol' ladies stuck around."

"So you're the only ones that kissed ass to her specifications?" Kit asked, crossing her arms over her chest and eyeing the five of them. Wasn't exactly a ringing endorsement.

—Ya think? Give them those minis I see in the middle of the rack and have done. Dude's stuff never fits over your hips right anyway.—

Now there was an idea…

"Yeah, because we're the only ones without any other options," the brunette by the mirror spat, tossing a long lock of hair over her shoulder. "I'm sure you can't relate, but kissing ass is preferable to what some of us have got waiting for us out there. You think we're here because we wanna be?"

"Jessie is," the woman with the dreads muttered, still packing.

The brunette rolled her eyes. "Jessie's Jessie."

"And that's Becca," Triss stage-whispered to Kit, nodding at the bitchy brunette by the mirror. "She and Kelsey were besties."

Kit's stomach dropped. Great.

"I wouldn't say that." Becca sighed, running a hand over the dress. "But I did tell her opening her mouth was gonna get her into trouble. At the time, I was talking about her badmouthing Nikki, but her putting Grim's dick in it had the same result, now, didn't it?" She strutted back over to the rack, returning the dress and looking at another. "Whatever she got, I'm sure she had coming to her."

Kit frowned, bristling at the bitch's cavalier attitude even if she did agree with it. "I wasn't aware that speaking your mind was a capital offense, but I can guarantee messing with Grim will be."

"We'll be gone, so it won't matter." Becca slid a hanger over, snapping it to the side.

"That's on you." Kit shrugged. "As long as you keep your hands off him and the other brothers that are spoken for, I don't have an issue with you staying."

—What?!—

The five mollys and Triss stared at her, obviously wondering the same thing.

"Look," Kit said. "I came here for sanctuary, same as you. I don't even wanna think about what would've happened to me if I'd run into Nikki first instead of Grim. If she'd kicked my ass out..." Kit shook her head. "I'm not gonna put another woman in that position unless they give me reason to."

The five mollys exchanged glances ranging from disbelief to hope and outright suspicion. Triss was beaming, bouncing on her toes. "Guys! I told you! She's really super nice!"

—Yeah, too nice. I guarantee this is gonna fuck you.— Kat grumbled. *—Nothing good ever comes from letting your enemies walk.—*

Kit sighed. *They're not my enemies.*

—Maybe not, but they're sure as fuck not your friends.—

No, they weren't, and judging by the calculating expression on Becca's face, she wasn't ever going to be, but... *We're setting a precedent, right?*

—Goddamn. You just love throwing that shit back in my face, don't you?—

"So..." Becca drawled, "aside from Grim being off limits, how do you see this working?"

"First of all, like I said, it's not just Grim that's off limits. If you wanna stay, you keep your hands off any brother with a mate, claimed or otherwise, and that includes Stitch and Deuce."

Triss sucked in a sharp breath and all the eyes in the room flicked to her. "No, you don't have to—"

"The hell they don't," Kit snapped. "If they want to keep being assholes, they can go find some strange elsewhere instead of rubbing their mates' noses in it."

Becca laughed. "That's gonna go over like—"

"Like it's a direct order from your queen?" Kit snapped back.

—Oooh! Burn!—

"That's actually how it worked before Nikki got here," one of the mollys that'd been packing said. She was the oldest of the lot with sandy hair that feathered around her shoulders. "If one of the brothers wanted to stray, they had to do it somewhere else." She shrugged, dumping her bag out. "I don't got a problem going back to that. Was a better system, in my opinion."

Kit blew out a breath she didn't realize she'd been holding. "And you are?"

"Candace," the molly said, standing and bobbing her head at the woman that had been packing beside her. "This is Lisa, and Pepper and Rae are there on the bed. Jessie and Lena are still in the bar."

"How many of you were there?"

Candace shrugged. "That stayed here? Maybe five or six other regulars. Cat House was a hell of a lot cushier before the feds raided it."

"Not as safe," Lisa whispered, thumbing the strap of her bag. Her thick dreads hid her expression, but not the livid white burn marks crisscrossing over her shoulders and down her arms.

Kit's lips pinched together, her stomach churning at the memory of Grapple holding her while Reaper spat in her mouth. Abruptly aware that she'd gotten off easy. Were all of the women here running from monsters? What about the others that'd left? How many of them had gotten caught by them while Nikki was playing queen? How many of them had been fucked over like Kelsey?

—Girl, I dunno, but you know what you gotta do, and for the record, I don't fucking like it.—

I do, and the rest of it's too damned bad. "Whoever wants to come back to Mayhem is welcome as long as they follow the rules and contribute something to the club. Doesn't have to be pussy."

—That isn't gonna go over well.—

You think I give a shit right now?

—I'm just sayin'…—

"And if someone breaks the rules?" Becca asked, not looking at anyone.

Was this bitch for real? "Then you'll be wishing you had rent in Ottawa to worry about."

Becca nodded like that's what she'd expected Kit to say. "I'm only asking because Jessie's not smart enough to remember who's off limits. She won't mean anything by it, but…" She shrugged.

Triss's brow furrowed. "She really isn't."

"We'll help her," Candace said, looking at the other mollys. They gave nods of varying enthusiasm.

Great. Well, at least Kit knew who was going to be the problem. She eyed Becca. Two of them, in fact. Kit ran a hand over her face, empathizing with Grim's headache. This shit was too heavy; she needed to lighten the mood.

—Um, yeah! Girl, you're getting married!—

Kit bit back a smile, the racks of gowns making it abruptly real. Holy crap! She was! "Right, now that that's settled, why don't the rest of you pick out one of these dresses to wear so I can get married? I've only got Triss and Chanté to stand up there with me, and I'm sure Grim's gonna have to have the whole table up by him."

Becca's eyebrow just about arched off her face. "You want a bunch of club whores as your bridesmaids?"

Kit shrugged. "As far as I'm concerned, anyone who wants to put on a dress can stand up there with me." Because Mr. Asorav was right. This was about bringing the shifters together. Kit didn't need this wedding to know Grim was hers, but their sect needed it to know that she was their queen.

The voluptuous molly that'd been sobbing on the bunk wiped a hand over her eyes and laughed—Pepper? "Easy for you to say, I'm not exactly an off the rack kind of girl." She frowned, running a dimpled hand over her generous curves.

"No, and none of these are gonna look any good without tailoring." Becca sighed, flipping through them again.

"You're right." A smile tipped up Kit's lips. "So I suspect it's a damned good thing that I've got mad shifting skills."

CHAPTER FIVE

GRIM STALKED through the bar and out into the clubhouse's parking lot with Bones right behind him. The two of them stopped cold on the front stoop, trying to take it all in. Jesus fuck.

"This vamp's shit is legit outta control."

Grim frowned, hands on his hips. "Ya think?"

Three huge tents had been set up at right angles to the clubhouse, making a kind of square with a raised dance floor in the middle. Off to one side a DJ was setting up, the screech of his mic check slicing through Grim's head. For the love of… This day was not getting any fucking better.

"How many edwards does that *cabrón* have?"

Another thrall went by wheeling a full-sized helium tank. "Too fucking many."

Bones snorted his agreement, watching them bustle around, setting up tables and stringing tiny, twinkling lights like tinsel over everything. "Well, I guess we don't need to worry about the vamp suckin' on brothers considering he brought his own buffet, but I do know a couple of guys in cuts that wouldn't mind that witch on her knees."

"Do not even go there," Grim said with a hand to his head, wincing.

"Why?" Bones snorted. " 'Cause she's all dude looks like a lady?"

Grim shot him a look. "Watch it."

"Hey, I ain't throwing' shade! You remember my cousin, Miguel? They're Mariah now. Went full-blown snip snip and looks like a million bucks. Hell, I'd bang her if we weren't blood. I'm just pointing out a fact, not that I think half of the brothers care what gets their dick wet—well, maybe the old timers, but who knows. Stitch is a kinky fucker. I swear I caught him with a pair of panties once that were way too big to be Doc's."

Grim snorted. Like that was the only woman the man was tapping. "Maybe not, but he's busy with her now."

Bones's look of horror summed up that situation. "Tell me he's not railing her up the ass in the kitchen again. I haven't been able to eat pork chops since the last time."

"No, I'm not sure where they ended up."

"That might be worse."

Grim grunted his agreement. "Look, anyone disses Kit's bestie and there's gonna be hell to pay, so just do me a favor and remind brothers that Chanté's not a damned molly. Not that she can't take care of herself, but I don't need her fucking up brothers for stepping out of line."

"Can do... Jesus. How much you think all this shit costs?" Bones asked, gawking at the huge urns of fresh flowers sprawling at the corners of the tents. Smaller versions decorated the tabletops and patio heaters studded between them, raising the outdoor temp enough for Grim to start sweating.

"Too damn much." He stomped past the setup to the edge of the parking lot, scratching his stubble. Yeah. The heaters were the problem. Not Hellspawn being en route, or all of Asorav's bullshit messing with Grim's head. Christ. Was all this high class fuckery really what Kit wanted?

—no. wants a porcupine—

Dude. She doesn't.

—lies—

Jesus fucking… He wasn't having this conversation again. *Fine. After this.* Grim frowned, glancing at the bend in the drive. Judging by the rumble of bikes getting closer, Asorav and Chanté had let Hellspawn in. Hopefully there was room to park back by the garage, because there sure as hell wasn't any up here.

The first bike rounded the corner and Grim snorted. Figures Lars was so fucking pissy if him and his ol' lady had ridden up the eastern seaboard in one straight shot on a Fat Boy. The rest of Hellspawn followed, his officers pulling up behind him as he coasted to a stop in front of Grim. Christ. Looked like he'd mobilized his entire MC.

—stinks like dog—

Because he is one. A Cane Corso, if Grim was remembering right, and one mean fucking beast when he shifted. Man was roughly the same age Clay had been, his dark, tatted skin crisscrossed by tattoos and a battery of scars from the cage matches Hellspawn was known for putting on.

The sinewy woman behind him climbed off his bike and Lars spat to the side. "Well, well. Would you look at this, Rox?" he yelled over the rumble of bikes. "Little Mayhem's all grown up. 'Course I suspect you were little Vengeance back then."

Christ, this guy was a prick right out of the box. No wonder Clay'd hated him. "Lars. Roxy."

The Alpha's mate was also in her late fifties and all lean, corded muscle over bone. She eyed him up and down with a snort, a gap where one of her back teeth used to be. "I'd fucking say so. Last I saw you, you were knee high to a dragonfly, wrasslin' with them two degenerate littermates of yours for table scraps. Don't look like I can count your ribs now, but I'd sure as hell like to try."

[CRINGING]

—scary—

Yes, she is.

Her eyes flicked to Bones. "You, I don't know."

"Name's Bones, ma'am," he said extending a hand.

She eyed his tats. "You know what they say about givin' a dog one of those…"

"Mind yourself, woman," Lars growled, glaring at them as she laughed. "The fuck you got goin' on here?"

"We got a wedding planned," Grim said. "You're welcome to stay for—"

"Bathroom and then blood," Roxy interrupted, pulling off a pair of gloves. "Where can me and my girls take a piss?"

"Inside. First door on the right," Grim said.

She grunted and made a round 'em up motion over her head. A dozen plus women dismounted from behind brothers to follow her. No doubt about it, Roxy was something else, and Grim wasn't entirely sure that was a compliment.

He shook his head and turned back to Lars. "Rest of you are welcome to pull around back. We're a little cramped for space at the moment."

Lars snorted, looking over the tents. "I'm assuming this gentrified pig roast is part of what went sideways?"

"S'not even the half of it."

Asshole's lips twitched like he was trying not to laugh.

"The fuck, *mijo*, you can't even say hi?" a woman's voice called out.

Bones turned. "Oh hey, Zoe—" He grunted, catching her helmet to his gut.

"Hey yourself." She laughed, tossing a thick black braid over her shoulder and pointing at him, walking backward into the clubhouse with the other women. "You're mine later."

"Bring it!" He grinned back at her, cracking his knuckles. "Hey, Grim, if you got this, I'm gonna go take care of what we talked about earlier. Sooner they're here, the better I'll feel."

He nodded. "Good luck."

Bones jogged off, saying something in Spanish and crossing himself.

"A wedding…" Lars mused, pulling off his sunglasses. A nasty slash cut across his right eye, the whole thing milky as a poached egg. "Yours?"

Grim grunted in the affirmative.

"Well, ain't you just lockin' down the queen any way you can." Lars said it like it was a power grab or some shit, sawing at Grim's already frayed nerves.

"Wasn't my idea, but yeah. Something about the blessed event reuniting our sect. By the way, Navarro's on the guest list too."

"The wolf's comin, huh?" Lars sucked on a tooth. "Then maybe we will stick around."

"You two assholes decide to go at it, I'll put a bullet in you both. This shit falls under *hospitium*. You feel the need to settle a beef, you can do it on the other side of my gate."

Lars grinned, leaning back to look at Grim. "You got a pint more piss in ya' than your old man ever did, now, don't ya? Feel like goin' a couple rounds? Friendly like, on account of your *hospitium*."

"I'll pass. Look," Grim said, jamming his hands deeper into his pockets, "I dunno why you and Clay butted heads—"

"Not me, I was just along for the ride. Roxy was the one with a problem. I mean, don't get me wrong, I thought Clay was a piece of deadbeat shit for letting Reaper and those two little fuckwits of his beat on you after that cunt Abigail hanged herself, but…" Lars shrugged, scratching his jaw. "Whatever. Wasn't my business. Roxy didn't agree. Then, after all the shit that went down with Maria—"

"I'm sure Clay had his reasons." Goddamn, that canned line sounded pathetic. Grim pursed his lips, rocking back on his heels. Didn't know what the fuck those reasons were, but maybe after this shit show he could escape to that tree stand and figure out why Clay's will was pointing him there.

Lars snorted. "I'm sure he thought so. Asshole always figured he was the smartest man in the Goddamned room. Don't change that fact that he—"

"Nope. It doesn't, and it's done. I'd ask you not to speak ill of the dead when you're standing in the house he built," Grim interrupted, crossing his arms over his chest. The edges of his vision had started pulsing in time to the throbbing in his head again. He needed to wrap this shit up.

Asshole chuckled. "Yeah, definitely more piss. I like you, Mayhem."

"Name's Grim, and the feeling's not mutual, but like I said, you're welcome to pull around back and stay for the festivities." He nodded toward the tents. "Looks like they're starting to put out food."

Lars's grin got wider. "My boys would appreciate that, but if you don't mind, I'm more of a business before pleasure man, myself. I'd rather sort out what I came up here for first."

Grim grunted. Fine by him, then hopefully, they'd leave. "I'll have Nikki brought out to the garage for you to settle up. You can toss whatever's left to the wights in the woods."

"Yeah. About that. Shit's fucking unnatural," Lars muttered, his eyes on the group of the nasty things.

The original one hadn't moved, and more had joined it. Grim absently ran a hand over the tingle zinging up his forearm. Had to be two dozen of the raggedy, decomposing creatures standing there. A town car with dark tinted windows pulled up, blocking their view and a moment later Asorav and Chanté got out and moved to the edge of the parking lot, staring at the creatures. The vamp made some weird hand motion at them then frowned. Guess whatever he was expecting to happen, didn't. That couldn't be good.

"Having those two on your payroll ain't natural either," Lars muttered. "You wanna explain how you recruited the Darkling and a fucking witch to play for our team?"

"I'm not paying 'em, and I sure as hell didn't recruit them. They're friends of Kit's."

"Friends," the man said like Grim was full of shit.

"Friends," he confirmed, not giving a fuck.

"All right then. Can't wait to meet Her Majesty." Lars put his sunglasses back on and wheeled his bike back a few steps, then revved the engine. "Guess we'll go find that parking."

—hate that guy— Darke muttered as the prick and the rest of his MC pulled around the back of the clubhouse.

Grim raked a hand through his hair, trying to will his head to stop throbbing. *Yeah, I'm not a fan either.* He sighed, pulling out his phone and calling Brick.

"Yellow," the enforcer answered.

—idiot—

Don't start. "I need you to bring Nikki out to the garage for Lars to play with, then do me a favor and round up a crew to keep an eye on him and the rest of Hellspawn, would ya?"

[GRUMBLING]

—stupid cum-slut...—

"On it."

Grim killed the call and shoved his phone back into his pocket. *Right, let's get this shit over with.*

Darke's proverbial ears perked up, whiskers vibrating. *— porcupine?!—*

Yeah, you dumb ass. It's time to get your fucking porcupine.

KIT RAN a hand down the back of Candace's gown, the material shifting to alternately loosen or tighten over the woman's body for an exact fit. Kit bit back a pleased smile, having the hang of it now, well, when Kat cooperated.

—What? I'm cooperating. I just don't fucking care. It's not like I'm gonna be wearing one of those things, and as far as how they look on a bunch of mollys? Whatever.—

Well, they care, Kit murmured, surprised to find she did too and stupidly pleased by the women's reactions to the gowns. With the exception of Jessie, they'd all chosen fairly modest cuts and, all dressed up, the women looked like something you might find at a country club instead of an MC. Becca and Rae were doing the other mollys' hair, and Triss was killing it with the glitter-free makeovers.

"I think that's it," Kit said, straightening up and casting a critical eye over Candace. The older woman was really beautiful, and the fact that she had to be close to forty wasn't a detriment. The way she glowed in the gown she'd chosen, she was... stately or something. Before, she'd just looked tired.

Candace ran a hand down the gown's strapless apricot bust and blinked furiously at herself in the mirror. "This is... thank you."

Kit shrugged. "I didn't do anything but take it in and let it out. None of this was my doing. You'll have to thank Mr. Asorav."

"You're really friends with a vamp?" Rae asked, her flyaway curls tamed into sleek pipettes framing her long face.

—*No.*— Kat snorted.

Quiet, you. "We're not exactly friends," Kit said, drifting over to the rack of wedding gowns. She still couldn't believe he'd done all this for her. "I used to walk his dog."

Rae rolled her eyes. *Okay,* she mouthed with an exaggerated wink.

"Is that what the cool kids are callin' it now?" Pepper snorted. "Hell, I'd walk his dog, his friend's dogs—" she winced as Lisa tugged her hair into place. "Ow! Watch it, bitch, else I'm gonna tie those dreads of yours to the bunk frame."

"The hell you are. You do, and I'll cut a chunk out your ass."

"No, there really was a dog. I saw it," Triss said. "One of

those little, fluffy teacup ones." The room broke into awws. "But I'm pretty sure it's dead."

"Cecelia's not dead," Kit said at their cries of dismay. "At least, I don't think she is. The last time I saw her she looked fine, though the witch king was feeding her wasabi peas… shit cannot be good for a canine…" she murmured, then glanced up at the abrupt silence, everyone staring at her. "What?"

"You know the witch king?"

Kit's cheeks flushed. "Um, no. Not really, but he's Chanté's dad—"

"Wait," Becca said, leaning in the bathroom's doorframe and brandishing a curling iron. "You're talking about the witch that was with you earlier? The—"

"My best friend?" Kit interrupted "Yes, *her.*"

"Ah." Becca made a face and went back to Jessie's hair. "Just checking."

—Girl's gonna get checked all right,— Kat muttered.

For real. Kit went back to flicking through dresses. It was totally weird that she could alter them to be exactly what she wanted on the fly. Color, cut, fit…as long as it was close… She squeezed her thighs together with a little shiver, her options for consignment couture abruptly infinite. *See, I knew I should have picked up those YSL heels…*

—The ones a half size too small?—

Yeah.

[SHRUGGING]

—Well, next time you'll know.—

Kit frowned, her eyes going back to that blush gown. Strapless, nude fitted bodice flowing into a profusion of gossamer ruffles and then falling in soft waves of tulle silk to the floor and trailing behind. It was ethereal, like it belonged in a fairytale, not in Flatts, NY. She rubbed a bit of the material between her thumb and forefinger, loving the way it slid. *So frickin' gorgeous…*

—Girl, agreed, but we both know your boobs ain't gonna even play at staying in that and you're too damned short to do it justice. Altering it will fuck it up, and unless you plan on walking down the aisle as a six-foot, pin-thin model wannabe, that dress is gonna wear you.—

And turn me into a squat little troll playing peek-a-boob. No, I get it. Kit sighed, flicking past it to the next. Kat wasn't—

Hello. Her breath caught.

—That's the one.—

Oh, yes. Yes, it was. Kit ran her fingers over the intricate—

Behind her, the door banged open. "Holy—the fuck is going on in here?" A woman snorted.

Kit sighed. What now?

"I thought this was supposed to be the Goddamned shitter, not Barbie's Dream Salon." An older, whip-thin woman sucked in a gasping breath and fell back, her eyes wide as Kit turned. "Maria?"

Being called her mother's name was a gut punch, and there was something about her… "No. Kit. Maria was my mother." *Is her mother.* Whatever, didn't matter whether she was still breathing or not, she was gone.

The woman steadied herself and ran a tatted hand over her face. " 'Course you are. Right. Ah…bathroom?"

"And you are?" God, what was with these people? Had exchanging names fallen by the wayside, or were they just so full of themselves they figured everyone knew who they were and they didn't need to?

"Roxanne Underclaw. Lars' ol' lady." She didn't make a move to come closer and looked nervous for some reason. Behind her was another group of women murmuring amongst themselves. They glanced at Kit askance like she was some kind of freak. What the hell was that about?

—I dunno, but the way they're looking at us, the next time that door opens, we should charge admission.—

For real. And their ogling wasn't doing a damned thing for

Kit's anxiety. "Through there," she said, jerking a thumb over her shoulder at the bathroom.

Roxanne nodded, then paused like she was going to say something before rushing past Kit. A dozen plus tatted-up biker chicks followed, looking just as nervous as their leader had.

"You have any idea what that just was?" Kit asked as soon as Becca squeezed past the last of them, exiting the bathroom in their wake. She didn't quite slam the door behind her, holding onto the handle behind her back with pure shock etched over her face.

"Um, weird?" Triss said, oddly subdued, chewing on the side of her thumb. "I thought Hellspawn's supposed to be like this super badass MC..."

"They are, and Roxy Underclaw?" Lisa shook her hand out like she'd touched something hot. "She's a legend in their cage matches. You watch her bouts, the woman does not get ruffled."

"She did right then. Looked like she'd seen a ghost," Pepper said, batting Lisa's hands away from her head. "What did she call you? Maria? You said that's your mom? Did she know her?"

Kit shrugged, something about the woman's name niggling at her... She shook it away. Probably just sitting through *Chicago* too many times with Chanté. Kit took the gown's hanger from the rack and draped it over her arm. "I dunno. Reaper shot my mom in the head when I was eight and she's been a vegetable since. Think I'm gonna go take a shower. Come get me when they're ready to start, okay?" The mollys turned to glare at Pepper and she held out her hands like, "What?"

"Kit, Pepper didn't mean—" Triss brows drew together at whatever she saw on Kit's face, and she sighed, nodding. "Yeah, okay. You sure you don't need me to—"

"No. I'm fine. Thanks."

—No, you are totally full of shit,— Kat muttered as Kit fled the dorm and headed up the steps.

Whatever. I just—you know, today's the one fucking day where I just really wish she was here, okay? Kit sniffled, wiping an eye.

—I got you. I mean, I don't, but I do. I guess I wish I'd gotten a chance to know her like you did.—

Jesus…you didn't, did you? She closed her eyes feeling like an absolute bitch. *She was your mother too, and you never got a chance to meet her.*

[SHRUGGING]

—I mean, no, I didn't, but she wasn't, not really. Genetics wise, yeah, but it's not like she could shift. Claymore was the closest—It doesn't matter. It is what it is.—

What it was, was shitty. *I really am sorry.*

—Why? It's not like I know what I'm missing. You do, which I think is worse.—

Kit didn't know about that but—her hand froze above the keypad on Grim's door. She pressed her forehead to the wood. Damn it. She'd forgotten about that stupid thing.

—So? Shift it open—

Kit laughed. *Right? Duh…* The deadbolt clicked back, and she was in. *Guess breaking and entering is now something we do.*

—Girl, if I had hands I'd be rubbing them together. Can you say level-up?— Kat chuffed. *—I'd like to see Auntie Jojo keep us in a closet now.—*

Mmm. Kit frowned, opening the door. She'd prefer to never see her Auntie Jojo again. Damn. She waved a hand in front of her nose. The room reeked like sex.

—Better than freesia and patchouli.—

But is it really? Kit hung the gown on the back of the bathroom door before opening the window. It was cold but felt good after the cloying stuffiness of the mollys' dorm. Outside, the tents had become even more decadent. Fine china chargers studded the tables, profusions of flowers, strings of lights… A bower had been set up at the far end of the dance floor with a dove-gray carpet leading to it and rows of chairs on either —

She squinted. Was that a decapitated head on a pike off to one side?

—*Sure looks like it to me.*—

Kat, I can't even. But apparently the string quartet warming up beside it could, their notes lost beneath the rumble of motorcycles pulling around the back of the clubhouse.

Grim stepped from behind one of the tents, a hand at his temple. Yep. She definitely could relate.

"Hey there, handsome!" Kit called down, leaning out the window.

He looked up and grinned. "Careful, I thought I was supposed to be bad luck. Triss'll kick your ass if she thinks you're tempting fate."

"What else have I got to do?" Kit put a hand to her forehead, batting her eyes. "I mean, aside from showering. It's too bad you can't join me..." She raised a hand to unclasp the back of her halter, the other arm across her breasts, catching the material as it fell.

Grim's eyes darted around the yard, a hand running down the front of his pants. "Are you seriously gonna tease me right now, Kitten?"

"Tease you? No...I'm just..." She shook her head, teeth pinning her lip and pulled her arm away, arching her bare breasts as she stretched. "Whoops..."

"Oh, it's gonna be whoops all right." He ran toward her and leaped as he neared the building. She fell back with a little scream, laughing as his hands slapped over the sill and he pulled himself inside the second-story window.

"What? How the heck did you do that?" She laughed again, backing against the wall. "Oh my God, Grim, you can't be in here—No! Don't look in the bathroom!" He turned his head, and she jumped at him, slapping a hand over his eyes.

"There better not be a dude in there—"

"No!" She laughed. "You can't see my dress!"

"Trust me, I did not come up here to see you dressed." He caged her in, breathing heavy, one palm against her throat, the other cupping her breast. "And as a matter of fact, I'm thinking you need to be more undressed," he murmured, pinching her nipple taut as his mouth claimed hers, swallowing her groan.

Kit melted against him, her hands cupping his jaw, fingers sliding to bury themselves in his hair. His tongue traced hers, sucking it into his mouth with a low rumble. "Christ, I missed you."

"It hasn't even been an hour, and you have people here."

"That's too fucking long, and I don't give a shit. I told you I wasn't done with you. Hands behind your head, baby." His lips trailed down her throat, burned hot against her breast. He dropped to his knees, suckling, the zipper at the back of her skirt sliding down, his teeth moving to graze her hip bone. "You're so Goddamned sexy..." Her skirt dropped and his eyes flew up to meet hers. "You went downstairs without panties?"

She wet her lips, standing there before him, fingers laced behind her head, in just her high-heeled booties, totally bare. "I shaved for you."

"I can see that." His irises darkened to slate, pupils blowing out. "Turn around and face the wall, Kitten."

"What are you going to do?" the question husked from her lips.

He smiled at her, and her thighs grew slick. "Face forward, palms flat. Good girl..." he said after she'd obeyed, running a hand over her ass. "Slide them down the wall until your back is flat." Grim stepped behind her, hand at his belt, and toed her feet apart. "Mmm...so pretty."

Kit swallowed, her eyes on the floor, anticipation clenching her core. His hand skated over her cheeks, and her lids fluttered shut with a small moan. They flew open at whisk of leather through denim and the crack of his belt against his thigh, her breath coming fast.

"And such a fucking brat. You think it's fun to tease me?"

—Hell yeah we do.—

Oh my God, Shut up! Kit pressed her lips together and shook her head. The belt snapped against her backside, and she cried out.

—See what you get for lying?—

Don't you have something else to do?

[FRUSTRATION]

Kat chuffed. *—Normally I'd be diddling myself to all this, listening to Darke talk dirty, but since I can't hear him, you got my undivided attention.—*

Grim rubbed at the stinging welt striping her ass. "Use your words, Kitten."

She bit back a moan. "No, sir."

"Mmm. I don't think you're telling the truth." The belt landed another line of fire across her opposite cheek and her knees buckled. "Are you lying to me, Kitten?" His lips brushed her ear. "Choose your words very carefully. I'd hate for you to have to walk down the aisle a wet, aching mess because you weren't allowed to come." His fingers slid over her sodden folds, and she rocked toward them.

Kat chuffed. *—Now he's a damned liar, too.—*

His touch stayed just out of reach, brushing with no real contact. Kit moaned, a sob slipping past her lips.

"How long do you think I can edge you? How close can I get you?" he murmured. "How bad do you think I can make it hurt, Kit? Tell me the truth and then beg me fill up that aching pussy."

"Yes," she burst out panting. "Oh, my God, yes, I love teasing you. It gets me so hot when you're rock-hard, and you can't do anything about it."

His fingers went away, and the belt licked over her clit. She screamed at its wet slap, then moaned, a tremor going through her. Grim fisted her hair, pulling her head back. "Naughty. I didn't say you could come. Open." He jammed the leather between her teeth. "Your palms don't leave the wall, and that belt stays in your mouth, understood?"

She nodded, and he knelt behind her. His palms skated over her sensitized cheeks, the prickle of his beard delicious torture around the wet heat of his mouth. He kissed over the globes of her ass, his tongue flicking out over her rosebud, face dropping to bury his nose in her folds. He inhaled with a growl.

"I love smelling myself in you," he murmured, tongue sweeping the length of her slit. "Mmm. Tasting my cum mixed with yours when I eat your pussy." His lips closed around her clit. Kit cried out, tipping her hips back, legs splaying farther apart. Her eyes rolled back, breath fast, the musky tang of leather and her own desire heavy against her tongue.

Wet, oh God, she was so damned wet…so ready for him… she whimpered.

He chuckled, his hands cupping the backs of her thighs. "That's it, baby, rain for me. Show me what I do to you," he rumbled, his thumbs separating her folds, the warmth of his breath clenching her core, honey dripping. Grim lapped at it. Slow. Like he had all the time in the world. "So bare and so fucking pretty. You have any idea how much I love teasing your little pink hole?" He rimmed around it, thumbs spreading her wide and tongue dipping in. Kit mewled, squirming for more. "Watching it stretch to take me…" He added a finger and she writhed.

"Please, Grim—" she moaned around the belt.

He took his fingers away. "What's the matter? Don't you like it when I tease you? When you're all sloppy and dripping and can't do a thing about it?" he asked, kissing her pussy. "That's funny, 'cause I fucking love it. It gets me so hot."

— *Damn, he's a bastard.* —

"I'm sorry!" she choked out around the belt. "I won't do it again!"

"Mmm. You will. And when you do, I'm gonna sit just like this, watching your cunt drip for me, hungry for something to fill it up." He blew over her fevered flesh, his fingers returning to stretch her wide, scissoring. Kit cried out, her knees buckling. "You want that, baby? Or do you want me to fuck you full of my cum?"

"Please, oh please…" she sobbed, so damned close…

Grim stood, unzipping his jeans. "Then get on your knees. That lipstick's going around my dick first." He took the belt from her mouth and encircled her throat with it, jerking it snug and tipping up her chin. He traced her lips with his thumb, pushing in. "Suck."

He fisted his cock, pumping it, his gaze not leaving her mouth. Kit's eyes rolled back as she abandoned any pretense of control.

"Good girl." He popped his thumb from her mouth, the head of his cock at her lips. "Lick the tip. Taste what you do to me." Kit flattened her tongue and swept it along his slit, lapping. She moaned at the salty musk of his pre-cum, leaning forward to take his swollen crown into her mouth.

"Greedy girl." He tugged at the belt around her neck and her spine went rigid. "You look at me when you have my dick in your mouth, understand?"

She nodded, and he thrust deeper, one hand pressing to the wall behind her and his stance widening. Her nostrils flared as he hit the back of her throat, and she fought not to gag.

"Relax and open up for me, beautiful. That's it. I know you can take more, and you look so fucking pretty swallowing my cock."

Kit moaned at his praise. He pushed into her throat, his breath speeding as her nose hit his abs. "There's my dirty girl. Show me how bad you want to make me feel good." He withdrew, then slid back in, pistoning, his eyes locked on hers, a muscle in his jaw popping as he fucked her face, his breath growing ragged.

Kit squirmed, her core throbbing. She dropped a hand from his thigh, and he drove himself deeper. "Did I give you permission to touch yourself?"

She sobbed around him. *Oh God, please...*she rolled her hips, her pussy aching.

He grinned at the pleading look she sent him, tears tracking down her cheeks, ropes of saliva spattering across her chest. Grim dusted his knuckles down the side of her face. "Goddamn, you're so fucking gorgeous. You need something, baby?"

She bobbed her head, whimpering.

"Huh." Grim cinched the belt around her throat tighter. "Too bad brats don't get fucked. They get punished." He slowly pumped his cock between her lips, brows furrowing on the retreat. "You still wanna be a brat?"

Kit shook her head, sniffling.

"Christ, it feels so good when you cry around my dick." He rocked his hips, long and slow, abs rippling as he worked his cock in and out of her throat, then pulled out. He stroked his hand over his wet length. "Stand up and put your hands back on the wall."

The head of his cock brushed through her folds. "Please, oh please..." Kit whimpered, tilting her ass to take him.

"Is this what you want, Kitten? My rock-hard cock in your wet little cunt?"

"Yes!" she rasped out.

He speared into her without warning, pulling her hips against his with a groan. "Then take it...fuck, you're so fucking hot and tight...so Goddamned wet..." he growled, punishing her pussy. Kit cried out, her tits slapping together as he railed her hard against the wall. "I need to ruin you, Kit.

Make you all fucking filthy," he breathed, lips brushing her ear as his body covered hers. "All fucking mine."

His teeth fastened onto her nape and Kit moaned as he bit down, canines piercing her flesh. He lapped over the rapidly healing wounds. Her eyes fluttered, giving up control, letting him use her body, lost to the rhythm of his cock battering her, pleasure coursing, legs shaking, small muscles tightening.

"Mmm. So damned sweet. Good girl," he murmured, his fingers dropping to strum her clit. Her walls trembled, tightening around him. "All of it belongs to me. Let me feel it, Kitten. Come on my cock. Get me all fucking wet."

Kit's breath hitched and she cried out, the pressure building in her core coalescing and exploding outward in bursts of staggered ecstasy. Her pussy pulsed around him, and he groaned, cock swelling, his thrusts more urgent. His fingers tightened on her hip, and he bellowed, his weight falling forward, pinning her against the wall as he plunged deep, groaning.

The distant rumble of motorcycles approaching sounded in the distance, and Grim swore. He nipped at her nape again, taking his belt from her throat. "You're keeping it in you," he murmured, picking her up and carrying her to her bed.

Kit blinked at him sleepily. "What?"

"My cum. It stays in you." he said, laying her down on the bed, her legs over the side. He knelt between them, his fingers spreading her open.

Kit slid a hand down her belly, and he glanced up at her, the intensity of his quicksilver eyes through messy bangs stopping her cold.

He licked a trace of her blood from his lips, his gaze dropping to watch his fingers slide in and out of her. "I like you bare. Your pussy's so fucking pretty. So pink and soft for me. Wet."

"Grim." She glanced toward the open window as the motorcycles grew closer. "People are coming."

Outside, someone sounded an airhorn, and he winced. "I don't give fuck." His eyes locked on hers as he lowered his mouth to kiss her clit. "You gonna be a good girl for me and come again, Kitten?" He slid his fingers through her folds to push the hood of her clit back. His tongue flicked over her exposed nub, and she gasped, her breath coming fast.

Someone hit that airhorn again, and Grim growled.

"I don't know, you gonna take your pills?" she asked.

He frowned and slapped her pussy. "How about you don't worry about that."

"Hey! But Kat says—" Kit's eyes rolled up into her head, her protests cut off by Grim's swirling tongue and the suction of his mouth. Her passion crested from zero to sixty. "Oh God, yes, I'm gonna come again…"

Her walls spasmed, thighs clamping over his ears, back arching as she cried out.

"Mmm. That's it, baby," Grim rumbled, nuzzling at her through the aftershocks. He tucked her legs up into bed and pulled the comforter over her, then kissed her gently. "I want you to stay just like that, understand?"

Kit sighed, but was too blissed-out to argue as he stood, zipping his pants and retrieving his belt. "Where are you going?"

"Pretty sure Hellspawn's working over Nikki, and it sounds like Navarro just got here." Grim smacked the top of his dresser and the side opened up. Well, Kit guessed that was one way to get to those two bottom drawers. He pulled out a box of ammo and reloaded the magazine. "Him and Lars do not get along, and Cantone'll be here any minute. I gotta play chaperone before this shindig kicks off."

Kit sighed. "And your meds? Kat's worried. She says it's like there's a wall around you, and she can't hear Darke."

"He's fine. A pain in the ass, but fine." Grim frowned again, rubbing a temple. "And trust me, right about now I wish I could medicate, but if I take one of those, I'll be flat on my back snoring in under twenty minutes. I can't afford to be down for the count. I will after this."

"You promise?"

"Yeah, baby, I promise. Hang out here for a few, okay?"

She nodded, and he kissed her again on his way to the window. "Open or closed?"

"Open. The fresh air feels good," she murmured, her lids heavy.

"Then open it is. Sweet dreams, Kitten." His lips brushed against her temple, and she was already asleep as the door closed behind him.

CHAPTER SIX

GRIM WADED through the crowded bar, the clubhouse absolutely packed with brothers. Looked like the rest of Mayhem had shown up, and they didn't seem to have a problem partying with Hellspawn or Navarro's pack. The girly little tables were gone, and somebody had dragged back the couches and the pool table, the clacking of balls barely audible over the crowd and some bullshit country twang blaring through the room.

Despite the shitty music, brothers looked like they were enjoying themselves. Grim was positive that the infusion of mollys had something to do with that. Hellspawn had brought up more than a few and, if that chick Juliette was anything to go by, the wolves had too. But the majority of them he recognized as regulars of Mayhem. They sat on brothers' laps and hung off their arms, all of them wearing fancy pinky-orange dresses with their hair done up like it was the prom or some shit.

—Kit's stuff—

Yeah? Can't imagine that's gonna go over well. Grim scratched his jaw, not about to enter the fray. *You'd think her kicking Nikki's ass would've given them a heads up. Damn.* As alpha female, Kit was gonna have to sort out the women in the club. If a bunch of mollys had invaded instead of leaving when she told them to—*You know what? Not my problem.* He had enough of his own, and she was more than capable of laying down the law.

And speaking of which, his ears perked up at a woman's familiar voice tearing somebody a new one over the blaring stereo's twang. Nice. Hanna was back, which meant Miser was somewhere around here, too. The club's treasurer was gonna shit a brick when he saw all the cash the vamp was laying out for this shindig. Grim snickered, pushing through the last of the crowd behind the bar, and went into the kitchen.

Hanna was with a handful of Mayhem's ol' ladies, cornering an edward. They circled him, brandished cutlery, while Hanna got in the thrall's face.

"I don't care what your 'Master' told you to do. Figure out how to do it somewhere other than my kitchen!" She scowled, cracking him over the head with a massive wooden ladle.

"Hey!" Grim called out, grinning. "Go easy on him. Dude's just trying to do his job."

"Grimdarke James!" she said, her gray, chin-length hair flaring out as she spun around, sweeping her eyes over him. "You wanna explain to me what hell is going on around here?"

"Hell?" He jammed his hands into his pockets. "I dunno. Pretty sure it's frozen over."

"Was that a joke? Since when do you have a sense of humor?" She shook her head like she was concerned. "But you can say that again. I'm expecting a pig to fly past the window at any moment. I swear I just saw Lars Underclaw and Craig Navarro shaking hands, Bones says Doc and Stitch are holed up some place fuckin', and what's this I hear about you getting married? To Reaper's girl? Since when?"

Grim shrugged. "Since I claimed her as my mate and the Darkling's paying for it?"

"Oh, well, that just makes everything else all the more plausible," one of the ol' ladies muttered.

Another snorted. "Yeah. About as plausible as this new queen of his inviting all of Mayhem's mollys back and reinstating the old rules. I can't figure out if she's a genius or a complete idiot not vetting them first. There's more than one that's gonna give her trouble."

"If Reaper's really her daddy, she's probably as batshit as he is," a third chimed in.

Grim's eyebrows shot up. Well, the molly thing was a surprise, but regardless of them giving Kit trouble, it was gonna make his life a hell of a lot easier. "Kit's not batshit, and I hadn't heard about the mollys, but I haven't talked to her recently, either. Triss says I'm supposed to be off limits until after the ceremony."

"Mmm hmm." Hanna sniffed, frowning. "Funny, don't seem like that's stopped you from fucking the shit out of her upstairs just now. You know the whole damned bar can hear you, right?"

"Not to mention he smells like he bathed in pussy," another ol' lady muttered.

He shrugged again, a stupid smile on his face.

Hanna's brow cocked. She crossed her arms, that wicked ladle bobbing against her shoulder. "Huh. I didn't know those lips of yours could twist into a shit-eating grin, but it's nice to see something other than a glower on 'em. Now tell me you didn't fuck her on my bar while I was gone."

"Nope. God's honest." He made a show of crossing himself. Not yet at least, but it was definitely on the bucket list.

Hanna narrowed her eyes like she knew it.

He grinned again and rubbed the back of his neck. "Right. So, is everyone back who's coming back?"

She looked at him a moment longer and then shook her head. "Mostly. Don't know about some of the brothers that went nomad, and a few others with families are keeping their tails tucked until they see Reaper's cold, dead body nailed to the clubhouse wall. Riding back through Flatts...he's definitely holed up somewhere close. Man poisons the damned air around him, and I swear I can feel him and that other brother of yours out there, seething." She waggled the ladle at Grim. "Ain't nothing good's gonna come of them being allowed to fester."

He grunted. "Agreed, but putting them down's not happening tonight. I enacted *hospitium* and anyone who comes through the gate is welcome."

They looked at him like he'd lost his mind.

—facts—

"You serious?" Hanna asked, raising her hand to press against his forehead.

He flicked it away. "Yeah. This wedding doesn't need to be ruined with shifter politics. Like it or not, Reaper is Kit's dad. He wants to walk her down the aisle, I'll be the first to shake his hand." At which point, he planned on shifting the motherfucker into that gray place and putting a bullet in him, but they didn't need to know that.

—won't work—

It's gonna work. And given the number of ol' ladies that'd just heard that proclamation, news of Reaper's supposed safety would be all over the compound and beyond before Grim stepped out of the kitchen.

Trap was set; now he just had to wait for the man to show up and spring it.

Darke sent Grim an image of his foot stuck in a bear trap. Him falling into a stake-lined pit. A rock on a rope, swinging to crush his head—

Okay, asshole, I get it. You're not a fan.

—idiot—

The long look Hanna was giving him said she was of the same opinion. Whelp, time would tell on that front. *It's gonna work.*

[SERIOUS DOUBT]

"It true you killed Grapple?" one of the other ol' ladies asked, breaking the terse silence in the kitchen.

—NO—

Grim snorted. "Darke did."

Hanna shook her head, the lot of them exchanging glances the way they always did when his cat came up in conversation. They edged away from him as a unit.

—know I'm a God—

No, they don't fucking trust you.

Hanna's eyes flicking over his shoulder to watch Roxy saunter into the kitchen. The corners of her mouth tightened. "Good. That monster needed to be put down. Now if you'll excuse us, we need to put this kitchen back to rights. Fucking edwards screwed everything up. Who the hell stacks dishes with the pots and pans and cutlery in the glasses?" The other ol' ladies murmured their agreement, drifting off to see it done.

Grim slipped out the back door, feeling oddly better than he had in a while. About the club, about the whole stupid wedding idea. Like he had a modicum of control over shit again. He had a plan to get rid of Reaper. Hanna was back to running a tight ship, Kit sounded like she had a handle on the mollys, and *hospitium* seemed like it was working. Maybe Chanté and the vamp had the right of it, and this was what the shifter sect needed. Not that he was gonna fucking tell them that, but still. If there was a win somewhere in there, he sure as fuck was going to take it.

The normally barren stretch between the clubhouse and the garage was packed tight with delivery trucks and motorcycles. Grim squeezed through them to the one clear cut path between the two buildings, toward the sounds of a rabid crowd behind the garage.

Christ. What the—

He sighed, shaking his head at the clubhouse's back forty. The wide-open space was roughly the size of a football field.

Fire pits and a couple little outbuildings dotted one side, and a makeshift shooting range was on the other.

Or there had been.

Now it was a freshly shorn lawn sprinkled with fucking guest yurts. Whelp, he supposed that filled the need for more housing while Reaper was still breathing, but if they'd trashed the club's smoker, he was gonna be pissed.

Grim scratched his head, hoping Cantone's helicopter still had room to touch down. There definitely wouldn't be if the assembled crowd was still playing with Nikki.

Despite the swanky temporary housing, the entire affair had a definite keg party vibe. Brothers and mollys clumped together in small groups around a ring of members from Lars's MC. In the center of it, it looked like a bunch of the women that'd ridden up with him were taking turns kicking the shit out of what was left of Nikki's ass. More than one of Mayhem's ol' ladies cheered them on from the sidelines. Grim frowned, scanning the crowd for Doc. Way she'd hated Nikki, you'd think she'd make it a point to get off Stitch's dick long enough to throw a punch or two.

Grim eyed the brothers standing around, watching the action with their phones out. Well, he guessed she could always catch the video. Hopefully no one would be stupid enough to post it.

Christ, he might as well wish in one hand and shit in the other and see which one filled up first. Zhu's kid was definitely going to earn that retain—

What the—Grim shook his head, doing a double take. Jesus fuck. Hanna hadn't been hallucinating. Lars and Navarro were off to one side, lazing back in lawn chairs, bullshitting like they were old friends. Grim headed over, not believing it. The last time they'd been in a room together, Navarro had been the one to fuck up Lars' eye.

"Don't you two look cozy," Grim said, taking a red plastic keg cup from a passing edward's tray. Because thralls serving beer off silver platters was apparently a thing. That he could get used to.

"Maybe, but I rather have a slice of whatever you been havin'." Lars sniffed. "Smells like prime pussy."

Grim took a long swallow of beer, glaring at the grinning asshole.

[GROWLING]

—hate that guy—

Yeah, me too.

Navarro glanced between them, not quite rolling his eyes. "Mayhem." The alpha wolf tipped his cup at Grim. "Invite wasn't one I could refuse, especially not after our last conversation. I've been telling Lars about Kraelle. He made his move last night. Half his crew hit the safe house you'd been in, and the rest went after private residences. Fucker halved my pack, and I ain't just talking about the men."

Jesus. Grim pulled over another lawn chair. "He went after women and kids?"

[GROWLING]

Navarro grunted, his face hard. "What's left of them are here. The ones we could find, at any rate. I hope to hell more went to ground, but while we sort that out, I figured you wouldn't mind returning the favor by keeping an eye on mine considering we put up yours."

"Yeah, of course." Grim waved a hand at the yurts, pissed as hell. *You didn't go after females and kids.* "Grab whatever you need for as long as you need to."

"Appreciate that."

—good. all shifters ours—

What?

—Kit-Kat's queen. makes us king. all shifters ours—

Grim snorted. *And here I thought you were already a God.*

[CHUFFING]

—am. God king—

Whatever you say, buddy. Grim rubbed his temple. How the

fuck could someone eighty-six kids? Well, unless you were a totally psychopathic piece of shit like Reaper. Grim pulled his phone, checking the time. It was almost two. If Bones wasn't back soon, he needed to put Brick on it.

Lars let out a loud burp and slapped the alpha wolf's shoulder. "If Mayhem's got your pack square, I ain't got a problem extending this little revenge-cation to help you take out more trash." He cracked his knuckles. "Shifters trucking with witches is un-fucking-natural enough, but if Kraelle's using their bullshit magic to win his challenges and fucking with natural selection—"

"He is," Chanté said, sauntering up beside them with a plate of appetizers. Grim offered her his seat, and she got a funny little smile on her face as she took it. "Oh, I like you." She settled in, selecting a pastry from her plate and popping it into her mouth. "Mmm. Shrimp," she murmured like someone had asked, then, "Kraelle's also currently at the gate with a large contingent of your sect. Since his attempt to roll right in didn't go so hot, he's taken the opportunity to issue all three of you a challenge via the nightly news crews camped out there."

"How large of a contingent?" Grim asked.

Chanté shrugged. "Couple hundred?"

"And he wants to fight us all at once?" Lars snorted sounding impressed. "Man's got some fucking balls on him."

"You would too with a bunch of witches backing you up," Grim muttered.

"The fuck are you talking about? Lars' stones are knocking between his knees as is. Motherfucker wouldn't be able to walk if they got any bigger," Navarro scoffed. "And I guarantee you he's gonna take the maniac up on it."

Lars nodded, grabbing another beer. "I do love a good tag team."

"I believe Mr. Navarro was his top pick to start," Chanté broke in. "But I can't say as he sounded real choosy."

Grim laughed, his headache creeping back. He dumped a couple more aspirin into his palm. Of course, Kraelle hadn't. Sounded like he wanted to be at the top of all the packs, prides, and any other flavor shifters came in. Good fucking luck admin-ing that. Whatever, what was a wedding without at least one good brawl?

Grim shook his head and crunched on the bitter little pills, washing them down with a long swallow of beer. "Yeah. Sounds great. Might as well let them in with everybody else. We're already over capacity; what's a couple hundred more?"

"Don't tell the fire marshal." Lars snickered into his beer.

"They don't all need to come in," Chanté said, fiddling with a strawberry. "But I was going to allow him to crash the party with a dozen or so friends. Otherwise, I'm pretty positive the triad of Bléda doing a shit-ass job of hiding out in his ranks will make it a moot point. And not for nothing, but if I had to read a room, I'd say the majority of Kraelle's posse does not want to be there. Once he's inside, who knows what'll happen in their ranks?"

"I can attest to that," Navarro said. "From what we got out of one of them last night, he's holding hostages from every pack he's taken somewhere out by Heart Lake. They've got no choice but to follow him while he's got their people, but as soon as someone cuts the head off that snake, the rest will fold."

Lars let out a loud burp. "Putting this prick down just keeps sounding better and better."

Grim frowned. They weren't gonna want to hear it but… "Feel free to go out and meet him, but he passes through the gate, *hospitium* applies."

"Are you fucking serious?" Navarro growled. "I just told you the asshole massacred women and kids!"

"Yeah. And before you get your panties totally in a twist, that means that until this wedding is over, I can't shank

Reaper or Shiv, either. If Kit's gonna be queen, we're going back to the old way of doing things."

"Oh, you mean when we had honor?" Navarro asked dryly. He scowled, but seemed mollified by the explanation.

Lars spat, shaking his head. "Whose bright fucking idea was that?"

"Asorav's, but he's not wrong. Speaking of which, where the hell is he?" Grim asked Chanté.

"Tending to the wights. He says they're not behaving properly." She gestured vaguely over her shoulder, plucking a phyllo dough triangle off her plate to inspect before nibbling on it.

Grim's gaze went in the general direction of her wave. Another group of the nasty things were clustered at the edge of the woods, staring at them. He rubbed his forearm. Jesus fuck, what the hell was that about? "They gonna be a problem?"

She shrugged, abandoning the triangle for another shrimp puff. "I'm not too worried about it while it's still light, but once it gets dark, Mikhail's will is the only thing keeping them confined to the woods. If he can't continue to exert his control, we'll have to banish them once the sun sets. Fingers crossed that doesn't happen, seeing how not a damned thing is getting through that donut and that's the way we want it." She trapped Grim's eyes with hers. "You feel me?"

"Funny, I can't help but notice nothing's getting out, either," Navarro said, waving down an edward for another beer. He passed one to Grim and another to Lars.

Chanté paused, pursing her lips around a smile. "Glad someone's paying attention. Oh, and before I forget, there's also a very vocal Asian woman at your gate threatening to file an injunction against the media outlets covering 'today's big story.'" She finger-quoted. "She says she's your lawyer."

Grim groaned. No, that had to be his lawyer's kid. Christ,

he had enough problems without paying to keep one on retainer. "Haul her ass in here before she—" His stomach dropped. "Where did the feds end up?"

"We had them loaded into one of the delivery vans and brought inside." Chanté waved that same vague hand back toward the clubhouse. "Somewhere that way."

Grim pinched the bridge of his nose, definitely not imagining his headache intensifying. "You said there were Bléda in Kraelle's pack. Do we need to worry about them? Do you?"

"Aww." Chanté pouted at him. "You are so sweet. Nah, Boo. I can take care of them and myself."

Grim gritted his teeth, trying not to see Lars and Navarro snickering at the stupid nickname. "Okay, and if they go running to Sama, blabbing about where you are?"

Chanté waved away his concerns as she finished chewing some other dainty. "Oh honey, if I was worried about my mother showing up, I wouldn't have used her credit card to pay for all of this." She smirked, waving that damned hand again, way too fucking pleased with herself.

Grim's jaw dropped while the other two alphas blanched. "Wait, this was you, not Asorav?"

She held up a hand as she finished chewing. "Now, don't get it twisted; Mikhail helped to make it happen. The man is a certifiable logistical whiz, but the queen witch definitely financed this venture."

Grim laughed despite himself, dragging a hand down his face. Fuuuck...they were fucking dead. "So, any bets on whether she's gonna nuke the compound before or after the wedding?" he asked the two alphas. Christ, where was Brick when you needed him to make odds? Grim's money was definitely on sooner rather than later.

"Well, look at you, going all drama." Chanté *tsk*'d, getting up and smoothing her dress. "She'll get over it, and as long as

I'm here, I wouldn't worry about her nuking anything. Kit in your room? I didn't see her downstairs, and she needs to sit for the hair and makeup."

"Yeah, she was taking a nap last I saw her."

"Mmm. A deep dicking will do that to a girl," Chanté said, deadpan, smiling as Grim's ears went hot. The two assholes next to him snickered into their beers. Whatever; fuck them.

"Why the hell shouldn't I worry about your mother? Didn't she throw your ass in the Spire?"

"Facts. But aside from the positive PR boost she's gotten with her largesse, I don't think Shamir would be down with her offing me."

Grim snorted. He wouldn't put a fucking thing past the witch king, even if he was Chanté's dad. "What makes you think he'd care?"

"Who do you think slipped me Sama's card before Kit smuggled me out?" Her smile widened and, for a moment, the family resemblance between Chanté and her father was uncanny. "Oh no, honey. All this here? It's been written in the stars, and if there's one thing my father loves, it's a wedding."

A COOL BREEZE teased Kit's skin and she frowned at its metallic flatness, groping for the comforter. *Mmpf.* Where the heck... Her brow furrowed, the steady murmur of a party going on below her filtering up through the floor. She snagged the blankets and pulled them up under her chin, drifting. Trying to ignore the clinking glasses, the low rumble of conversation, and some guy singing about a sexy tractor.

Her brow furrowed. Wait, what?

—Yeah, and a minute ago they were saving horses by riding cowboys. Girl, forget about the tractor and haul your ass out of bed. Take your damned shower and put on that dress. You know your

hair and makeup's gonna take forever, and we got like two hours, maybe. I think I heard this soiree kicks off at sunset.—

Ugh, fine, shut up, Kit groused, rubbing her face in the pillow. All she wanted to do was lay there and enjoy feeling like jelly. *How are you so frickin' chipper?*

—You ever have a dream, and it's super crazy real?—

Um, yes? But usually those were of the Texas chainsaw variety, and she woke up sweating.

—No not that kind. This was a vision, Katherine. I saw it, and it was magnificent.—

What the hell are you talking about?

—My porcupine. I've never seen one so big!—

Are you fucking kidding me right now? Your whole mood's gone all one-eighty because you had a dream about a frickin' porcupine?

—Um, yeah. Tell me you wouldn't be gaga over an eight-carat Cartier engagement ring?—

No, because I wouldn't be able to put my damn hand in my pocket...but four? I could definitely do four. Kit rolled onto her back and stared at the cobwebs on the ceiling undulating in the breeze. She sniffed, trying to place the weird smell lingering in the room. Whatever it was, it wasn't sex. So much for her rage cleaning plans today, but after this she was gonna need a tanker truck full of bleach.

—Worry about cleaning later. Back to my vision and your lie, because you know you ain't turnin' down a diamond over fucking pockets. And hate all you want, but my dream was prophecy. You know, you're not the only one gettin' married today, and Darke is gonna do me proud by deliverin' an eight-carat porcupine with wings.—

Wings? You know what, I can't with you right now. Kit sighed, pulling the comforter around her and shivering as she sat up.

Her eyes landed on the bureau at the end of Grim's bed. Hmm.

She crawled forward and smacked the top like he had. It

took a couple tries to get it right, but when she did, the side popped right open.

—What were you saying before about breaking and entering?—

Quiet. If we're getting married, then what's mine is his and vice versa, right? Married couples don't have secrets.

[MANIC LAUGHING]

Whatever, shut up.

Kit dropped onto the floor, peering inside the hole. More boxes of ammo, gun stuff, fifty-six dollars in cash, a pill bottle full of quarters, and way in the back...

Photos. Kit pulled out a handful of loose ones and a thin album. She set that to the side and flipped through the ones that'd been on top.

A bunch were of the crew. The first was of a teenaged Brick, holding a scowling Wrench in a headlock while Deuce laughed. The camera had caught a super skinny pre-teen Triss mid-air, launching herself at his back. Grim stood off to one side, hands jammed in his pockets.

The second was of a rail-thin version of him and Claymore. The older man had a wide smile on his face and an arm around Grim in the same stance as he'd been in the first picture. The rest of the loose photos were similar, and Grim looked miserable in all of them.

—Well, I guess we know how he earned his name.—

Kit frowned, not knowing him like that. *Yeah, he looks grim, all right.* She set them to the side and picked up the photo album. It looked a lot older, the cheap binding crackling when she opened it and pictures sliding out from beneath the clear plastic sheets to land in her lap. Kit swore, trying to tip it and not totally screw up their order.

Ugh, I hate these stupid albums; nothing ever sticks under the cellophane the way it's supposed—

Her mom.

Kit ran a trembling finger over a Polaroid of her mother on the back of Claymore's Indian. Her smile stretched to her ears below dark Hollywood-sized sunglasses. In another, Clay gazed down at her like she was his entire world. Page after page, they looked…happy.

Kit turned the pages, Kat reminding her to breathe.

I don't…I don't understand. Why would Grim have this?

—Why wouldn't he? It's the entire club back in the day. You're just seeing the pics with your mom…see, Stitch is in that one.—

Kit snorted, squinting. *You sure?* Whoever it was could've given Deuce a run for his money.

—Yeah, same glasses, and I recognize that tattoo on his forearm. I bet that's Doc next to him.—

Whoa, okay. Yeah, that Kit could see, once she got past the long blonde hair and the fact that the woman was plastered to Stitch's side and smiling. Kit's brows drew together. *I remember her, and those two women there. They knew my mom. I think they were all friends? Well, until we moved out to the house. I didn't see them after that.* She bit her lip, a snippet of memory surfacing. She was very young, and a pretty red-haired woman was holding her on a hip.

"Stupid bitch is gone again," she said, storming into the clubhouse kitchen. Her tone pricked Kit's eyes with tears. "And she left Kit locked in her room again. She hasn't eaten and the poor girl peed herself. If Clay ever found out…"

"Maybe he should," Banana said, turning from the sink and drying her hands to sweep her chin-length hair behind an ear. She smiled broadly at Kit and held out her arms in invitation.

The red-haired woman passed her over, going to talk with Demi, the blonde drying plates. Neither one of them was as nice as Banana. Kit buried her face in the crook of the woman's neck.

"There's my Kitty-Kat. You wanna cookie?"

Her belly rumbled and she nodded, thumb in her mouth.

"Nah, nah, too big for that," Banana chided.

Kit hid her face again, sniffling. Banana tsk'd, rocking her as she hummed around the kitchen, the other women's voices barely audible over the soothing sound.

"I keep telling her this is not gonna end well for anybody —"

"And?" Demi snorted, picking up another plate. Her tummy was big and round with a baby. "I said the same when Clay showed up with her. There's some strays you just do not bring home, and Maria? Case in point."

"She can't help what she is," the red-haired woman murmured, "but after Abigail fucked him and Reaper so damned hard, you'd think they'd be able to walk away when another one of them showed up."

Demi frowned. "Don't work like that. Not once they've gotten a taste."

"Taste of what?" Kit asked, looking between them.

"Of cookie, baby," Banana said, breaking the awkward silence and handing her one. "Boys just love cookies."

Kit blinked the memory away, chewing her lip. Had her mom been a molly? Was that what they were talking about?

—Doesn't make sense from what you've told me. You said she hated them.—

My mom? Yeah. She did... Kit frowned, holding the blurry pic closer. *Doc was Demi back then, and that woman with the short hair, Banana, her name was really Hanna,* Kit said, tapping her finger over the third woman. *And the redhead was Roxy. The woman downstairs that called me Maria. That's why her name was bugging me. She knew my mom, and so did Doc. Why didn't uber-bitch ever say anything?*

—Didn't exactly seem like they were in lockstep back then, and somewhere along the line Doc obviously had a lobotomy, lost the California girl appeal, and morphed into an uber-bitch.—

Kit flipped to the next page. *But that's so weird...I swear I remember her being really fun. Like, enough to explain Triss.*

—Whoa. So when did shit go all Twilight Zone? Didn't exactly sound like the Maria you remember either. I thought it was just Aunti Jojo that locked us up, but if that memory is true, it sounds like Maria maybe wasn't the best mom?—

I-I don't remember her like that, but it could be true. Honestly, I don't remember much about growing up here, just bits and pieces that come back when something triggers them.

—Um, yeah,— Kat muttered, —*because that's how trauma works.*—

Seeing your mother shot point blank in the head will do that to you.

—As shitty as that was, I have a hard time believing it completely erased seven years of your life, and you remember *everything from the house.*—

Kit frowned, turning to the last page in the album. A single photo, older than the rest, had been shoved into the back. Two teenagers. One was unmistakably Claymore, and the other—

—*Girl, that's Reaper.*—

Kat was right. He had his arm draped over Clay's shoulders and the two of them wore shit-eating grins, posing for the camera. One light and one dark, they look like brothers. *Stitch said they used to be tight.*

—Look, I'm seeing, but I still ain't believing, and we got a wedding to get ready for. We can visit your bizarre lack-of-memory lane later.—

Yeah, no, you're right. Kit took one last look at the photo, not understanding how a woman could drive a wedge so deep, even after she was dead. She put the album and the loose photos back where she'd found them and went to close the side of the bureau.

—*Missed one.*—

Hmm? Oh. Kit plucked up the wallet-sized print that'd slid partially under the bed. It was a baby picture, the kind that chain department stores did with cheesy backgrounds and props.

[LAUGHING]

—*Is that your boy?*—

I dunno, who else it would be? Grim was in a diaper and someone had put a pair of wings on him. He'd pushed up onto his chubby forearms. The look on his face was pure indignation and if that wasn't an Anne Geddes Pinterest fail, Kit didn't know what was. "Oh, Grim, baby, I'd be pissed too."

Well, that was going right back where it'd come from. Lord have mercy if Brick ever got his hands on it. Kit bit back a laugh, flipping it over and looking at the back.

CHECK MOTHERFUCKER

THE WORDS WERE WRITTEN in bold block letters in the center. Sweet baby Jesus, she'd expected a name and a date. Why the hell did everything have to be so damned cryptic? She winged the photo in with the others and closed the bureau. Right. Bathroom.

She froze before she'd taken the first step.

A perfect, blood red long-stemmed rose lay on the window sill. Kit smiled, wandering over to pick it up.

—*Your boy's upping his game.*—

How did he get it in here without me waking up? The door would've beeped.

[SHRUGGING]

—*Maybe he put it there the same way he came in earlier? I dunno, man's got skills.*—

Kit laughed. He did at that, and it'd been hot as hell, but she didn't think it was conducive to silently delivering flowers. He'd made one hell of a thump when he'd pulled himself in. She held it to her nose, her brow furrowing. That weird smell from earlier lingered on its petals. What the heck was that? She tapped the flower against her cheek as she slipped into the bathroom, needing to take that shower she'd come up here for.

Ugh, and to un-ball Grim's hand towel again. She put the rose down next to the sink and flicked the stupid towel out, hanging it over the towel rack to dry properly. *I swear he does that just to piss me off.*

—*No comment.*—

What! Are you serious? Why, what did Darke say to you? [SHRUGGING]

—*Nothing. He hasn't said anything to me all day.*—

Kit frowned, bothered by that. She flipped on the water in the bath and took off her necklace with Grim's ring and the key. Whatever the latter was made out of did not like getting wet and she didn't particularly care for rust between her boobs. She laid them next to the rose, searching for the ends to untie the dick scarf from her wrist. *Don't worry. As soon as he takes his meds and kicks this headache, you'll be able to talk to him again.*

—*I guess, but it still doesn't feel right.*—

Agreed. Kit's fingers stilled. She turned away from the mirror above the sink to face the bathroom door. That blush dress she'd drooled over hung from the back of it. *What? I thought we brought the other one up?* [CONFUSION]

—*So did I.*—

Would Grim have swapped it out?

—*Are you for real right now? That boy couldn't give two shits about what you put on your body apart from how he's going to rip it off. Is the other one behind it?*—

Kat had a point. Kit chewed her nail. *No, and I'm gonna be really mad if it's fucking gone.* A surge of rage went through her. *It was perfect! Ugh! No. You know what? Just no.* She slammed off the water and threw open the door.

—*Whoa there, what're you doing, Bridezilla?*—

I'm gonna go find my damned wedding gown! Kit looked around the room and threw her hands up. And her clothes were gone. *What the fuck?*

—Guess we're wearing that blush dress since you've been banned from parading around in bedsheets.—

Kit stomped into the bathroom and ripped it off the back of the door. *It would serve him right if I did.*

—More like you wanna give him a reason to paddle your ass raw.—

She stepped into the voluminous skirt, thighs squeezing together at the thought. Kit laughed, not even gonna play. *Yeah, that too.* An unrelated moan slipped from her lips as she pulled on the dress, the silk tulle a sensual whisper against her skin. A puff of that weird smell tickled her nose. What was that? Whatever. It would air out, because God*damn.*

Okay, so maybe I'm not wearing this for the wedding, but I'm totally lounging in it. Crap, I didn't even look. Did you see who the designer was?

—There wasn't a tag, but you see that stitching? This is definitely bespoke.—

Kit shimmied her girls into the bodice and pulled up the side zip. Whoa. She wouldn't have thought it possible, but they were staying in place, and it didn't look like she had a uni-boob.

—Mmm. We all about the lifting and separation of assets.—

Yeah, but how in the hell? It was like it'd been made for her. *Fuck it. If this looks even half as good as it feels, we're wearing it.*

[ANXIETY]

—Kit, what if Grim didn't leave the dress or the rose.—

What, like you mean— Her movements slowed, and she swallowed, her gaze darting around the room. *If it wasn't him, then who the hell was in here?*

—I dunno, but I think you need to take it off.—

The dress?

—Yeah, the dress,— Kat said, just shy of full out panic. *—I-it's just a feeling. I dunno. I can't place whatever it is, but my fur's standing straight the fuck up.—*

Okay, fine, where did I put the comforter?

—It's—oh, shit. Did you do that?— It was draped over the edge of the tub, thoroughly soaked.

I...I guess I must've? Kit reached in and turned off the water, her mouth dry. Wait, hadn't she already done that?

—Let me shift, and we'll go in fur.—

Fur's murder, Kit said, trying to keep her shit together. Kat's anxiety on top of hers was freaking her out. She *had* turned off the water and there was no way she'd draped that over the side of the tub. Add to it, the only time her other half had lost it like this had been the last time they'd been in the gray. Kit's eyes snapped down to the blush dress. She raised a handful of fabric to her nose.

Shit. That flat, metallic smell. That's where it was from. Who or what had been shifting this stuff in here?

Okay. Yeah. Now she was definitely freaking out. Crap, don't let Kat know…Kit put a hand to her abdomen. Breathe, Kit, breathe…

—Fur's not murder when I'm still wearing it, you cunt. And it's not like that stopped you from rocking that full-length chinchilla genocide last fall.—

No. She needed to know. *Fine, you have a point, but can't you smell it?*

[GUILT]

—I was wondering when you were gonna notice that.—

What? Why didn't you say anything!

—I didn't want to freak you out!— Kat snapped back.

Hello? That ship has fucking sailed, and I'm not go anywhere near the gray, not to shift your ass or otherwise; especially not if it's making guest appearances in my Goddamned bedroom! Kit stormed to the door, holding the stupid skirts up so she didn't trip over them. She blew a strand of hair out of her face, a total flustered mess. *Claymore's room is just down the hall. Like two dozen steps away, and I'm out of this as soon as we get through his door! This gown is on the floor and we're going to find Grim.*

[RELIEF]

— Yeah. That works. —

Kit shook her head and reached for the doorknob.

Something sharp jabbed into her arm, and she stumbled, strong arms catching her as she fell forward, her vision fuzzing into a long tunnel, and everything going black.

CHAPTER SEVEN

GRIM CHUGGED the rest of his beer as Chanté slipped away through the crowd. The hell did she mean, Shamir never missed a wedding? Was that the asshole coming here, to this one? Ugh. Fuuuck, the pounding in Grim's head upped another notch.

"So let me get this straight," Navarro mused, watching Grim pull out his bottle of aspirin. "*Hospitium* lasts until the wedding is over, but that death donut we came through is gonna be closed all night long?"

"Yeah. So whoever's here, is here, I guess." Grim crunched pills. Christ, he could practically hear his kidney function declining. Better have another beer to help push that shit through.

—idiot—

That was sarcasm, shithead, Grim muttered, grabbing a full cup off a passing edward's tray.

"That's what I heard her say, which is why I'm Googling what constitutes the official end of a wedding," Lars murmured, intently tapping his phone's screen. He grinned at Grim. "Nothin' like shooting fish in a barrel. I'm guessing the ceremony is Catholic?"

He didn't give a fuck, but Kit? "Ahhh...probab...maybe?"

The two alphas looked at each other and laughed.

"You don't have a fucking clue, do you?" Lars wiped his

good eye. "Damn, that pussy's got to be legit! You've known her for what? Four days?"

Grim scratched his jaw. "Five."

"Kit's his mate," Navarro growled. "Amount of time he's known her doesn't matter; it's fucking fated. Written in the stars, just like the witch said, and I suggest you stop talking about our queen's pussy before we got a problem, you dirty fucking dog."

Lars barked, his grin totally unrepentant. "That I fucking am." He went back to scrolling through his phone. "Whelp, looks like regardless of denomination, as soon as the bride and groom are introduced, the wedding ceremony is finished, and the reception begins. Pretty sure *hospitium* just applies to the ceremony."

"You would be wrong."

The three of them looked up to see an incredibly tall, painfully thin Asian woman with a buzz cut, wearing a pinstripe pantsuit and holding a lime-green briefcase.

Oh, this was gonna be fun. Grim sighed. "Shen Zhu?"

"Accurate. And based on your mugshot, I'm assuming you're Grimdarke James. Pleasure to finally meet you." Her lips pursed like it was anything but. "I'd shake your hand, but I don't condone gratuitous physical contact."

"Germaphobe?" Lars asked.

"No, I don't need your chi infecting my wah."

His brows knit. "Is that a thing?"

"It might be. I'm Chinese and very mysterious." When Navarro snickered, she arched a brow at him. "Regardless, to answer your non-question, *hospitium* applies to this event in its entirety, so unless you plan on going all *Game of Thrones* and pulling a red wedding, the ceremony, reception, afterparty, and the breakfast you're holding tomorrow morning for your guests, all fall beneath that umbrella."

"Damn," Lars muttered into his beer. "I loved that

episode. So you're saying we can't slit anyone's throat, shoot them full of crossbow bolts, or stab them in the gut?"

"It's a free country. You can do whatever you'd like, but I would advise against broadcasting your intentions prior to, or getting caught."

Lars grunted like those were entirely new concepts.

"This is your lawyer?" Navarro asked.

"No, this is my lawyer's kid," Grim said, standing. Jesus, she was taller than he was. That made her what? 6'7"? 6'8"? And she was in frickin' Converse. "Look, you can set up in the office, but we need to talk about that retainer. Clay specifically hired your father—"

Shen held up a hand, her mouth sour. "Yes, and I am very aware of the penalties listed for his breach of contract. I'm hoping that unlike the rest of my father's clientele, you'll be amiable to renegotiation instead of demanding restitution."

—?—

I dunno and now's not the time to ask. "Sure. We can talk about it later."

She gave a sharp nod and turned to leave, her eyes wary, like that'd somehow been a trap. "Then I'll go find that office and continue to work on your case."

"Yeah, you do that," he said.

She nodded again and marched away, arms swinging.

—*weird*—

Yes, she was. Deuce was gonna have to take a look at that contract, stat.

"Well, I dunno about you two, but I gotta bolster all this beer with something," Lars said, pushing out of his chair with another burp. He stood and slapped Grim on the back, looping his arm over his shoulders. "And if I were you? I'd be making my final rounds through the mollys. Set yourself up in one of them yurts and hold yourself a casting call, if you know what I mean." He waggled his eyebrows, grinning.

Dickhead. "Yeah. I'll think about doing that right after I take a piss."

"Good man." He slapped Grim's shoulder again, pushing off and away.

—hate that guy—

Right there with you, buddy. Whaddya say we go find that porcupine before I break my own hospitium?

[JOY JOY JOY]

—YES!—

Navarro gave Grim a half-assed salute as he left, his attention on one of Lars's crew rolling the wheelbarrow toward the woods. Guess they'd finished up with Nikki. Didn't mean they were done sparring though. Two mollys had squared up in the makeshift circle. Damn. They were good, too. As much as Grim would've loved to stay and watch them beat the hell out of each other, he had shit to do.

First and foremost, he needed to take that piss. Grim ambled off toward the tree line. Beers were going right through him. He unbuckled his belt—

The fuck? He bent down and flicked aside a clump of grass. What was Stitch's vape doing out here? Damn. A better question was how high did the man have to be if he'd dropped the damned thing? Grim'd never seen him without it. He looked along the tree line, into the woods.

A group of wights stared back at him. Goddamn, that was creepy, and he wasn't in the fucking mood. He shoved the vape into his back pocket and sent a steaming stream of piss in their direction. "Fuck off."

They jerked like someone had pulled their strings and loped away.

Riiight. He was just gonna leave that alone. The wights were Asorav's problem. Kraelle was Navarro's, and if Lars wanted to get involved and blow shit up, who was Grim to deny him the pleasure? In fact, now that he was thinking about it, none of this shit was actually his problem. Reaper and Shiv would show up or they wouldn't, and until then, the only thing Grim had to do was stand up at that altar and say, "I do."

Christ. He was gonna stand up at an altar and say I do.

He rubbed a temple and started back toward the garage, pulling out his phone to call Bones.

"*Sí?*" he answered on the third ring, a steady stream of a woman's diatribe in Spanish rolling through the background, punctuated by a dog's high-pitched yipping.

Christ, having that around was gonna suck. Shit was like an ice pick through his brain. "I'm assuming that's your *abuela* and her dog? You back at the clubhouse?"

"Yeah, we're—*Abuela, no, detente, por favor! No más lejía*—fuck. Dude, I gotta go."

The line went dead.

Grim pulled the phone away from his ear and stared at the screen. *Lejía?* Wasn't that bleach? What the hell were they doing with bleach? Jesus, whatever. They were back, that's all that—

The low drub of a helicopter thumped over the general fuckery. Grim knocked the phone against his forehead, grimacing. Shit. Cantone. That was his fucking problem. He pocketed his cell and pinched a hand across his temples. That was it, damn it. The last fucking complication. After Cantone and Kraelle got here, no one else was coming, no one else expected. Well, aside from Reaper and Shiv, maybe. Jesus, there wasn't any room for anyone else. Where Cantone was gonna put down his chopper...

Yeah, apparently that was right on top of what Hellspawn had going on. They cleared out at the last second, widening their circle to gawk as the rotors slowed to a stop and a broad-shouldered, olive-skinned man in a cream suit disembarked. Jesus, stereotype much? He turned to help a woman down after him in similar Miami corporate wear. Grim bit back a snort. No way in hell were those heels gonna make it through the back forty. From her resemblance to Cantone, it had to be one of his sisters, and Grim was going to bet it was her kid Reaper had put the hit on.

Great. Grim frowned, walking up to meet them. Another fucking thing he didn't need.

Cantone was in his late fifties, but held himself like a much younger man. He ran a hand over his oiled scalp, scanning the crowd from behind gold-rimmed aviators. A blindingly white smile slashed across his face as he spotted Grim, and he held his arms wide like they were old friends.

"Mayhem! I hope this isn't an inopportune time for my visit. I didn't realize you'd be entertaining." He extended a hand for Grim to shake, heavy gold rings glinting on his fingers.

Grim wiped his palm on his jeans and shook it. Wasn't like he'd just held his dick with that hand or anything.

—lies—

Wise it. "Cantone. Neither did I, but apparently I'm getting married in a couple of hours. You're welcome to join the festivities."

"Ah." He nodded sagely. "Locking down the queen? Smart move."

Again with that shit. Grim forced the scowl from his face. "Locking her down was never my intent. She's already my mate. Ma'am." He nodded at the woman. Up close there was zero doubt she was related to Cantone. Christ, they might even be twins.

"My apologies," He stepped back to put a hand at the small of her back. "Grimdarke James, allow me to introduce my sister, Marian. Ruffino was her boy."

—called it—

Yep. "I was sorry to hear about your loss," Grim said, trying to dig up his manners. That's what people said when a kid got nixed, even if he was a banger, right?

—idiot—

Thanks for the support.

"And I yours," she murmured back, her voice molten. She cast an appreciative eye over him as he shook her hand, her fingers lingering against his palm. Damn. Woman was a straight-up cougar and shifting had nothing to do with it. He fought the urge to wipe his hand against his jeans.

[GROWLING]

—not our mate—

No, she's not. Grim cleared his throat and took a step back, much to her apparent amusement. He ignored her smirk and scanned the crowd for Deuce or Brick, not seeing either of them. Shit. Grim pulled out his phone. "If you give me a sec, I can have your guest brought up—"

Cantone waggled a finger. "No, no. This is a special day. A man takes a wife…he gives his heart." He inhaled, spreading a hand over his chest. "True love. It's a beautiful thing. Precious."

"Indeed." Marian arched a brow, the "I'm going to eat you, little boy" vibe she was putting off intensifying.

"Um. Yeah." Grim toed the dirt, feeling too many eyes on him.

The crime boss's face went stern. "You do love this woman?"

"I-yes." Grim's head jerked up to meet Cantone's eyes. "Yes, I do."

"*Bueno.*" He slapped Grim's shoulder. "Then you honor us with your generous invitation. We'd be delighted to witness your nuptials."

"Uh, cool." Crap. Grim's gaze locked on a pair of familiar pigtails bopping through the crowd. Sal-fucking-vation, "Hey, Triss!"

Her pigtails froze, then dropped out of view. A moment later, she popped out from the crowd between and rushed over like she needed an alibi. "Oh my gosh, *there* you are! Um, so, I don't want you to freak out, but—"

Grim put his arm around her and pulled her in front of him like a shield. Marian's smirk deepened. "Cantone. This is *my sister*, Triss."

Her eyes flicked to his, and then to Cantone and Marian, her brain visibly switching tracks. The train engaged, and Triss's smile widened to megawatt status. "Yeah. Yup. I'm his sister, but I prefer to be called Beatriss, actually." She twirled a pigtail around one finger, cocked a hip, and offered Cantone her other hand.

Was she fucking kidding? The look on Marian's face said Triss better be. Shit. Grim glanced askance at Cantone. Judging by his expression, he was of the opposite opinion, his gaze roaming over her appreciatively. Damn…but, Grim had to admit, Triss looked good.

Like, maybe too good. She was in one of those peachy dresses the rest of the mollys were rocking. This one didn't have any straps and the bottom was high in the front and low in the back. She'd paired it with black fishnets and combat boots and, because Triss was Triss, the combo somehow worked in a weird 80s throwback kind of way.

Cantone certainly seemed to think so. He took her hand and dusted a kiss over her knuckles. "Pleased to meet you, Beatriss."

She preened. "Not yet, but you play your cards right, and you might be," she said, taking back her hand and fanning a coy smile with it.

Cantone chuckled, way too Goddamned amused, and Marian looked like she was about to swallow her teeth.

Grim gritted his so hard his jaw popped. The hell was Triss doing? "She'd be happy to get you both settled and show you where they're setting everything out."

"I could definitely eat." Cantone fingered a button on his suit jacket. "But it'd be a shame if you couldn't join us. Would you grant us the pleasure of your company, Beatriss? And please, call me Gio."

"Why, I'd be delighted to, Gio." She grinned, glancing past his shoulder.

Ah. That's what she was doing. Grim didn't need to turn to see who was there. The waves of visceral rage searing into the back of his head were enough. Triss shoved something into Grim's hands and then slipped her arm through Cantone's, leading him and his sister back toward the club house. Woman was definitely gonna break an ankle.

Grim opened his hand to see what Triss had passed him. It was the necklace he'd given Kit with his ring and that key. Why would Triss giving him this make him freak? He shoved it into his pocket, looking back toward the clubhouse. Shit, should he freak?

"Are you fucking kidding me?" Deuce growled as soon as they were out of earshot. "You seriously introduced Triss to that…that, perv?"

"To Cantone? Yeah. I introduced him and his sister, to Triss as *my* sister. Trust me, Marina wasn't impressed, and with her playing cockblock, you don't have to worry about anything."

Deuce shook his head. "No, trust *me*. Soon as she sees a brother she likes, she ain't sticking around, and I know his type. He's a fucking predator."

"No shit, he's a predator. He's the head of the biggest crime syndicate on the US/Canada border. Kind of goes with the territory." Grim's fist tightened around the necklace in his pocket. Should he go check on Kit? Triss would've said something if she'd thought so, wouldn't she? He took a deep breath. Yeah, of course she would've. He looked toward the clubhouse again.

Maybe.

"You know that's not what I mean," Deuce growled. "Goddamn it, if he fucking hurts her, Grim…"

He shoved the necklace deeper into his pocket. "Jesus Christ, he's not gonna hurt her. Cantone needs us as much as we need him, and I've got something he wants. You wanna speed that up, feel free to set him up in the playroom with Weasel as soon as I take these fucking vows. In the meantime, Triss can hold her own with a human."

Deuce wasn't buying it, his face all screwed up as he stared after them, one hand pressed to his gut. Man's daddy issues were messing with him hard.

"Dude, you ever consider going to—"

Deuce spun at him, jabbing a finger in his face. "Don't. I'm this fucking close, Grim. This. Fucking. Close." He glowered, pushing past him and disappearing into the crowd.

"Well, that's not ideal," Brick said from out of nowhere. Asshole strolled over in a tux beneath his cut, munching on—was that an *empanada*?

"How the fuck do you do that?"

"Do what?" He took another big bite, smacking his lips as he chewed.

"Just show up like that."

The enforcer looked up from his plate like he was thinking real hard about it. "I walk, mostly. Sometimes I use big steps. Other times, small."

Grim rolled his eyes. Fucking Brick. "Where'd you get the *empanada*? Seems a little low brow after what I saw on Chanté's plate."

"Psh. Snob. This is way better than that foo-foo shit. Bones's *abuela* made a big batch for the guys in the bar. Think she's got *patatas bravas* coming, too."

"Why the hell is she cooking? Chanté's got all of that fancy catered shit."

"Trust me, ain't nobody complaining." Brick shrugged, starting on another. "She said something about it not having a soul, and Bones took away her bleach, so it was kind of a compromise. I tried to tell her to chill the fuck out, and she tagged me good. Check it." He pulled up his sleeve to show a massive welt over his bicep. "Between her and that little rat fuck dog of hers, she's got all of Mayhem's ol' ladies churnin' 'em out assembly line style."

Grim looked at him like he was crazy. "Even Hanna?"

"Didn't see Hanna."

Great. So much for her getting her kitchen back to normal. "Hey, you didn't hear anything about Kit when you were in there did you?"

"I heard plenty about you fucking her a while ago." He offered his knuckles to bump and Grim obliged. "Props, man."

"Yeah, thanks." He squinted at the welt on Brick's arm. "Why does that look like a flip flop?"

"Nah, ya fucking *gringo*, that's from a *chancla*. My *bisabuela* had one too, and her backhand was no joke. Woman was lethal. So, you ready to do this thing? Got your tux in the office."

"I'm not wearing a tux," Grim said flatly.

Brick shrugged. "Whatever. You wanna look like a scab standing up there, that's on you." He straightened his lapels and eyed the crowd. "Me, I'm set to mop up all the lonely ladies. Damn, I love fucking weddings, and I gotta say, there's a lot less tension here than I was led to believe there'd be. Guess that *hospitium* shit works. Only dude worth following around is Deucey playing stalk-arazzi with Triss, unless we got more incoming?"

"Yeah. Last I heard, Chanté was about to let in Kraelle and a bunch of his crew. Dude's a real winner. Last night he murdered a shit ton of women and children from Navarro's pack, and just challenged all three of us. Oh, she let in Zhu's kid too, and Shen's a fucking piece of work."

"Real tall, toothpick skinny?" Grim grunted and Brick snickered back at him. "Yeah, I saw her in the bar and when I asked her if she played basketball, she said no because Koreans didn't believe in jumping."

"They don't believe in...what kind of horseshit is that? And I thought she said she was Chinese?"

Brick shrugged again, taking another bite of his *empanada.* "I dunno know what her deal is. When Bones's *abuela* tried to conscript her into cutting up potatoes, she said she couldn't because Japanese women only worked in kosher kitchens. So, this *hospitium's* a front, right?"

Damn, this chick was just getting weirder and weirder. Deuce definitely had to look at that contract. Grim rubbed a temple. "Nope. *Hospitium's* legit, and I expect you to enforce it until the wedding is over."

Brick scratched his head. "When's that?"

"That, my friend is the question of the day. Shen seemed to think it's when all wedding activities are done, including some bullshit morning-after breakfast I didn't know I was having."

"Mmm." Brick took another bite, talking around it. "Is that breakfast like the pill, and it makes it all go away?"

"Doubtful." Grim frowned. But it sure as hell would be nice if all this shit disappeared. He rubbed his aching temples. "Maybe whoever's officiating has a better answer."

"Nah, I don't have a clue, man."

Grim stared at him, his stomach dropping. "What do you mean *you* don't have a clue. I was talking about the priest or whoever's gonna do the ceremony. Like, the actual marriage."

"Yeah. That's me." Brick grinned, chomping into another *empanada.*

"Jesus fuck, tell me you're—" No. Nope. He wasn't kidding. Fuck. He had to be—Christ. No. There was no way he was kidding. Grim's headache was abruptly that much worse. "How? I know you're not a priest."

"Ordained fucking minister, baby." He put an arm around Grim's shoulders and took a deep breath, exhaling with a perverse amount of satisfaction. "You know how long I've been keeping this card in my back pocket? I figured I'd be whipping it out for Deucey, but damn." He laughed. "You've got no idea how satisfying it is that the higher calling I felt way back when to sanctify the polygamous love of several Vegas prostitutes and a weredonkey would serve me so well now. I mean, granted, it's only legally binding in the state of Nevada, but all love starts somewhere."

Grim groaned, his head throbbing. "Christ, make it stop… whatever I did, I'm fucking sorry…"

[GROWLING]

—hate Brick—

So do I buddy, so do I.

"Nope. No. I'm not buying it." Grim laughed, shoving Brick away and rubbing a temple. "Even if you were, there's no Goddamned way Chanté approved this shit."

"Whatever you gotta tell yourself, Grimmers." Brick tossed his plate onto a passing edward's tray and popped the last *empanada* into his mouth. He dusted off his hands. "Guess you'll find out in another hour and a half, now, won't you?"

"Yeah, I guess I will."

"Yep, you will." He grinned.

"Dude, fuck you. You're not really—"

Brick pulled out a clerical collar, whistling an off-key version of *Losing my Religion* as he put it on, walking backwards. "See ya up there, Grimmers." He winked, flashing finger pistols at him.

Motherfucker.

Grim frowned and headed toward the garage. Fuck Brick's shit and all the rest of it.

—porcupine?—

Yeah. Porcupine. Let's go nuke the fucking thing and haul it up to Kit.

KIT FROWNED at the annoying buzz in her ear. She hugged her pillow tighter, ducking deeper into the blankets, but it wouldn't go away.

—Kit. KIT. Wake up! Seriously, wake the fuck up!—

Damn, that was Kat. *What?* Kit scrunched up her nose, the air still and dead. It pebbled her skin, all cold and metallic. *Umph.* She snuggled down again, pulling the blankets closer. All she wanted to do was sleep, and it was still so dark…

—Open your eyes!—

Her eyes? Oh. Her eyes. How… One popped open and then the other. That shouldn't have been as difficult as it was. She blinked, heavy lashes fluttering. She waved a hand in front of her face. What the—ew. Falsies. Gross. She reached up to tug one off, and it didn't budge. What the hell?

—Girl, that and the nose piercing are the least of our problems! Haul your ass upright, we got to move!—

Why? Where? Wait. Nose piercing? She pushed upon a decadently soft mattress, a hand to her face. A little stud was through her nostril. *What the fuck?* She flicked the airy white duvet back. The blush gown had ridden up around her bare legs, and a weird iridescence coated her skin. She paused, staring at the French pedicure and the delicate gold chain around her ankle. Serpentine bracelets cuffed around her right wrists and upper arms, and a heavy golden torque rested against her collar bones. Rings of the same decorated her fingers and her nails had been buffed and polished.

What is all this?

—You mean aside from sketchy as fuck? No clue.—

The dick scarf was still wrapped around her left wrist, though it looked like someone had tried to mess with it. They'd also taken blood, if the cotton ball and Band-Aid at the crook of her arm was any indication. Kit frowned, her pulse ticking up as she absently tucked in one of the scarf's loose ends, long earrings brushing her shoulders as she looked around the room.

—It's not a room, it's a bed in a box.—

Kit's brow's knit but the description was accurate. Aside from the mattress, there was nothing. Not even a door. Light came from the walls, illuminating the space with a strange twilight that softened reality. Kit put a hand to her forehead. Was this real?

—Oh, it's fucking real and any second those motherfuckers are gonna be back.—

What motherfuckers?

—The ones that roofied your ass, kidnapped you, bathed and primped your unconscious body, then left you in here for God knows fucking what, Katherine.—

Anxiety spiked through her, remembering the arms that caught her as she fell. *What? Oh God, they didn't...*

—No. I dunno what happened to him, the rest of it was all some kind of Stepford shit.—

Kit pulled the dress down around her legs and wriggled back against the wall, pulling a pillow into her lap. *Can you shift?*

Kat laughed. *—If I could, they sure as fuck wouldn't have walked outta here.—*

Where do you think we are?

—I don't know for sure, but it smells like the fucking gray.—

Kit's heart rate ticked up, her mouth going dry. *No one knows we're here, do they? Like, they don't even know we're gone. You haven't been able to talk with Darke all day, and we locked Asorav out of our brain. How are they gonna find us?*

—Since when do we need a Goddamned man to save us?—

Okay, yeah, but not for nothing, there was a time and place for feminism, and right about now she just wanted someone to ride in and save her ass. Her stomach churned. *Kat, if it's the gray, then those motherfuckers of yours are motherfucking fairies.*

—Oh, they're not mine, but yes, that was my take on the situation.—

Kit shook out her hands. *Breathe in through your nose, out through your mouth... Right...okay, okay, okay...if this is the gray, and we focus our will, we should be able to go wherever we want, right?*

Kat snorted. —*Sure. Have at it.*—

Kit frowned, trying to focus on Grim, the clubhouse, Mr. Asorav, Cecelia, anything. *Ugh! This is just like when we were under Sama's table, and I couldn't shift out.*

—*Shamir was doing something then, wasn't he?*—

He was, but she hadn't a Goddamned clue what or how to get around it. *Can you hear anyone?*

—*No. It's like we're in a vacuum. Even when those Stepford bitches were in here, I got nothing. They were all creepy fucking silent.*—

Aside from her own stuttered breath and the pounding of blood in her ears, it was still creepy fucking silent. Kit wet her lips and hugged the pillow tighter, then took a deep breath and stood. *There has to be a way out.*

—*Not if this is the gray.*—

Kit ignored her, running a hand over the wall. It was cool, smooth, and slightly moist, like refrigerator plastic.

—*Well, that's disgustingly accurate.*—

She wiped her hand down her skirt before raising it again to trail down the length of the wall. *Yeah, it's not great.*

It was also entirely fruitless. So was searching under the bed, then jumping on it and tossing pillows at the ceiling. They were literally stuck in a sealed box.

—*Bright side, if that's the case, we'll die from asphyxiation at some point.*—

How is that the fucking bright side?
[SHRUGGING]

Kit put her back to the wall and snagged a pillow to hug. *I was supposed to be getting married.* She laughed and then a surge of panic went through her. *Oh God, I left Grim's ring on the sink. Do you think he's gonna think I just left him?*

—Umm… no?—

Thanks. Kit rolled her eyes. *Real fucking helpful. Do me a favor and try that again with a bit more conviction.*

—How the hell am I supposed to know what your man will or won't do? Now Darke, he'll know something's off.—

Yeah, then he'll freak out, won't be able to verbalize what's wrong, and Grim'll lock him down, none the wiser.

[ANNOYANCE]

—Oh, now who's being a ray of fucking sunshine, Katherine.—

Look, I'm agreeing with your bitchy ass. She scanned the room again and took a deep breath, hugging the pillow tighter. *We are definitely on our own.*

CHAPTER EIGHT

"THE FUCK DO you mean it's gone? How the fuck can it be gone?" Grim scrubbed a hand over his face, trying to keep his shit together. Darke's pacing and teeth gnashing had officially spiked Grim's headache and spiraled it straight back into migraine territory.

—STOLE IT!—

Calm the hell down, nobody stole your fucking porcupine.

[HISSING]

—*gone. your fault*— Darke spat at him.

"Jesus, Wrench," Grim pinched the bridge of his nose. "You've been holed up in here all day, avoiding people. Do you remember anyone coming in?"

"Brick snagged the wheelbarrow a while ago. Then brought Nikki through. Other than that, no. Trunk was popped open and—empty—when I got out here," Wrench grunted, his legs twisting as he torqued on something beneath the sports car. It and the Lincoln were parked in the garage behind the clubhouse. Metal thunked and the mechanic swore as the heat shield clanged onto the concrete. "The fuck possessed you to take a Miata off-road?"

—*you owe me*— Darke growled.

"Talk to Triss; she was driving," Grim muttered at the mechanic. *How the fuck is this my fault?*

—*left it unprotected*—

He bit back a laugh. *Dude, it was a squashed, stinky, dead thing. Excuse me for thinking it'd be safe locked in a trunk in the middle of our compound, surrounded by wights and whatever else is going on in those woods.*

[SEETHING]

—WAS FOR KAT!—

Grim winced. Jesus, Darke was pissed. *Yeah. I know. Look, we'll get her another one.*

—won't be as big— he muttered.

Christ, then get her two of the Goddamned things! Grim pinched the bridge of his nose at Darke's grousing, officially past the point where he should've grabbed his meds. Goddamn, he should've listened to Kit and screwed the consequences. Screw that Goddamned porcupine, too.

And what was more concerning about the situation, was that Grapple's head was also gone, and how the hell did you put out a BOLO for that? Missing, one head. Decapitated and ugly as fuck.

Whatever. Maybe Brick could pray for its fucking return. Christ, that this was what his life had devolved into… Grim slammed the trunk shut—

And gripped his temples, wincing. Jesus, that fucking hurt.

—pills, stupid—

Yeah. It was definitely time to get his meds. Shit was gonna knock his ass out, but that was better than not being able to function, and it would get him out of taking whatever fucked up vows Brick came up with. Kit would understand. He spun on his heel, wobbling, and staggered out of the garage—

Sunlight seared into his brain.

Nope, fuck that. Grim slumped back against the far corner of the building paralleling the woods. A wight stood there, because of course the creepy fucker did. Grim squeezed his eyes shut, grimacing. "Don't you have a fucking donut to patrol?" he muttered. It was too damned bright, halos of light bleeding into one another. He lifted a hand, shading his eyes and trying to blink them away.

A whiff of nasty teased his nose, and his stomach lurched. Whatever that was sure as fuck wasn't helping matters. He turned his head, the urge to vomit abruptly that much worse with the motion.

A round hole in the ground gaped beside the garage. Shit, the manhole cover he'd tossed into that gray whatever was still missing, and all that rancid funk from the culverts was coming up. Stank like hell and with his luck, some drunken asshole would fall in and sue his ass. Wasn't there a stack of pallets somewhere? He gritted his teeth and went to push off the side of the garage—

And staggered beneath a crashing wave of vertigo. Nope. Not happening. Grim turned toward the clubhouse with a pained grunt, bile rising in his throat and his head lolling back against the garage's siding, trying to keep upright—

And landed on his hands and knees, dry heaving. Ugh… He dragged his arms beside his head, eyes scrunched shut, face in the dirt, wanting to die. Bill had come due whether he wanted to pay it or not.

Christ, that'd escalated quickly.

Three sets of heavy boots crunched across the gravel drive and stopped in front of him. A low chuckle grated at Grim's ears. "Well, well. Would ya look at this here, Shiv? A more a pathetic lump of sinner I ain't never done seen."

[BLIND PANIC]

—Reaper!—

Stabbing pain shot through Grim's temples with Darke's terror, and his stomach heaved again, the world spinning. *Fuck, you stupid asshole, calm down, that just makes it worse!* He groaned.

A steel toe dug into Grim's ribs, kicking him onto his back. He threw an arm over his face, sprawled across the sharp gravel, blinking. Trying to bring the shadowed forms leering down at him into focus.

[CRINGING]

—run, need to run—

Calm the fuck down!

"Mmm. I'm afraid I have to concur, he is a sad piece of cheese," Shiv said, the blurry shadow on the right crouching down beside Grim. He could *hear* the asshole smiling. "It looks like he's having one of his migraines, doesn't it? And I venture to say, it's a nasty one at that. Pity, what will your pretty, pretty princess do now that her white knight has been relegated to the disabled roster? Perhaps it's time for your beauty to meet a real beast."

—NO!—

Grim tried to say, "You motherfucker," and it came out as a sad groan.

Shiv chuckled, his lips close to Grim's ear. "Don't worry, she's in good hands."

[PANIC]

—he'll hurt them. hurt us—

"This is what took out Grapple?" the third shadow asked in a deep, unfamiliar voice, his tone calling bullshit.

"Oh, now, Kraelle, everyone's allowed an off day," Shiv *tsk*'d, pulling back. "Let's add to brother Grim's, shall we?" Metal chimed—

—NO. NO CUFFS! NO, NO, NO! STAY AWAY!—

Darke erupted out of Grim's form, bowling Shiv over and tearing into the woods. Shouts arose from behind him as he flew past the wight and kept going, running faster than he ever had. Miles fleeting, his paws ate up the ground.

Deep in his psyche, Grim moaned, curling into a tighter ball, pressure beating down on him, the energy around him throbbing and angry—

POP

Darke burst from the witch's donut and into the woods,

birdsong and the small chittering of mammals punctuating the late afternoon. He slowed, chest heaving, lungs burning, the wind flicking through his fur. Maw open, he tasted the air.

Alone.

He chuffed, turning his attention inward. —*stupid. said it wouldn't work—*

The fuck? Grim uncurled from the depths of their shared psyche. *That pop. My headache's gone. Like completely. What the fuck was that?*

—*told you. stupid—* Darke picked down a gully. He'd come out to the east of town, headed deeper into the mountains.

Dude, shut up. Something just happened. Try to talk to Kat.

Darke paused, cocking his head. He flicked an ear back, trying to listen for her, then sent out his thoughts—

And ran smack into a barrier. He shook his fur out, rippling it down his body to the tip of his tail. —*can't. wall—*

That's what Kit said. That Kat felt like you had a wall around you.

Darke's lip curled. —*I know. magic—*

Wait, I thought you meant the fucking wight donut.

He shrugged. —*that, too—*

So let me get this straight. Someone's been using magic on us? Grim made it sound like Darke had been keeping something from him. Hadn't. Wasn't his fault if his man was too dumb to figure it out.

[EYE ROLL]

—*yes—*

And you didn't think that was important enough to tell me?

—*aid I hated it—*

You're a fucking idiot, and we need to get back to Kit.

Darke paused, licking an errant patch of fur. No. His man needed to get back to Kit. Darke needed to hunt. He lifted his head, drawing in air over his tongue. Squirrels. Tinge of bear spore. Maybe a moose. His ears tipped forward. Moose were mean. Big too. It'd be better than a stupid deer...meh. He'd already told Kat he was getting her a porcupine. Darke sneezed, then sniffed the air again. No porcupines. Talking was definitely overrated.

His lip curled over a canine. How was he going to prove to Kat he was her rightful mate without an impressive kill? He chuffed, starting down the trail again. Stupid thief. He bet it was Brick. He really hated that guy.

Dude, Brick didn't steal your porcupine or Grapple's fucking head. What I want to know is who the hell was using magic on us and why?

—not on me. on you—

Whatever. Same thing.

—not—

Grim's disagreement colored their psyche. *Hey, wait, take that offshoot. We're near the tree stand.*

Darke meandered in the general direction, his paws silent on the packed strip of earth, his lean mountain lion form threading through the bushes. Huge sentinel pines rose up above. He jumped from a rock to one of their lower branches, skulking upward, through the trees, to the elevated platform above.

He clawed his way up a stretch of trunk then made the final leap onto tree stand twenty-one. It was one of the higher ones in the area, which is why Clay had liked it. It swayed in the breeze, trees creaking around it, scent of pine thick in Darke's nose. Their father had always seemed at peace up here.

He did, didn't he? Let me look around.

Darke retreated and Grim took over their form.

They hadn't been up there since Clay's death. It was somehow wrong that nothing had changed. The view was still something else. Steady wind still flicked his hair against his cheeks. Grim sighed, hooked it behind his ears, and traced the scarred twenty-one scored into the bark, gobs of resinous sap dripping from the number.

The platform was built off the southern side of the tree, one hundred percent old school instead of like the newer ones that looked like someone had bolted a ski lift onto the trunk. Nope. This was all plywood and two by eights reinforced with steel eyes and cable, just big enough for a pair of full-grown men and a cooler. It was also too high for anyone to actually peg a deer, but they'd never come up here to hunt.

Grim set his forearms on the rail, looking out over the valley. With all the foliage gone, the rocky landscape was stark, large granite boulders and deadfalls dotting the landscape. What the hell did Clay want him to see?

Grim stepped to the other side of the platform, the position subtly changing the same view of nothing. He ran a hand over his jaw. Thinking of how many times he'd come up here with his father and never asked the questions he most wanted the answers to.

And now he never could.

Why the fuck did you want me out here, Clay?

Christ. Maybe he didn't. Maybe this was just one last fuck you from MK. Grim snorted, straightening up. Well, that was that then, but what had he expected? Some magic vault of knowledge? A pre-recorded explanation, putting his entire life into perspective? Shit didn't fucking work like that. Grim wiped the moisture from his cheeks and pulled Stitch's vape from his back pocket, hitting the button to warm it up. He plunked his ass down on the platform, back against the pine's trunk, and closed his eyes. Hearing his father's voice the first time Clay took him up here…

"When you close your eyes, what d'you see?"

Grim shrugged, not sure what he was supposed to say.

Clay took a swig of his beer. "Go on, first thing that comes to your mind."

"I dunno…my eyelids? Darkness?" Was this a trick question to make fun of him?

His father nodded like he'd said something profound. "Most people do, but you're not most people. What do you want, Grim? Think bigger, out of the box, of all the infinite possibilities. That darkness is a blank canvas, and you and Darke…one day, the two of you will want the same damned thing so damned bad that when you open your eyes, your heart's desire'll be right there in front of you. You'll manifest it, son. Go on, try it. What do you want? Tell me what that looks like."

Grim snorted. Like that was gonna happen. Furry asshole and him could never agree on anything.

His doubt must've shown on his face because Clay grinned, taking another pull off his beer. "Oh, I promise you, it'll happen. You'll both make it happen…"

It was stupid, but every single time they'd come up here, Clay had asked Grim the same question. *"What do you want?"* Then, *"Tell me what it looks like."* Over time, the answer had changed, no longer darkness or his lids. A million dollars. A new carb for his bike. A bullet with Nikki's name on it.

Darke always wanted a dead rabbit.

[SHRUGGING]

—*taste good*—

Stitch's vape buzzed, and Grim took a hit, his eyes still closed, tears leaking into his beard. That pressure in his head was back, but different this time. Instead of crushing his skull, it was like it wanted out. He gritted his teeth, wishing he could just ball everything he was feeling up and toss it. *You know what I fucking want? I wanna open my eyes and see Clay sitting on the other side of this dammed stand with one of his shitty beers, grinning at me like he told me so.*

[AGREEMENT]

—*loved us. miss him*—

Grim growled, shoving all that emotion and buried rage away from him, along with the renewed throbbing in his head. *Yeah, buddy. Me too,* he said, oddly deflated, his words tinged with exhaustion. Goddamn, he was so fucking tired. Grim sniffed and ran a hand under his nose. Wishing Kit—

"How about you suss out the one that's been granted before you go and get greedy?"

Grim's eyes popped open. On the other side of the platform, Clay toasted him with a bottle of shitty beer, his mouth twisted into an *I told you so* smirk.

———

KIT FOUGHT to keep her eyes open, her head nodding then jerking back up. Being in the bedroom box was a weird kind of torture. Nothing about it had changed since she'd awoken, everything in limbo. Light still emanated from the walls, casting the room in a twilight glow; the same stale metallic smell filled her lungs, and her ears rang with absolute silence.

The whole thing was an experiment in ennui, the plush mattress and comforter calling to her. It would've been so easy just to curl up and sleep. To forget about everything outside of the sterile square space.

—Oh, no. You know I'm gonna say fuck you, right? Because, girl, FUCK YOU. Stand the hell up and make some Goddamned noise! Don't you let them shove us in here and forget we exist!—

Kit sighed, pulling herself upright, her head falling back to knock against the wall. She huffed. *Explain to me how that's gonna make the situation better?*

—I don't give a fuck about improving the situation. It's solely to address my own personal angst. You know, since I don't currently have a fucking body. So do me a solid before I start screaming inside your damn head and make some fucking noise!—

Yep. Kat was definitely losing it and apparently, it was catching. Kit laughed, her listlessness succumbing to the lunacy of the situation. She grinned manically at the ceiling, trying to appeal to some higher power. *Noise. You want noise? Here's some fucking noise!* Kit screamed, arching away from the wall, the sound tearing out of her throat and echoing around the hollow cube.

She fell forward onto her knees, punching into the comforter. "Let me out of here, you fucking twats!"

—*Hells yeah, just like that!*—

This is so frickin' stupid. Kit snickered, but she couldn't deny it felt good to shake her fist at the glowing walls. "I'm supposed to be getting married!"

—*Mmm hmm, preach!*—

She stood on the bed, gasping for breath as she laughed at the ridiculousness of her predicament. Who the hell got locked in a backlit box on their wedding day? She bounced, the mattress bobbing beneath her bare feet. "I'm the fucking queen, asshats! You can't do this to me!"

"Actually, we can."

That voice.

Kit stumbled, falling backward into the airy linens. They poofed up as her ass hit the mattress, hiding her view and then drifting down to settle.

When they did, a doorway had appeared in the far wall. Between it and Kit stood Uber-bitch in a lab coat, taking notes on a clipboard. What the hell was Doc doing here?

—*Nothing fucking good, that's for sure.*—

She frowned as she scribbled, her mouth all puckered up like she'd rather be scrubbing toilets. Her pencil jabbed down with finality, and the woman's serpent-green eyes flicked up to stare at Kit, deadpan over the top of her clipboard. "You done?"

—*Hell no, you traitorous bitch,*— Kat snapped. —*We ain't even close to being done.*—

Is she fucking serious? Kit put a hand to where she'd been jabbed back in Grim's room. She'd been the one skulking around the room while Kit slept? "That was you? How?"

"How do you think? I had help," Doc muttered, flicking through papers. "Don't worry; now that you're clear, you'll be reunited soon enough, and trust me, he can't fucking wait."

[SEETHING]

—Cryptic much? I wanna know exactly who can't fucking wait, and if she gives one more answer that's not a fucking answer…—

Agreed. Kit's temper spiked. "Who can't wait and clear of what?"

Doc rolled her eyes. "You're not knocked up."

Kit blinked back tears, her hand going to her abdomen. Why did that hurt so bad to hear?

"Fucking Fae." Doc snorted. "All you fairies are so Goddamned keen to dig your claws into our alphas."

Did she really just call us a fairy? What the hell is she talking about?

—I don't know,— Kat said, sounding just as confused as Kit.

"Excuse me?"

Doc tossed over a packet of papers from her clipboard. "Read your labs if you don't believe me. Your bitch mother had Fae blood and so do you. Congratulations; you're officially a menace to society."

—She's lying.—

Kit swallowed past the lump in her throat, flipping through pages of test results that meant absolutely nothing to her, but the ring of truth in Doc's voice sure did. *I don't think she is.* "I don't understand."

"Abigail. Maria. *You,*" Doc sneered. "Every single problem that's ever strutted through Mayhem's door has had a pair of fucking wings attached to it. I thought Abigail was a one-off the way Reaper and Clay lost their shit over her, but to have it happen again with Maria?" Doc shook her head, her face all screwed up. "Unfortunately for you, the dumb bitch wasn't as cagey as Abigail and ran her mouth. It's in your fucking blood, and as soon as they get a taste of it, they're hooked."

Kit's hand rose to cover the marks from Grim's bite the last time they were together.

"…so damned sweet…"

Her mouth went dry as she tried to process that bomb. "But if Abigail had Fae blood, then Grim does, too."

"I know," Doc said, snatching the paperwork back from Kit. "And how fucking fortunate that the witches developed a pill to suppress that."

—*Jesus… that's got to be what they're feeding him for his headaches.*—

And I tried to get him to take one of the damned things. Kit's stomach dropped with a sick certainty. "What have you been doing to him?"

Uber-bitch cocked a supremely satisfied eyebrow and then her face went stormy. "Saving him from himself, until you started giving him Goddamned infusions. Now get your ass up and let's go."

She waited until Kit had gotten to her feet before prowling from the room.

—*Wait, then Doc's in cahoots with the witches? How the fuck does that work?*—

I dunno. Kit paused in the doorway, a standard medical facility's hallway beyond. Revulsion churned in her gut, the flat metallic pall of the box bedroom lacing with the sanitary funk endemic to hospitals and long-term care. She took a deep breath, fighting not to gag, and forced herself to cross the threshold and step onto the gray and green checkered linoleum. Kit shivered at its cold slickness beneath her bare feet.

The hallway was wide, lined with heavy doors fitted with card readers. Gurneys were haphazardly pushed against the walls between them, IV stands and wheelchairs scattered into the mix. One of the ceiling's long florescent lights flickered farther down the hall where Doc had stopped to note something else on her clipboard before moving on.

Kit really didn't want to move on.

Her footsteps slowed, the blush gown soundlessly trailing along the floor behind her. She frowned. Doc's voice and the *scritch* of her pencil had been the only things Kit had heard in this place, aside from her own voice. It was weird. Like wherever she was didn't really exist. The *clop* of Doc's boots should've echoed through the hall the way she was marching through it.

—*There was no sound in the gray, either.*—

No there wasn't, was there? Kit chewed her lip, glancing around the hall. *Help me for a sec.*

—*What are we trying to do?*—

I feel like they're pulling an Oz on us, and I wanna look behind the curtain. Whatever is keeping us from shifting, it doesn't feel as heavy here.

—*Yeah, okay. I got you.*—

Kit concentrated on the sharp line of a doorway ahead, mentally slipping her fingers beneath it and wrenching it aside. A ripple coursed across the hallway and Doc stopped cold. Sweat broke across Kit's brow. *Shit. Now what?*

—*Now we do it fucking harder!*—

Right. The seam where the door frame meets the wall, on one, two, three!

Their combined focus went to where Kit's had just been, and they yanked. Doc ran back toward them, her face enraged as she pulled hypodermic from the lab coat's pocket.

Oh no, fuck that... Kit stepped backward. Somewhere nearby, doors slammed open. *Shit, shit, shit...*

—*Do it again! Harder, Katherine!*—

Kit set her mental fingers into the seam and screamed, her fists clenching. A violent ripping went through the hallway, juddering through reality. She staggered as the floor tilted, gurneys and medical equipment rolling across the way. The hallway in front of her folded like an accordion, taking Doc with it, and Kit was standing before a plane of gray shrouded mist.

Yelling came from behind her, and she looked over her

shoulder. The hallway was still there and hospital orderlies were pushing through the upset equipment to get to her.

—Move, move, move!—

Kit gathered up her skirts and sprinted into the mist. Its dead tendrils swirled around her, grasping and cloying. She coughed, choking on it, groping frantically for something, for anything—

Grim.

She could feel her name in his thoughts. Her focus snapped to him, and she threw herself into the shift—

He grunted as she landed in his lap. Kit threw her arms around his neck, sobbing.

"Jesus fuck, Kit, what the hell? Are you okay?" She shook her head. Nodded. Shook her head again. "Christ, don't do that. You scared the shit out of me." He sighed, his arms tightening around her, lips pressed against the crown of her head.

"Goddamn. Now that was worth coming back for."

Kit froze. Claymore? But...she pulled back from Grim, throwing a wary glance over her shoulder.

—Holy fuck. It is him. Right down to the scruffy flannel beneath his cut and that stupid man-bun.—

Kit laughed, pretty sure she'd officially lost her mind. *I always liked the man-bun...* "But you're dead."

"That I am." He grinned, taking another sip of beer.

"Thank fuck you can see him too," Grim muttered, settling Kit onto his lap. "I thought I was hallucinating from whatever the hell Stitch has in this damned vape."

Kit eyed the ebony stick. "Why do you have Stitch's vape?"

"Found it at the edge of the woods, though I can't imagine he's fucking Doc out there."

Her breath caught. "No, he's not...she was in the gray just now, with me."

"You better start talkin', Kitten." Grim's eyes narrowed. "Fast."

CHAPTER NINE

"SO LET me get this straight. Both my mom and Kit's were part Fae? How does that work when up until a couple days ago, I thought they were all dead?" Grim asked, scrubbing a hand over his face.

"More like disenfranchised." Clay shrugged at the look Grim and Kit were giving him. "Hey, you want answers, I get it. But the fact of the matter is, so much Goddamned time has passed, no one knows exactly what happened aside from the humans somehow managing to banish the Fae. As far as I can tell, they trapped all the purebloods in the gray, but there's plenty of their by-blows kicking around."

Grim pinched the bridge of his nose. Goddamn, this shit was getting weird. "Which is why Doc's been drugging me to suppress my blood? What the fuck does that even mean?" he asked, his gaze going from Kit to land on Clay. "And Jesus fuck, but how are you even here?"

His father shrugged, toying with the label on his beer. "You called, I answered."

"So the stuff she said about Fae blood? It's true?" Kit asked, leaning back against Grim's chest so she could snuggle into his jacket. He wrapped it and his arms around her, an eye on the setting sun.

"Yeah, it's an amplifier, which is why your cats are separate in every way but skin. All shifter royals have Fae blood, and I'd venture to guess the same is true for the other sects as well. But that extra infusion from a claiming bite…it amplifies everything, flaws included. That's why I never made Maria my queen. I loved your mother, Kit, but after seeing what claiming Abigail had done to Reaper—"

"Liar," Kit gritted out, huffing deeper into Grim's jacket.

Clay hung his head. "It's true, but I can see how you'd think it wasn't. And I'll admit, I was chicken shit; so afraid of what it would do to me I only saw the bad and none of the potential for good. I didn't…neither one of us handled our relationship well."

Kit snorted but didn't say anything else.

"Reaper was always more than a bit off, but after he bit Abigail…" Clay shook his head. "The man went officially fucking batshit. Everyone thought it was her keeping his nuts in a vise and spewing poison in his ear, but it was more than that. Abigail…she was a lot like Nikki. Vain, self-centered. Obsessed with power. Then fucking Shamir foretold she'd be the one to bring the true shifter queen back into the world—"

"But that it had to be with you, so she commanded you to fuck her," Kit finished.

Grim started. *Wait, what? How did she know that?*

She glanced up at him and shrugged. "I made Stitch tell me."

"Then your command overrode mine for him to keep his fucking trap shut." Clay frowned. "But yeah. And long story short, Reaper and I had a huge falling out over it. Club split, I fucked her out of spite, and then issued a command for her to hang herself if she didn't have a daughter."

"Are you fucking kidding me? Then it's true, you did kill her."

Clay met Grim's eyes. "Wasn't one of my finer moments."

He snorted. "Ya think?"

"There was a lot more to it, but Christ, it's fucking done, and by the time you were born, Satan's Vengeance was firmly established as Mayhem's rival. That Abigail hanged herself just solidified their animosity."

"Then why the fuck did you leave me with him?" Grim's pulse thrummed through his temples, the question acid upon his tongue. Kit squeezed his thigh, and Grim dropped his nose to her updo, breathing her in and blinking the sting from his eyes. Fuck, he was a Goddamned pussy.

Clay looked away, shaking his head. "Didn't want to. You gotta believe that it killed me every fucking minute of every fucking day knowing Reaper had you...but in all the Goddamned futures Shamir saw where I'd claimed you, you died before you became a man."

"So what? At least I would've..." Grim growled, riffling his hair. "Whatever. Doesn't fucking matter," he muttered.

"Okay, now hold up," Kit said, leaning forward with a finger upraised. She turned to Grim. "Yes, it does," and then she looked at Clay. "And you're talking about the same Shamir that flat-out lied to Abigail? The one that's been fucking with both Grim and me on a consistent basis?"

"That last part sounds on par."

"Um, then you get why he's pissed, don't you?" Kit laughed. "Why would you listen to that man?"

"Because he doesn't lie. Ever. Abigail heard what she wanted to, not what he said, and if you look at everything Shamir's done, all of it has been to bring the sects back into balance."

"Right, right. It's all about the greater fucking good," Grim spat.

"Mmm...I don't know if that's technically true. Some of it has just been *really* fun," the witch king said, abruptly before them, arms out at his sides and balancing on the deer stand's railing. "Doot doot doodle doo do doot doot do do..." he sang like he was in a circus, walking a tightrope, the toes of his emerald green slippers curling upward.

"Does this thing have a weight restriction?" Kit asked, pressing back against Grim.

Shamir *psh*'d her with one hand. "Not to worry. I'm not really here, much like the deceased Mr. James. Though I do suppose I'm not dead yet. Sorry about that, champ."

Clay shrugged. "It happens."

"Only if you're lucky. Anywho, astral projection does have its benefits in situations like these. No need to worry about exceeding weight capacities or falling to my doom." He jumped up and down on the rail and the stand bounced. Shamir's arms windmilled as he caught his balance, then froze with a confused look on his face. "Oops. Maybe I am here. Damn. I hate it when that happens."

[CHUFFING]

—idiot.—

Glad I'm not the only the only one in the room. Grim pinched the bridge of his nose. "Why are you here, Shamir?"

"Speak of the devil and he shall appear! Muah hah hah!" he said, throwing his head back and then windmilling to catch his balance again. He looked down at the ground like he was somehow impressed. "No, but seriously, my ears *were* burning. That, and I thought you'd appreciate a heads up that either your wedding or World War III starts in just under fifteen minutes. I'm good either way, but it is your special day, so I figured you two should have the honors. My gift to you." He turned to them, bowing with a wide grin, and way too pleased with himself.

Kit glanced over her shoulder at Grim. "Imma go with wedding."

"Yeah, but I'm not going anywhere until I hear all of it." He glowered at Clay. "What about me living is for the greater good, because growing up with Reaper sure as fuck wasn't for my benefit."

"Do you think I'm too old to learn the aerial arts? I feel like I may have missed my calling. Perhaps one of those bouncy tightrope acts," Shamir mused, pumping his legs and making the tree stand bob again. "Have you ever seen them?"

"No!" Grim and Kit both yelled.

Shamir looked surprised, dropping to sit on the railing like he wasn't forty feet in the air. "Remind me to invite you next time we go to that Cirque du Whatchamacallit. It's fascinating. Well, aside from the clowns. I can never follow their storyline."

"Shocker," Kit muttered. "And yes, you're too old. You gotta learn that acrobat stuff straight outta the womb."

"Mmm. Rather like dealing with psychopaths, I'd suppose, but overall, how disappointing. I think I'd cut a rather dashing figure soaring through the air in bedazzled spandex." He hopped back up and struck a wobbly Superman pose. "Wooo!"

—?—

I don't get it either.

Kit flinched. "My God, he's like a frickin' toddler. Sama needs to get him a leash."

"Oh, I have several." He grinned. "She's quite the lady Domme. It's one of her more redeeming qualities."

[VOMIT NOISES]

Nope. Didn't need to know that.

Clay cleared his throat and Grim's eyes flicked from the train wreck that was Shamir to his father. "What was your gut reaction when you saw Kit at Skin?"

"Darke and I both wanted her. And how the hell do you know I saw her there?"

Shamir started whistling his circus music again, back to walking the tightrope.

Jesus. Grim pinched the bridge of his nose, feeling like he was going to throw up. "You went there knowing you were gonna die. That's why you were so fucking distracted."

Clay drained the last of his beer, somehow less substantial than he'd been. "If I hadn't, Kit would've met Shiv instead of you, and he would be very busy playing with his favorite pet right about now," he said, glancing at Kit.

[GROWLING]

Agreed. Grim kissed her temple. Fucker wasn't getting anywhere near her.

"You need to watch out for him." Clay frowned. "It skipped Grapple, but Shiv's got as much Fae blood as you."

Kit went very still. "Can he travel through the gray?" she asked.

Clay nodded. "It would be safe to assume so."

"Wait a minute." Grim's eyes narrowed. "Asorav said that Shamir was the only one beside Kit who could do that."

"And you believed him?" The witch king laughed, dabbing an eye. "Ahh...and people call *me* crazy."

"Oh, God." She put a hand to her mouth. "Then that had to be him. In our room, while I slept. He was the one that left me that rose, this dress..."

"Yeah...about that," Clay said, pinching his lips together. "It looks a hell of a lot like the one your mother was wearing when I picked her up on the side of the road."

"What?"

Clay nodded. "Her and your Aunt Jolene were on the lam. Something about an arranged marriage I never did get the full story on. But I'm pretty sure that, or something just like it, was supposed to be her wedding gown."

Kit's fingers trembled against her lips. "Oh, God."

"So where does Doc come into play with all this?" Grim asked. "What the fuck would possess her to work with Shiv and the witches?"

"She said that all Mayhem's problems had wings attached to it," Kit murmured.

"Aside from Nikki, she's not wrong." Clay grunted. "Doc never did like Maria. Fucking hated Abigail." He shrugged. "I dunno, maybe some misplaced loyalty to the club...when I brought you back, well, you know."

Yeah. Clay might've been the one that'd gotten Grim to come back to two legs, but Doc had been the one that nursed him back to health. She'd been constantly at his bedside, helping him through physical therapy, feeding him, making sure he took his meds…

Jesus fuck. The blood drained from his face.

All those times a medication made him sick as hell and they had to swap to something else. The weird diets, fucking therapy sessions…that bitch had made him her lab rat.

[GROWLING]

"What's wrong?" Kit asked, looking up at him, her brows knit.

Grim shook his head. "Nothing. Just…" Just another fucking person who didn't actually give a shit about him. He scrubbed a hand over his face. "So what the fuck about my blood were those pills suppressing?"

"Well, obviously we can't have any unleashed royals running about, but aside from my sect wanting to keep the shifters gelded, I'd venture to say necromancy," Shamir said, looking up from buffing his nails to jerk a thumb at Clay. "Which, by the by, was why humans got a wild hair across their asses and banished Fae into the gray. Totally skeeved them out. I'd advise you to ixnay on the whole ecromancy-nay."

Kit went pale. "Fairies are necromancers?"

"Manifesters and healers, actually, but they think of necromancy as a bit of both and then caduceus cubed. And no, it's far from common, but it only takes someone trying to subjugate the planet with an undead army once, and hello! Guilt by association. Nope. Zombie apocalypse? Zero stars."

Kit looked at him like he was a complete idiot. "That never happened."

"Hasn't it?" A Cheshire cat grin slid across Shamir's face. "Huh. Well then, back to the matter at hand. I'd venture to say surviving that wight's bite has also given Grimdarke's ability a boost."

He scratched his jaw. Shit. Was that why Asorav's wights weren't listening to the vamp? That one had fucked off when Grim told it to...

"And you two claiming each other did the same." Clay sighed, the sides of the tree stand clearly visible through him. "That's why I waited until that night to introduce you. Once the two of you'd met—"

"A twisting of fates was destined to occur! And what a conjunction it was!" Shamir said, his clasped hands beneath his chin and a look of adoration on his face. "So many threads flowing together, tying up, splitting anew, the tapestry changing... I couldn't have done a better job if I'd planned it." He tapped his lip. "Oh, wait..."

"But why?" Kit asked.

Shamir waggled a long, golden finger at them and mimed locking his lips. Then he tapped his wrist and disappeared, taking what was left of Clay with him.

"I'M ASSUMING that was a reminder that we have to get back to the clubhouse and avert World War III," Kit said, rubbing her cheek against Grim's chest. Was she a total bitch for just wanting to stay up here and watch everything implode?

—Nope. View would be killer.—

It would at that. Kit cast an eye toward the side of the elevated platform. How high up were they? She snuggled closer to Grim, not a big fan of heights.

"You okay?" he asked, tucking a stray tendril of hair behind her ear.

Kit laughed. "Are you?"

"Not even a little." He tipped his head back against the pine tree. "You believe all this Fae bullshit?"

She shrugged, her gaze running along the strong column of his throat. "Considering how the rest of my week has gone? It's not the craziest thing I've heard."

Grim snorted. "I dunno, me summoning the dead is pretty high up there." He cracked an eyelid to peek at her. "Watch it. I can feel it when you look at me like that."

Kit wet her lips, fighting not to smile. She turned, straddling his lap. "Look at you like what?" She shivered as his hands slid up her thighs to knead her rear.

"Like you wanna eat me," he murmured, his lips dusting over hers, fingers sliding over her thighs. "Damn. I really like the way this dress feels."

"I know, but doesn't it weird you out that it was probably my mom's?" Kit's head tilted back, his mouth hot on her throat.

"Nope." Grim's hand moved to her breast, thumb and forefinger finding her nipple.

Kit let out a little cry and arched into his touch. "What about the fact that Shiv left it for me to wear?"

"That pisses me the fuck off." Grim pressed his forehead to hers, his quicksilver eyes intent. "So does the fact he put a stud in your nose, even if it is sexy as fuck. He didn't put anything anywhere else, did he?"

"I…" Kit squeezed her thighs together. *Crap. I dunno, did he?*

—Not that I know of, but tell the man he's free to check.—

"Tell me he didn't fucking touch you," Grim growled, his hand tightening on her hip.

"Kat doesn't think so. They injected me with something. I didn't wake up until later."

The rumbling in Grim's chest got deeper, and he shrugged out of his jacket. "Put it on."

"But—"

"And if you don't want that dress shredded, take it the fuck off. I need to see you, and I need to see you now."

Kit stared at him, her mouth dry and her core throbbing.

His gaze locked on hers, he traced the swell of her breasts just above the dress's bodice. "I said, take it off."

"You do it," she whispered.

A wicked smile tipped up his lips, and he tongued a canine. His fingers tightened in the blush gossamer silk, then tore the dress asunder. Kit gasped at the suddenness of it, tattered fabric pooling around her waist, the cold brush of air pebbling her skin and tightening her nipples to diamond-hard points.

Grim's eyes remained locked on hers. His hand cupped her breast, thumbing across an aching peak. Watching her face. Her quick intake of breath.

She wet her lips again, her tongue darted out, and he mirrored the motion, dipping his mouth to claim hers. Kit let her arms float up around his neck, tangling her fingers in his hair. Their tongues dancing languorously. The brush of his beard chased the softness of his lips. He splayed his hand between her shoulders, sliding to her nape, tugging gently with the other. She crossed her ankles at the small of his back, pulling him closer.

He leaned forward, lowering her to the platform, reaching down to grasp her hem, raising it, his palm running up her thigh. Kit tugged his shirt from his jeans, her fingers smoothing over the ripple of his abs, then at his belt.

Grim chuckled as she pulled it free. "Mmm, you think so, do you? What have you done to deserve that?" he murmured, teeth nipping at her jaw, his mouth meandering. A long, hot line of kisses trailing down her throat. He licked around her areola, the cold breeze a sensual torment.

"Please, Grim, don't tease." She moaned, arching for him.

He grinned against her skin. "I always tease."

"But we don't have time—"

He silenced her with a kiss. "We've got all the time in the world, Kitten, because I don't give a fuck if everything burns as long as I've got right now with you."

Kit stared at him, her breath stolen by the intensity in his eyes. He sat back on his heels, gripping the waistband of her dress and tore the rest of it free. She lay there, in her nest of tattered blush silk, bare to him. One leg rising to press against the other as her hips rolled, a heated dampness growing between her thighs, slick with her desire.

The heat of Grim's gaze slid over her body, a hand going to the rigid length straining his jeans. He popped the button and unzipped. "Goddamn, you're fucking beautiful," he murmured, pulling his cock free and fisting it. "Open up and let me see."

Kit's knees rose, legs splaying. He stroked himself slowly, giving a deep rumble of appreciation. Her fingers trailed down her sternum, over the rise of her belly to the dust across her clit.

"That's it, baby, touch yourself for me. Show me what you like."

"I like it when you put your mouth right here," she said, swirling a fingertip around her nub.

He grinned, raising a brow. "You asking me to eat your pussy?"

"No. I'm telling you to. Lie down."

"As my queen commands." Grim smirked. He balled up a hank of her dress and positioned it beneath his head as she straddled him. Gripping her thighs, he pulled her forward, running her dewy slit over his cock with a low rumble of pleasure. "Now what?"

Kit fell forward, slapping a hand onto his chest to catch herself. "Now I'm going to sit on your face, Grimdarke James."

He pulled her down for a kiss. "Do it, Katherine James."

She gave him a look. "I'm not your wife yet."

"Yeah, you are. We just don't have the paperwork. See? I've got our rings right here." He shoved a hand into his pocket and pulled out her necklace. His brow furrowed and the air around the ring waffled, blurring. A moment later there were two bands where it had been.

"How did you do that?'

"I wanted it enough to make it happen, and I told you, you're mine."

Kit held out her hand, her eyes hot. "Put it on me?"

"Not until you're sitting on my dick."

She laughed, scooching forward to rest her knees beside his ears. "Face first."

"Yes, ma'am," he murmured, inhaling along her honeyed folds, then parting her lower lips to lap her core. Kit groaned, one hand on the trunk of the tree and the other in Grim's hair, hips undulating. His mouth was hot and insistent, his fingers teasing. Her thighs shook, and she cried out, her pussy clenching.

Grim moaned at the burst of her desire, his fingers dimpling her hips, holding her in place as he feasted, then kissed gently. She slid down his body, and one strong arm held her to his chest as he pushed up to sit between her thighs. He raised her chin up, his mouth descending to share the taste of her heady bliss.

"That what you wanted, baby?"

"Mmm." She smiled with hooded eyes.

He kissed her softly, his hand dipping between them to drag his thick crown through her swollen folds. "My turn. You gonna be a good girl and come for me again?"

She nodded, arms around his shoulders, burying her face in the crook of his neck. Grim notched himself at her entrance, then held her hips steady, slowly pushing upward. Kit's nails scored him at the delicious stretch of him. She whimpered as he bottomed out, pressing so deep inside.

"Shhh...I know you can take it. You were made for me,

Kitten." He reached to the side and then took her hand in his. "My wife," he murmured, slipping a ring onto her finger where it shrank to fit.

She smiled, doing the same for him. "My husband."

"Mmm." Grim gave a satisfied rumble. "And I'm gonna have Bones ink your name right here." He raised his chin, baring his throat.

"Here?" Kit kissed over the patch of flesh, her tongue flicking out to taste him, drawing his skin between her lips.

"Yeah." Grim moaned, one hand raising to press against the back of her head, and the other delving between her cheeks, fingers pressing to her pucker.

Kit's hips tipped back, her canines elongated, scraping. His cock grew harder inside her. Fingers sloppy with her desire pushed into her back hole, and her eyes rolled up, teeth threatening to break his skin.

"Fuck," Grim panted, "You keep that up, I'm gonna barb this pussy again when I come and claim you all over again. You want that?"

Kit moaned, writhing on his cock as she bit down, copper filling her mouth. Grim went lax beneath her, holding her close until she lapped over the healing wounds, then grunted, fisting her hair, and pulling her head back. He struck like a viper at her throat, canines piercing through her flesh, claiming her, then ripped himself away, panting.

"Look at me when I make you mine," he growled, their brows pressed together, gazes locked. His brow twitched, furrowed, pace speeding. Kit cried out as he battered her inner walls, fingers stretching her back hole, his other thumb circling her clit.

His pupils blew out, and he thrust deep, lips parting with a moan. Heat pricked at her core, and her eyes went wide, a stabbing—

"Come with me," he growled, the dual resonance rumbling through her, triggering her satiation. Kit's pussy clenched around his throbbing shaft, sweet agony exploding through her. She sobbed and his mouth claimed hers, waves of wanton desire cresting and breaking around him. He groaned, his eyelids fluttering, the hot lash of his release scoring her womb with long, searing ropes of pleasure.

They fell back against the tree, Grim holding her to him, his breath coming fast.

Kit sighed, blinking slowly. "You're right. After that, I'm definitely your wife."

He laughed. "Brick's gonna be pissed. He was all set to do the ceremony."

"Brick?" She pushed up against his chest. "There's not a chance in hell I'd let that man marry a couple of gerbils, never mind officiate my wedding."

"Take it up with Chanté." Grim shrugged, "Apparently, she signed off on it."

"Trust me, I will." Kit shivered, putting her back to his chest and pulling her tattered dress around her.

"You ready to go?"

Kit looked out over the valley. The sun just beginning to dip below the mountains. "No. Not quite yet. You said we've got all the time in the world, right?"

"I did, and we do." Grim kissed the top of her head. "But you have to promise me something. Shiv's dangerous, Kit. The shit he does to women…mind-fucking Kelsey wasn't even the half of it. You need to stay away from him."

"I'd planned on it," she huffed, "but if he can just shift in from the gray—"

Grim scrubbed a hand over his face. "Yeah. I know. He needs to be put down. Him and Reaper. They were both at the clubhouse with Kraelle when Darke bolted." Kit raised an eyebrow and he sighed. "That damned migraine hit hard. Took me down just as those three assholes showed up. Shiv went for those fucking argents he keeps on his belt, and Darke took off. Then as soon as we got through Chanté's donut of doom, there was this, I dunno, a pop, and my migraine was gone. Darke says it was a spell."

Kit chewed her nail. "Just today's migraine or all of them?"

Grim went quiet, his pupils waffling. "He says both."

"So, then that means whoever's been messing with your head's a Mayhem regular. You think that was Doc, too? I mean, she's not like secretly half witch or something, right?"

"Not that I know of, but if they gave her the pills, they could've given her something else. Who the hell knows what magic can or can't do?"

"Chanté would."

"Yeah, you're right. She would."

"You think it's been fifteen minutes?"

"Easily. World War III's a lot quieter than I'd anticipated."

Kit giggled. "Chanté will make up for it when she finds out we eloped and don't need that ceremony."

"No..." Grim scratched his jaw. "And without the ceremony, there's no basis for *hospitium*."

"And everyone's still trapped in the donut."

"Unless Asorav banishes the wights when the sun sets. Fuck." Grim frowned, then dipped his head to kiss her. "Is it stupid that I'd rather stay up here with you than go deal with that?"

Kit smiled, kissing him back. "Nope. Not stupid at all. I'm assuming we're too far away to get back to the festivities on foot?" she asked, teasing her fingers through his hair.

"We are. Which means you're gonna have to give me a crash course on traveling through the gray." It was her turn to frown, and he tipped up her chin. "Hey, I won't let anything happen to you, Kit, but you need to stay clear of Shiv and Reaper, just in case—"

"I'm not," Kit said, feeling sick. "Doc did a test. She said I wasn't pregnant."

"Yet." Grim cupped her cheek, running his thumb over its

rise. "Females in heat don't ovulate until day four. That's tomorrow."

"Then why—"

"Priming the pump, baby. I wanna make sure there's plenty of my swimmers waiting, and after that second barbing, we're definitely having a litter."

She smacked him and he laughed. "Are you serious?"

He shrugged. "That's what I've heard. I dunno if it's true, but it was hot as fuck."

"Yeah, it was." She shivered, pulling his jacket closer. "But it's getting cold now."

"Then come on, let's head back and find Chanté. I want the two of you holed up in the bunker while this shit is going down."

Kit sighed, slipping her necklace and the key back over her head and wrapping her ruined dress around her waist. She stood, pulling his jacket close.

Grim took her hand. He raised it to his lips and kissed her knuckles. "Ready?"

No, but she was gonna do it anyway. She forced a smile for him, and they stepped through the gray.

CHAPTER TEN

GRIM SHIVERED as they walked through the desolate gray landscape. As far as he could tell, wherever this place was, there was literally nothing. Whatever it was. No defining features, no signposts. Just a flat, dead plane, churning with clouds of mist. He gripped Kit's hand tighter, not sure if it was his palm or hers that was sweating.

[HISSING]

—bad place. hate it here—

Agreed. "So how do we get to where we're going?" he asked, just above a whisper. His words hung limp in the damp metallic air, and he swept a hand in front of his face, scattering the feel of them.

"Um…you just kind of think of where you want to end up, or who you want to see."

—taking too long—

That's what I was thinking. His brow furrowed, watching Kit's nose scrunch up as she pursed her lips to puff at something. He stopped, reached over to wave her murmur away.

"God, that's weird. Thanks." She hiked her torn dress up higher and caught his look. "I'm trying to decide where to go. I'm not stepping a foot back in your room, Grim. Not after Shiv was in there."

Grim grunted his agreement. "Clay's, then. Tell me if I'm doing it wrong—"

"Wait. What if…what if your migraine comes back?"

Shit. She had a point. Grim riffled his hair. "I dunno. Then maybe we should go to Chanté?"

"That's what I was thinking, but I'm fixing my damned dress first," she muttered, glaring at him.

"What? You told me to." Her scowl deepened, and he laughed. It echoed discordantly through the mist. Yeah, that couldn't be good.

Kit had to have been thinking the same thing. She took her hand from his and smoothed down her torso, the gown reforming to her curves. He blinked. Damn, she'd gotten good at that. It must've shown on his face the way she cocked a brow, all smug, before taking his hand again. "What? I've had practice. Now let's get the hell out of here. Try thinking of Chanté."

Grim pictured Kit's statuesque bestie and a weird tugging sensation went through his gut, then the impression of moving very quickly over a great distance before the gray spat them out.

They landed on their hands and knees in what had been his father's bedroom, at Chanté's feet. She sat in a beautician's chair looking thoroughly annoyed while a woman buffed her nails.

Grim stood, cracking his neck as he turned to help Kit up. Next time they went through the gray, he definitely needed to work on that dismount.

—idiot—

Whatever. We're out, aren't we?

"Sweet baby Jesus, it's about fucking time!" Chanté snapped, snatching her hand away from the beautician to push out of the chair. "Do you have any idea how beyond ready people are for this wedding to start? An open bar and a big-ass rodent sighting only go so damned far. Now go clean your ass up so Brenda can do something with it."

The woman that'd been doing Chanté's nails waved. "Hey. I'm Brenda. Hair and makeup. I do beard cut ins and fades, too."

"Big ass rodent sighting?" Grim asked, ignoring her.

—?!—

Darke's ears perked up and Grim ignored that too.

"Yeah. According to Jessie, it's of the unusual size variety. I swear that girl makes dim bulbs look bright. She busted into the bar screaming about a giant spiky rat thing out in the parking lot and a whole bunch of brothers, drunk off they asses, mounted up posse style to hunt the damned thing down. We goin' all *Princess Bride* up in here. Pretty sure that nut job Brick's downstairs practicin' his lisp."

—go see?—

Dude, it's not real. Jessie's even dumber than you.

[GRUMBLING]

Grim and Kit exchanged glances, and he shook his head. No way in hell was he gonna be the one to tell her the wedding was off.

Kit sighed. "Chanté," she began, "look, we appreciate—"

Chanté rolled her eyes. "Oh, good lord, shut the fuck up 'cause we ain't got time for this. You eloped. Yes, I know, now get your ass into the bathroom and clean up. Five minutes and do not get your hair wet. Your dress is on the back of the door. Make sure you chuck that rag you're wearing out here so I can burn it." She turned to Grim. "And you, Mr. Darke and Delicious, come here, Boo."

Mr. Darke and Delicious? Jesus, suddenly boo wasn't so bad.

—you're not delicious.—

Grim sighed. *It's a figure of speech.*

—rodents are delicious. wanna go see—

Dude, in a minute.

Chanté made a come-hither motion with two gold enameled fingertips. "Come on. Lemme see what those big bad witches got on you."

Grim sighed and went over to where she was striking a pose.

"You know we eloped?" Kit's eyes narrowed as she backed toward the bathroom.

"I do, but all them out there don't, and we gonna baffle them with bullshit, else that World War's still on the table," Chanté murmured running her hands over Grim's chest and arms. The tingle of magic trickled over his skin, standing his hair on end. "Nice. Very, very nice."

"It is at that," Brenda murmured.

[GROWLING]

—magic not nice and not our mate!—

Yeah, no shit. He wriggled away from Chanté's questing hands. "Is that necessary?"

"No, but it was awfully satisfying. Lucky bitch," she yelled at Kit, past his shoulder. She giggled from the bathroom and her bestie flicked those long fingers of hers, the door snapping shut. "Whatever the spell was, it was on demand. It shouldn't be a problem anymore, but if you see anyone in the fetal position, they're the culprit."

"How so?" Grim asked.

"I hit you with a little rubber and glue." She rolled her eyes again at Grim's blank expression. "You know, the spell version of whatever you say bounces off me and sticks to you? They gonna be fuckin' with themselves."

He grunted. Nice. Grim glanced at the bathroom as the shower kicked on, and ran a hand over his beard, glancing at Brenda.

"Oh, sec." Chanté breathed out some weird syllables while waggling her fingers, and the woman froze. "You got a minute and a half."

Right. "Question for you."

Chanté's brow rose. "The answer's no, but I'm flattered you would consider me for your throuple."

Grim did a double take. There's no way he heard that right. "What?"

"Oh, my God." She laughed. "Your face. You really are grim, aren't you?"

He frowned. "Look, is there any way to lock the gray around here? Both Kit and me would feel a hell of a lot better if the potential for assholes popping in unannounced was non-existent." That, and if the donut was still up, he didn't want that motherfucker Shiv getting away.

"Hmm…" Chanté tapped a finger against her lip. "Technically, it's possible. The Spire has special rooms that are warded, but that's not something I can do on the fly."

"What do you need?"

Her lips pursed. "A few ritual implements, some herbs, and a shit ton of blood."

Grim held up his hand, flashing the dark metal band around his ring finger. "*Hospitium's* been cancelled. I can guarantee the last thing on your list's not gonna be a problem."

Chanté waved a hand at her face. "You keep talking like that, I might just join your throuple. Don't you keep waving those red flags at me."

Grim snorted. "The sooner you can do it, the better. He's already gotten to her once."

"I know, and I wonder if I can modify…yeah. That should work. I'll take care of the spell; you worry about delivering the blood. In case I didn't make it clear before, that girl in there? She's my ride or die. Anyone fucks with her, they fuckin' with me."

"Then we're on the same page." Grim scratched his jaw, needing to trust her and not real comfortable with that concept in general. "Look, the club's got a bunker—"

"You don't wanna do that." He did a double take at the

iron in her voice. Chanté held his gaze and shook her head real slow. "She goes below ground and she's gonna stay below ground, you feel me? I got anything she can't handle, and your job is to take out the rest."

Across the room Brenda made a little gasp and shook her head, confused.

Chanté planted her hands on her hips as she cocked one, looking him up and down, that weird finality gone from her face. "Now you're gonna do my girl proud by getting your fine ass downstairs and putting on that fucking tux."

Grim snorted. "Pretty sure trying to fix whatever's wrong with the wights before Asorav banishes them has higher priority."

"Nah, we good. Creepy ass things started hopping to right before y'all cut out."

What? "They did?"

"Mmm. And FYI, Kit's got a thing for man-buns."

"She's not the only one," Brenda murmured, back to whatever she was doing at her station.

"For man—really?"

Chanté dusted her knuckles against her chest. "Mmm hmm. Go get 'em, Darke and Delicious."

—kind of scary—

Yeah, she is. Grim left the room, closing the door behind him. He paused in the hallway, the sounds of a party in full swing below, and scrubbed a hand over his face. His gaze went back to the door behind him, anxiety churning his gut. Chanté would take care of Kit. Christ, Kit would take care of Kit. Meanwhile, he had to take care of all the other shit going down.

He pulled his phone and shot out a handful of texts calling everyone to table. They needed to be on the same page for this shit to work. Hopefully none of them had been hitting it too hard. Brick'd probably kept his shit together, but Deuce? The way he'd stormed off after seeing Triss with Cantone didn't give Grim warm fuzzies. His VP had the tendency to go on a bender when shit hit him hard.

Grim's thumb hovered over Stitch's name. Did Doc have him fooled too, or was he in on shit? His vape dragged at Grim's pocket. Nothing about that felt right. He looked at Stitch's number for another moment and then hit call.

He didn't pick up, and Grim didn't leave a message.

His boots hit the steps and he pushed through the crowd of brothers partying in the entryway and made his way into the bar. He'd never seen the club house so packed. Mayhem, Hellspawn, Navarro's pack; alcohol was flowing and hard rock blaring through the speakers. Air was dank with bud, and the crisper scent of tobacco rode over the musk of too many shifters in one place.

Mollys flitted through the crowd, leading brothers off to the side or dropping to their knees. One bent over the side of the pool table servicing three at once while another group of brothers played doubles.

Grim took their fist bumps and congratulations, along with a couple hits and a shot of whiskey on his way through to the door at the end of the room. He turned the knob and pushed through.

Shen sat at the head of the table speaking rapidly in some foreign dialect. Wasn't gonna even venture a guess as to what that was at this point. She ended the call quickly, looking flustered. "Mr. James."

"Shen." She ran a hand down the side of her close-cropped head, nervous. Christ, he could smell her anxiety. That couldn't be good. He sighed, his gaze falling on the tux hanging on the wall by the desk. Time to make the fucking donuts. "There a problem?"

She paused. "That question is entirely dependent upon your perspective."

"Agreed." He flicked the jacket, never having worn anything so fine. Goddamn it. "So am I fucked, or are you?"

She barked out a laugh. "I'd say we're both on the bell curve, but I'm definitely outperforming you after that call."

Grim grunted, dropping his holster on the desk and pulling his Henley over his head. "I need to get this tux on. If you've got an issue with that, now's your chance to leave."

Shen put her back to him. "I won't look, but I'd rather not leave this room, if it's quite all right with you."

"I'm gonna need you to clear out for table and then I don't give a shit what you do." He pulled the button-down off the hanger. A plastic bag with tiny onyx buttons came with it. Christ, rich people were fucking bizarre. Why the hell couldn't they just get them sewn on like normal people?

"My father's spiritual awakening has put my family in a rather difficult position," Shen said after a long moment. "That call was from my—"

"Don't care," Grim said, dropping his jeans. "I've got way too much on my plate to take yours into consideration. Hit me up after this clusterfuck if I'm still breathing." He stepped into the dress pants and made a face. Fuck, they felt weird. Slippery. "If I'm not, everything goes to Kit and/or our kid."

"Noted, and your candor is appreciated."

Grim grunted, tucking the shirt in and pulling his hair back. He slipped back into his holster and toed into his boots, drawing the line at those shiny pansy-ass shoes. "Christ. How fucking stupid does this look?"

"Rather mafioso," Shen said after she'd turned, her face stoic. "I'm assuming you'd be considered on the upper end of attractive."

"So does that mean it looks stupid or not?"

"No, you don't look stupid. Do you know how to tie a bowtie?"

"No."

She frowned, then got up and approached him slowly. "Don't touch me."

"Don't worry."

She pulled the bowtie off Clay's desk. "You need to do up the last two buttons."

"Then forget it."

Shen laughed, her smile showing short, even teeth and lighting up her face. "I begin to see why my father always spoke so highly of Mayhem. I think I'd like to work for you, Mr. James, if you're amenable."

"Like I said, we can talk after this. Feel free to claim the couch over there until then," he said, shoving his arms into the jacket, then pulled on his cut over it like Brick had.

She bowed her head. "Thank you."

"Don't. Kit and I eloped," he said, transferring all his shit to the tux's pockets and re-holstering his gun. He grabbed another piece from Clay's desk and shoved it into his waistband. Extra magazines went into his pockets. "There's not going to be a wedding, so *hospitium* no longer applies. As soon as table finishes with this room, I suggest you lock the door and barricade it."

Her expression faded to neutral again. "Understood."

"Good." There was a sharp rap on the door. "That's your cue," Grim said to Shen. She nodded curtly, packed up her briefcase, and left, passing Brick and Mouse on their way in.

"Grimmers!" Brick clapped his hands together and rubbed them.

Beside him, Mouse winced, sniffling. "Do you have to be so loud?" Kid looked like he'd gotten shanghaied on his way to the prom in his borrowed tux, but Grim supposed that was only to be expected. Between all the canines running around the clubhouse and how hungover he'd been, it was a miracle they'd been able to pry him out of his room in the basement.

"Yep. I gotta be me, Mousey." The enforcer slapped him on the shoulder hard enough to jostle the tech nerd's glasses. Mouse looked like he was about to puke. He stumbled away from the enforcer and sat at the table, planting his forehead on it and not even opening his laptop.

"He gonna make it?" Grim asked, turning to the door as Bones came in.

Brick shrugged. "His moms seems to think so. She made him get dressed and kicked his ass up the basement steps, yelling about how filthy the kid's place is. Woman's a firecracker." He grinned.

"No, she's an evil fucking harpy," Mouse muttered, then sat up, going greener. "Oh God, don't tell her I said that."

Bones shook his head, taking a seat. "Too late, my brother. Women like that, don't matter where they are. She heard you and there will be hell to pay. I'll pray for you." He crossed himself.

"I hear your *abuela's* taken over Hanna's kitchen," Grim said to him over Mouse's groan. "Your sister here too?"

Miser slipped into the room and pulled out his chair, snickering. "Fuckin' monkey suits."

"We stylin'." Bones flicked his bowtie, grinning at him. "Yeah, my sister's here. Ivie hooked up with Zoe and the two of them are playing quarters in the back. My *abuela*..." Bones frowned, muttering something under his breath in rapid-fire Spanish. "She's in the kitchen and when Hanna shows up, I ain't positive *hospitium's* gonna keep the peace. So tell me we're here to talk about killing Reaper so I can take the woman and her damned dog home. Miserable fucker bit me."

Mouse moaned, his head back on the table.

[GROWLING]

—hate dogs—

Yeah, I know. "Where'd Hanna go?" Grim asked Miser. "When I was talking to your ol' lady earlier, she was kicking edwards out and getting a handle on shit again."

Miser ran a hand over his liver-spotted head. "She disappeared with Roxy. Two of them used to be thick as thieves. Wouldn't be surprised if they were playing against Ivie and Zoe. Hanna's a demon at quart—"

The door slammed open, and Wrench half carried, half

dragged Deuce inside. Christ. Grim ran a hand over his beard. That's what he'd been afraid of. He shut the door behind them and Wrench propped Deuce against a wall, not even attempting to get him into a chair. Man slumped to the side, his face mashed up against a file cabinet.

"Jäger?" Grim asked.

Wrench nodded, looking like he wanted to spit. "I'm on the fence whether or not he's gonna need his stomach pumped."

"Nah, way we're healing now? He'll be fine," Brick said, tossing something into his mouth and chomping on it.

"He won't be fine. Trust me," Mouse muttered. "It doesn't work on hangovers."

Deuce mumbled something about a fucker, his head lifting then smacking back into the cabinet with a metallic *thud*.

"You took his gun, right?"

Wrench rolled his eyes at Grim. "Yeah. And his pocketknife and the brass knuckles."

"Way to follow standard operating procedure, my friend."

"I'm not your friend." The mechanic glared at Brick.

"Well, now that we're all here—"

"What about Stitch?" Bones asked.

Grim scratched his jaw. "Yeah…about Stitch." He pulled the vape out of his pocket and set it on the table. "He's not answering his phone, and I found that out by the woods. Long story short, Doc's working with the witches."

"Not for nothin', but I'm gonna need to hear that long story," Miser growled, his eyes locked on the vape. Grim sighed and gave them the condensed version.

"Jesus fuck," Bones muttered, rapping his tattooed knuckles against the table.

"That about covers it," Grim agreed.

"Shit." Brick swiveled in his chair, looking thoughtful. His throat bobbed. "She sure as fuck deserves it, but we've never had a woman down in the playroom. I know she's got a Mayhem tat, but dunno if I can do it."

They all looked at him like he was speaking Greek.

"What? I'll put a bullet in her, but that shit… Christ, even I have limits."

"Huh." Wrench tipped up his ball cap to scratch his forehead. "Who knew?"

Brick shrugged. "I know, it's a failing of mine. But who knows, maybe flaying Doc's what I need to get over that hump. So, she's dead woman walking, but what if Stitch turns up?"

"Stick him in one of the cells until we can figure out what's going on. Preferably one without rats… Hey, that reminds me, did Deuce ever take Cantone down there?"

"Yeah, man, and that's the reason he's so fucked now." Wrench shook his head. "They're gone, and Triss went with 'em."

"What? That doesn't make any fucking sense. She was all hot to be one of Kit's bridesmaids."

Wrench shrugged. "Dude, I dunno all the details. Man was sloppy when he finally texted me. I guess Deuce took them down there, Weasel ran his mouth, and that sister of Cantone's lost her shit. Had some kind of an episode, and they rushed her out of here in the chopper."

Grim frowned, but that actually did track if it was a medical thing. Triss would be the first to help. He looked over at Deuce, passed out and drooling all over himself. Probably for the best. "He say when she was coming back?"

Wrench shook his head, and Grim pulled his phone. Nothing from Cantone or Triss. He shot her a quick text and pocketed it again.

"All right, so all of that is fucked and none of it's what I called you in here for. Kit and I eloped earlier." Grim flashed his ring. "*Hospitium's* off."

"Dude, not cool. You fucking owe me for playing my card, Grimdarke." Brick scowled.

"I don't owe you shit, and Deuce is so wrapped up in his own damned drama there's no way he noticed yours."

The enforcer's face lit up. "True that. Then I forgive you, my son." He made the sign of the cross at Grim, then glowered at the table. "Any one of you fuckers ruins that for me, I'll kill you. And might I just add, yesss." He fist pumped. "Dibs on Ty. Fuckers been begging for another cue ball."

Grim frowned at him. "No dibs and no cue balls. Navarro's pack and Hellspawn are off the table. We're going after that piece of shit Kraelle, Reaper, Shiv, and anyone they came in with. Chanté says they've got a triad of Bléda with them, so watch your asses."

"You know, I'm really kind of loving an actual shotgun wedding for you two, but how do you see it playing out?" Bones asked. "We make like it's happening until it's not?"

"Basically. That'll get all of them in the same place."

Miser made a noise that wasn't agreement. "It also puts the women in the middle of it."

"I'm happy to escort them elsewhere once the festivities begin," Asorav said, materializing from the shadows. Christ, it was so fucking creepy when he did that. Grim scrubbed his face. Whatever. He wasn't even gonna get into it with the vamp.

"Dude!" Brick loomed at the vamp. "Fucking table's closed door."

"I'm aware, Sergeant Arroyo, and the door hasn't opened."

"It's Brick," he growled.

Asorav inclined his head. "My apologies, Sergeant Brick."

"Jesus, enough!" Grim yelled, just wanting to be done with all of it. "You got a handle on the wights?"

"Yes," the vamp said, brushing an invisible spec from his sleeve. "They're patrolling as intended and the, ah, donut, is secure. Which leaves me at loose ends, hence my offer of support." His smile wasn't reassuring, and his fangs a titch too long.

—hate that guy—

Dude, you hate everyone.

—not Kat. Kit's okay. don't like you—

Feeling's mutual. "Yeah, do it." Grim frowned. And then hopefully he'd fuck off somewhere. "Hey Mouse, you got a spare burner?"

"Actually, I was gonna give Kit back this one." He pulled out that red sparkly phone Aryanna had given her. "Tell her happy wedding or whatever, I guess. I wiped it just to be safe, but it was clean. It's just a seriously blinged-out cell. Only thing on it was a single contact for takeout. Went to some dive in Hoboken."

Asorav's eyes narrowed. "May I?" he asked, reaching for it.

Mouse shrugged and tossed it to him.

"A gift from my queen, yes? Mmm. She's partial to these ridiculous cases." The vamp unlocked it, flipping through screens with his thumb. His mouth soured as he set the cell on the table. "I'm assuming you didn't call it?"

Mouse snorted. "What, like use a phone, phone? No. Nobody does that anymore."

"How fortuitous. That 'dive' is located over a particular nest of the queen's. Summoning her pets would have been inadvisable."

Mouse paled. "Can you do that by text? 'Cause I might have sent one of those."

The vamp's expression went flat. "Oh, my. Well. I suspect we'll find out. Might I suggest I escort the ladies to the processional carpet? Sooner begun, sooner done...and inside."

Brick started whistling *White Wedding,* and Grim snorted. "Yeah. Let's do this."

KIT STOOD in front of the ecru mermaid gown she'd chosen from the rack earlier, running her fingers over the intricate lace bodice, seeded with pearls. The matching bridal lingerie had been in a box by the sink. Now it was piled with the jewelry from the bedroom box. Soon as she could, she was pawning it. Between that and what she had in the bank she'd have just enough to settle the debt Claymore had left Grim so he wouldn't have to sell the Indian.

—Aww. And here I thought you didn't give two shits about that bike.—

Kit bit her lip, shrugging. *I don't, but it would kill Grim to have to sell it.* She smiled. Grim. Her husband. She held out her hand and looked at the dark metal band encircling her ring finger. How had her life gotten so crazy? *This is not how I envisioned my wedding. I mean, it is. The pieces are all there, but—*

"Are you done in there yet?" Chanté rapped on the other side of the door. "We're on a schedule and that hair of yours is a fucking mess."

Kit unclipped the gown from its hanger. "Yeah, I'm just trying to figure out if I climb in this thing from the bottom or the top."

"Bottoms up, baby. Ain't no way your ass is squeezing through that bodice."

Woman had a point. Kit found the hem and dove in, wriggling into it and holding it up. Oof. Thing weighed a frickin' ton. "Okay, I'm in, but you're gonna have to button me up," she said, opening the door.

"Whoa, that's pretty," Brenda said, pausing her work to look Kit over. "I see what you mean now about the spray of pearls. It'll be stunning with her dark hair."

"Mmm hmm. That's what we going for. Start with her makeup while I do up these buttons." Chanté made a spinning motion with her finger. "You're gonna have to back up to the bed so I can sit. You're too damned short." Kit complied, wondering when the new mattress had been delivered. Her bestie started hooking and fastening, and Brenda came over with her brushes.

"You good with all this?" Chanté asked after a long, weighted silence.

Kit flicked her gaze to the beautician, zoned out on contouring. "As good as I can be."

"Bullshit," Chanté murmured.

"Girl," Kit said, "after the week I've had, I will take what I can get. I fully expect this entire compound to be a smoking pit in the next couple of hours, and your Manolos are on point, but trust me, you're gonna want something you can run in."

Chanté tugged the sides of Kit's bodice together, hooking another eye. "You think I can't run in these?"

"No, I know you can do a seven-minute mile downtown, but Flatts, NY, isn't exactly paved."

"Mmm." Chanté tugged another hook and eye together. "True that, but this Jovani ain't gonna work with tennis shoes."

Her dress was incredibly fierce. "I may have your rainboots somewhere around here…"

Chanté froze. "Girl, shut the hell up, you do not."

Kit laughed, then sneezed as Brenda applied powder. "Almost done, just a little shine…look up," the woman murmured. "And down."

"No, I don't have your boots." Kit said, closing her eyes for liner. "Pretty sure they got blown up, but I can't remember which time."

"You know that's fucked, right?"

"I had my suspicions."

That heavy silence descended again, lasting until Kit's face had been done and her hair was styled. Brenda retreated from the room, and Chanté sighed, taking Kit in.

"If that man's eyes don't fall out of his head when he sees you, there's something wrong with him."

Kit forced a smile, wringing her hands. The question that'd been eating at her forced its way past her lips. "Goddamn it. Chanté, how the hell do you see this going down?"

She went very still. "You askin' me how I see it or if I've 'seen' it?"

Kit's brow rose. "Is that an option?"

"I wouldn't have said so before, but…" She shook her head, going to sit at the edge of the bed again. "My dad talks about these things called conjunctions. They're… places in time that are like a switching yard for a subway. Depending on what switches get thrown, a train can end up on an entirely different track. I keep getting these glimpses…" She chewed her lip, glancing at the door. "You got your scarf, right? You need something blue."

"Yeah, I tied it to my garter." Kit said, her brow furrowing at how rattled Chanté seemed. What the hell had she seen? "Tell me one of those glimpses is of where my Doc Martins ended up," Kit said, trying to lighten the mood. "You might be up for heels, but I—"

Someone knocked on the door. "Hold that thought." Chanté got up and answered it, her shoulders relaxing when she saw who was on the other side. "I saw them in the other room. Imma grab them. Meanwhile, be nice."

She pushed the door open, and Roxy stood there with a slight, gray-haired woman in a voluminous patchwork dress. Her familiarity tugged at Kit.

—*That's gotta be your Hanna Banana.*—

Kit ran a hand down her abdomen, stomach churning. *Yeah. I think you're right.* Chanté slipped past them, and they came into the room like they were entering a lion's den. Roxy's lips pinched down white, and she went over to the window without a word, standing with her back to them and peering through the mini blinds.

The gray-haired woman's hand rose to her mouth. "Oh, my Kitty-Kat...look at you..."

"You're B-Hanna, right?"

She nodded with a broad smile, tearing up. "Yes. See, Rox, she does remember."

"Maybe you, but she sure as hell didn't remember me downstairs," the wiry woman retorted.

"Because you never let me eat cookies," Kit murmured, a jumble of images tumbling through her mind, all mixed up. The two of them. Her mother. Doc, back when she was Demi.

"Yes!" Hanna laughed, coming over to clasp Kit's hands in hers. "Oh, you have no idea how often I've thought of you." Her eyes flicked to Roxy. "How often we both have."

—I wanna know if Doc was part of that equation.—

I don't think so. Chanté said to be nice. Kit took her hands back. "I'm sorry, I can't say the same."

—Chanté told you to be nice. Me? I'm gonna be suspicious as fuck, and you best stay out my way if I need to cut a bitch.—

"No. You wouldn't. Maria..." Hanna wet her lips. "What do you remember about her?"

"I..." Kit's brow knit. "Very little, actually. Almost nothing from here. Cooking at the house. Her fighting with Claymore. She cried a lot." Kit's voice cracked, and she bit her cheek, but those were basically her only memories, and they were pretty fragmented. Tiny moments in time something usually had to trigger, like that photo earlier.

"Nothing about her family?" Roxy asked, still peeking through the blinds.

"Aside from my Auntie Jojo? No. Why?"

"Because they're dangerous," Hanna said, wringing her hands. "And if anyone let them know you were here—"

"Anyone like Doc?" Kit asked.

The two women exchanged glances, and Roxy threw up

her hands. "Christ, if you're gonna tell her, just fucking tell her. Your mother and aunt were on the run from those twisted fucks. Jolene got the fuck out of Dodge, but Maria—"

"We didn't get the whole story until after you were born."

"Please," Roxy said. "We never got the full story."

Hanna frowned. "That's not important right now. What is, is this." From the folds of her dress, she pulled out a small box. It didn't look special. Plain, worn wood, battered by time, the key in its base darkened with age.

But Kit's breath caught.

"That's..." The melody she'd forgotten. The one that'd teased her memory that first night back at the house. The notes danced in her head as she took the tiny piece of her past from Hanna and twisted the key at its base before easing the lid open.

The tune was ethereal, lilting and strange. It tinged from the bronze drum rolling on one side, a tiny porcelain woman with red shoes pirouetting in its center, and beside it a ring. Kit's brow furrowed, the markings around the dancer wriggled like they were alive, something pricking just at the edge of her consciousness...

"Why do they dance with her, Mama?"

"They're trying to tell you a story. If they ever start to whisper and I'm not here, you run and tell your Auntie Jojo, ya hear?"

Kit snapped the box closed, shoving it under a pillow on the bed. She wiped her fingers down her thigh, the box's creepiness sticking to them like webbing.

—What's the ring?—

The what?

—The ring you're strangling. Do it any harder and it's gonna pop out the back of your hand.—

Kit looked down at her clenched fist, opening it. A delicate silver band wrought with tiny flowers was pressed into her palm.

"After what happened to Maria..." Hanna's mouth

pinched down. "Well. Jolene said if you ever came back here to give you those. She made us both swear we would."

Kit's head jerked up, having totally forgotten about the two women.

"The box to warn and the ring to not abide," Roxy murmured from the window. "Suggest you wear it. Fae are supposed to be able to pull some voodoo mind shit over each other."

It was already on Kit's finger, sparkling like an engagement ring above the band Grim had given her, concentric rings of dark and light. "So how the hell is my Auntie Jojo part of the Humanity Pure movement? They test for this shit."

"Not for Fae blood," Roxy said. "It's too rare and not everyone who's got it presents it. Jolene didn't, but your mother did."

"Well, lucky frickin' me," Kit muttered.

—*More like lucky frickin' me. Sounds like I wouldn't have existed otherwise.*—

True. I suppose you're worth it.

—*Gee, thanks.*—

Anytime.

The door opened again and Chanté came in with Kit's boots, followed by Mr. Asorav.

"Ladies?" He gave them a deep bow. "It's time."

CHAPTER ELEVEN

GRIM STOOD at the end of the dance floor beneath a bower of roses and a bunch of other flowers he didn't know the names of, hyperaware of the line of sweat tracking down his spine. It was fucking stupid. He'd already married Kit. Why the hell was he so nervous?

—Reaper—

Yeah. That had to be why. He sighed and it was too loud. Someone had cut the music from the bar and the low murmur of voices filled the air. A laugh sliced through it, and Grim eyed the prick he was pretty sure was Kraelle.

The burly, white-blond alpha sat in the aisle seat of the middle row of chairs lined up for this shit show, looking way too fucking comfortable. Next to him were three other assholes Grim would put money on being Bléda, but both Reaper and Shiv were missing.

Yeah. Grim wet his lips. It had to be not knowing where they were or being able to put eyes on Kit that made him nervous as fuck.

Christ, especially not being able to put eyes on Kit.

The sun had set, and all the tiny lights the edwards had spent the day stringing twinkled silver and gold. The breeze picked up, swaying their strands and rippling the deepening shadows. The flames from the patio heaters flickered, dancing blue and tangerine.

Farther back in the crowd, Navarro leaned forward in his seat, his glare hot enough to burn a hole in the back of Kraelle's head. Grim'd run into the alpha on his way outside and filled him in on what was about to go down. Man was hot for Kraelle's blood and cool enough not to jump the fucking gun, but as soon as it went off, things were gonna escalate quickly.

No one had said anything to Lars. Roxy had finally appeared, along with quite a few of Hellspawn's other ol' ladies. He sat, beer in hand and pie-eyed at her side, blatantly ogling Bones's sister. Grim shook his head. Man was definitely a dog, and from the glare the wizened Spanish woman at her side was giving him, if he kept it up he was gonna get neutered.

The rest of the seats, aside from the first row, were filled by Mayhem. Hanna had also shown up and was settled next to a woman with forearms as big as Grim's. Damn, that was Mouse's mom? She dwarfed the rest of the women, and half the brothers beside them. All of them were watching the proceedings with keen interest. Weddings didn't happen often in an MC, and for it to be his wedding? No one'd ever thought that was gonna happen.

Shit, *he* didn't think it would happen.

Of course, on the off chance he did get married, he sure as hell didn't think it'd be held in the middle of a donut full of wights. Every once in a while, he caught a glimpse of one of their fish-belly white, emaciated forms slipping through the trees. Hopefully they stayed there. Grim vaguely remembered saying something to one of them about patrolling the donut. Were they listening to him, or had Asorav gotten them back under his thumb? Christ, as long as they stayed in the woods and weren't eating people, did it matter?

—*no*—

And Darke was in a pissy mood again. Great. *The fuck's wrong with you now?*

[SEETHING]
—ring for Kit, nothing for Kat—
Dude, seriously—

The breeze from the east picked up again, and the sweet scent of decay momentarily overpowered the florals. Grim's eyes flicked from the clubhouse door, to Grapple's impaled head.

Although Grim was relieved to know where it'd ended up, its placement wouldn't have been his first choice. Someone had jammed it onto a sharpened stick to the right of the bower where his groomsmen were standing. He frowned. That shit had to've been Brick. Fucking thing was disgusting. Psycho probably thought it was funny as hell.

—see? did steal it—

Grim rolled his eyes. Again with this fucking porcupine. Cat was a Goddamned pain in the ass when he fixated on shit, and he wasn't gonna shut up until he got one of the stupid spiny rats. *Maybe he put it in the fridge for you.*

—it'll ruin it. turns mushy—

Sure it does. Grim humored him, staring at the stake spearing through the ragged stump of Grapple's neck. Thing looked like a wight lollypop. Rigor mortis had frozen his bristled jaw open, the stub of his tongue rigid behind rubbery lips. Christ, he'd been an ugly motherfucker and death wasn't doing him any favors. His clouded eyes were open, and a bird had been at one of them, leaving a half-eaten gory hole behind. Yeah, there was no way Kit needed to see that.

[SHRUGGING]
—hated him, too. peed on her—

Huh. Darke had a point. And at the very least, Kat would be down with it.

—'cause she's cooler—
What? No, she's not.
—is—
Whatever, dude.

"How you feelin,' man?" Wrench asked, sidling up next to him and bumping Grim's shoulder with his. The mechanic snugged the brim of his ball cap lower, looking even more uncomfortable in his tux than Grim was in his. "You know Deuce is gonna be fucking pissed he missed standing up here with you, right?"

"Yeah." Grim shrugged, more upset than he should be that neither Deuce or Triss was here for this bullshit ceremony. But at least he knew Deuce was safe and relatively sound locked in the office with Shen. Well, safe from anything aside from alcohol poisoning. Triss hadn't texted back and that wasn't like her. That made Grim nervous, too. If Deuce was right and Cantone had done something to hurt her…

Wrench rolled his shoulders and fiddled with his cap again, rocking his weight from foot to foot. Standing up here had to be torturous for him. Man hated being anywhere remotely near the center of attention. "Always figured it'd be him, you know? Like, he'd finally pull his head out of his ass or some shit and do the right thing."

Grim grunted, having thought the same. "He turned down a molly earlier."

"No shit? For real? Huh. Maybe there's hope."

"What about you? You still talking to that human chick, Allie?"

"Some." Wrench shrugged, his head dipped low. "Gotta finish fixin' the axle on her Bug. Wants to go on some road trip for the holidays."

"With you?"

"Nah, didn't say that."

"She's a teacher, right?"

"Kindergarten." Wrench nodded, running a finger under his nose. "She's pissed the repair's taking so long, but I'm glad. If it'd been done, you assholes woulda fucked it up royal off-road."

"Yeah, and I bet you would've hated having a reason to talk to her while you fixed it again."

Wrench laughed. "Yeah, that woulda sucked."

"Not as hard as your mama did last night. Woman's a fucking vacuum," Brick said, slurping in his cheeks as he appeared between them.

"Fuck you, dude, my mom's in France," Wrench growled.

"Ah, a little OJT at the Moulin Rouge, huh? Cool. Tell her I'll still expect my volume discount, since that snatch should be payin' me for fillin' it up." He grabbed his dick and made what Grim really hoped wasn't his O-face.

"Do it. Call my mom a whore one more fucking time—"

"Whore."

Wrench went for his gun.

Grim slapped a hand over the mechanic's wrist and glowered at Brick. "Dude, you're dressed like a priest; try to fucking act like one."

The enforcer looked offended. "Ew. Nah, man, I ain't a pedo."

"No, that's not—" Grim pinched the bridge of his nose and the first strains of the string quartet sounded. "The fuck?"

"Oh, yeah, that's what I came over to tell you," Brick said. "We're starting."

Instant cold sweat. Damn. Grim swept a hand across his forehead, turning to face the clubhouse door opening at the opposite end of the long swath of gray carpet.

Where the fuck were Reaper and Shiv?

A couple of random kids toddled out of the clubhouse and down the aisle, doing a shit job of chucking petals from baskets. Christ, there were gonna be kids here? Grim hadn't figured on that. Women were bad enough. And speaking of which, by their ooh-ing and awww-ing, they were eating that shit up. One of the baskets ran dry midway and the kid started pitching a fit. The other turned to watch him, picking her nose. A couple of Mayhem's ol' ladies scooped them up and hauled them back to the clubhouse. Thank fuck. Hopefully they—

"Adorable, weren't they?" Shiv asked, leaning close. "I bet you can't wait for your own. Well, ones you actually get to meet."

[PANIC]

Don't you fucking dare. Grim slammed Darke down and turned to smile at Shiv. He stood at Grim's shoulder in the tux that was supposed to have been Deuce's. Just behind him, the rest of the crew went for their guns and Grim shook his head, holding out his hand to shake Shiv's. The guys stood down, but they sure as fuck weren't happy about it.

Grim wasn't either. "Yeah. Glad to see you made it."

The asshole's smile widened as he clasped Grim's hand, the faintest chime of silver cuffs from beneath his tux's jacket reaching Grim's ears as they shook. His stomach cramped, a wave of nausea going through him. Figures the asshole would bring those fucking argents.

—run, run, have to run—

NO.

"Of course I made it. How could I miss my little brother's wedding?"

"Half-brother," Grim growled, wishing Reaper would hurry up and show so they could get this over with. The endless fucking parade of mollys down the aisle was killing him. Half of them were taking this shit way too seriously and the others had the mistaken impression they were on a runway. That dumb blonde that'd tried to hit on him earlier twirled down the center of the aisle blowing kisses.

"Semantics aside, when I heard you were out a best man, I couldn't let you down."

[WHINING]

—hurt, gonna hurt—

Stop. I won't let him. "I wish you would've."

Shiv laughed. "You're always so sour. You know, there

was a time when we got on famously. Now that Grapple's feelings are no longer a consideration, I don't see why we can't go back to that. I've even brought a pair of rings should you be in need. I can size them for wrists, paws, perhaps an ankle?" He shrugged. "Whatever the occasion might call for."

Grim clenched his hand into a fist, dying to put a fucking bullet in the son of a bitch. "What you're gonna do is leave me and Kit the fuck alone."

[KEENING]

Jesus, SHUT UP! I need to fucking think!

"Would that I could. But I can't, so I won't. You know Reaper doesn't allow us to have nice things, and that Kitty-Kat of yours is very, very nice. She's also an extremely hot commodity right now."

Grim's head snapped around to glare at Shiv, and the prick tongued a canine.

"No, she's gonna be my wife, and she's also your sister."

"Half-sister," Shiv gleefully corrected. "And it's so incredibly dirty that my siblings are fucking. Not even I've done that."

Christ. "We're not related."

"Doesn't make it any less true, or her any less in demand."

Off to the side, Brick snickered and Grim turned to glare at him, but the enforcer was busy watching the blonde do one last pirouette. She bowed to the whistling crowd before taking her place at the end of the row of mollys. Bones and Wrench were intent on Shiv, and Mouse looked barely functional as he eyed the crowd.

And still no Reaper. What a fucking shit show.

"Regardless," Shiv said, rocking back on his heels, "my intent in standing at your side wasn't just to upset you, though I'll admit, it was a very large deciding factor. Should you continue to survive, I wanted to put a bee into that empty little head of yours. All this fervor over Katherine. You've followed the breadcrumbs up to a point, but what exactly do the witches or the vampires gain by subjugating the humans, hmm?"

Grim turned to Shiv just as Chanté appeared at the other end of the aisle.

"See, my sweet beedlebum, I told you, right on time."

"Don't call me that."

Grim's eyes shot to the front row where Shamir, Sama, and their two daughters had just appeared in their Sunday best.

Fuck.

Shamir saw him looking and waved like a three-year-old, because of course he fucking did. The women in his party were far less excited to be there. Sama glared at him and the two girls slouched in their seats, pulling out their phones. One struck a pose and took a selfie. She made like she was gonna take a pic of Grim, and he glowered at her. She snapped it anyway and shrugged, going back to scrolling.

"Well, isn't that gracious, inviting the woman who wants you dead," Shiv murmured. "But I suppose you can't have a royal wedding without inviting other monarchs."

"I didn't."

Shiv's grin spread to his ears. "No, you didn't, did you? Like everything else, you're just along for the ride."

"Why the fuck are you still talking?"

"Consider it a wedding gift." Shiv shrugged. "There's more at play here than you're seeing, and the Fae have an axe to grind. Now, try to keep up. Things are taking you too long to figure out, and I'm getting bored waiting for you to get to the good part."

Christ. That never ended well.

[CRINGING]

Enough. We just have to play along. "I feel for you. Being a narcissistic sociopath has gotta be a heavy cross to bear."

"Look at you, using big words. Indeed it is. Yet another drawback of being born with all the brains." Shiv glanced at

Grapple's head. "I'll taking what's left of our brawn with me when I go. Wouldn't want beauty stuck in aisle five with clean up."

Grim glowered at him. Fucking prick's head was gonna be right beside Grapple's if Grim had anything to say about it.

Shiv smirked like he was daring him to try.

Chanté finished her walk down the aisle with barely a glance at her family. Her sisters sat wide-eyed and blinking. One of them raised her phone for a pic, and Sama hissed, snatching it away.

Chanté's lips pursed around a smile, cocking a hip as the music changed, and everyone turned as one to the clubhouse.

And still no Reaper.

STUPID, stupid, stupid. Why was she so nervous? Kit took a deep breath as Chanté started down the aisle, closing her eyes and inhaling through her nose. Holding it. One, two, three. And a slow exhale through gently pursed lips. Her fingers tightened around her trailing bouquet of flowers.

"Don't move." Reaper's alpha command rippled through her with a weird tingling, and Kit froze in shock. Was that what it felt like? Her palms grew moist, and she adjusted her grip without thinking. Wait...she wasn't frozen? What the hell?

—Not that I'm complaining, but either Aryanna was full of shit about our progenitor's power over us, or that ring of your mom's works on more than voodoo Fae shit.—

Unless that royal queen control was voodoo Fae shit. Either way, Kit's shock spiked to rage. *Then nothing's stopping us from turning that son of a bitch into goo!*

—No, wait.—

Wait? He spit in my fucking mouth!

[SEETHING]

—Oh. I know. But don't you dare move, Katherine.— Kat growled. *—Motherfucker thinks he's got us dead to rights, and I want him to talk before I rip his fucking spleen out.—*

Kit growled deep in her throat, holding her position.

"That's my girl," Reaper crooned in her ear, his fingers softly stroking her nape. "You and me, we need t'have a little father-daughter chat before I walk you down that aisle."

—Goddamn, I can't wait to gut this creepy-ass motherfucker,— Kat hissed, pacing through their psyche. *—Come on, you bastard, run your fucking mouth.—*

"Don't touch me," Kit gritted out.

"Oh, my sweet, sweet summer child, you best believe I'll do whatever the fuck I want to you, then command you to ask for more." He kissed her cheek and smacked her ass as he pulled away.

Kit swallowed her outrage along with her surging bile, her nails curving into claws beneath the greenery of her bouquet.

Reaper grinned, running a hand over his greasy, gray-streaked goatee. His gaze slicked over her. "And don't you just look a picture. Yes sir, dress like that'll do things to a man. Pity I ain't that inbred, but it do help t'set the price. I don't believe your mama ever looked half as fine. Too bad she ain't here to see it."

Gag. "She would be if you hadn't tried to kill her."

"Try t'kill her? Nah. I just wanted to slow her down some. Soon as she got knocked up again, woman was all hellbent on shippin' you off t'her kin t'pay off some debt of her daddy's, an' there weren't no way that was gonna fly. Not when I'd gotten myself a queen."

[SHOCK]

—What did he just say? Do we have a sibling I don't know about?—

I-I don't know... Kit fought back her shocked revulsion as Reaper lifted a lock of her hair and sniffed it.

"So this here's how it's gonna go. That boy out there's

gotten far too big for his britches. And though I've prayed for him, and the Lord is faithful and just, sayin' if we confess our sins, *He* will forgive us and cleanse away our unrighteousness." Reaper shook his head, a slow smile spreading over his face, his eyes cold and dead above it. "I ain't the Lord."

He flicked a wicked serpentine blade from his back pocket and held it to the light. There was no mistaking the bright gleam of silver. "This knife right here's got some history. It's cut my one true love down from them rafters and brought the great an' powerful Claymore James to his knees, right before a bullet kissed him." Reaper's two fingers stabbed into her temple and he mimed shooting a gun. "Here."

Kit closed her eyes, her throat bobbing, and he laughed.

Please tell me you've heard enough.

—*Yes, but no. Hang in there.*—

"It's the end of a dynasty, and I shall make no covenant nor show no favor. If Grimdarke James ain't picked up the call and started breathin' the air of the righteous by now, he ain't gonna keep breathin' at all. And Lord knows I done my best t'save the boy, leadin' him to water I can't make him drink. Now be a dove an' gimme your hand."

Kit reached out and he snatched her wrist, holding her palm flat and tracing the blade over the lines crisscrossing her flesh. She fought not to flinch from the sensation of needles driving into her hand. Oh God, what had it been like for Grim to be shackled for so long with those cuffs?

Reaper pursed his lips, intent on her expression. He grunted like he was satisfied, and flipped the knife around, snugging the leather-wrapped hilt against her palm, and closing her fingers around it with his. His eyes fluttered shut, lips moving in prayer, then snapped back open, an alpha command rolling from his lips.

"You're gonna hold on to this. Hide it beneath them

flowers. And when that boy turns to you with love in his eyes, you're gonna cut it from his heart. You got me?"

—And, we're done.—

Kit's grip tightened around the hilt.

[ANTICIPATION]

"Oh, I got you."

"Ah…" He crouched down to look her square in the eyes with an evil gleam, one long finger trailing from the divot between her collarbones down her sternum to where the key nestled between her breasts. "But do you, Katherine?"

She didn't blink, driving the blade into the soft flesh beneath his jaw and up into his skull. "I do."

His eyes widened in shock, his hands fluttered up, and he gurgled. Kat pushed forward, Kit's nails extending to claws and swiping through his throat, then down, splitting the taut skin of his belly. Intestines spilled, gore spattering. It stippled the walls and pattered onto the flagstones of the entryway, a widening slick, pooling scarlet.

He hit the floor with a dead meat *thunk*, and Kit reached down to pull out the dagger, her skirts a sodden ombre, sopping up his death.

—Take his nasty-ass head off at the shoulders to mount on a pole next to the other one.—

Um, savage much? Kit grimaced. *Is this more of your precedence-setting?*

—Hold up, I'm savage? Okay, so number one, you're the bitch that just stabbed that fucker in the face, and two, you damn well better believe it, Katherine. I am so tired of pervy, man-splainin' assholes fucking with us.—

Well then, decapitation it is. Kit waved a hand, shifting and separating bones and sinew, swept up his head by a hank of greasy hair, and stepped out of the clubhouse as the string quartet started playing her song.

—Forget about the bride. Here comes the Goddamned queen.—

KIT STEPPED out of the clubhouse and shocked cries rent the air, seats pushing back as people got to their feet in a mass exodus. Women screamed, scattering like billiard balls in a clean break, and brothers dove for cover, flipping over tables and pulling their guns. Vases shattered, flowers trampled beneath the feet of the fleeing mob, alphas rallying their packs.

Grim stood rooted to the spot, his mouth dry as Mayhem assembled around him. Kit strode down the aisle like an avenging angel, untouched by the chaos. Creamy, skin-tight lace spattered with gore hugged her sinful curves, then flared at the bottom, its train trailing a crimson smear in her wake. In one hand she held a wicked silver blade, and in the other, a still-dripping, severed head.

Whelp, guess he knew what'd held Reaper up.

A broad grin split Grim's face. Christ, she was perfect.

[PURRING]

—*ours*—

Yeah, dude. Ours.

"I literally do not think a chick can get any hotter," Brick said, stepping forward and palming his junk. "Damn."

A burbling, manic laugh came from Shiv. "Brilliant," he said too loud.

Kit's gorgeous brown eyes jumped to him, and she bared her teeth, storming down the aisle.

"Oh, she's going to be *fun*," Shiv breathed.

Before she'd gotten halfway, a howl split the twilight and the snarling of wolves filled the air. Goddamn it. So much for *hospitium*. Grim pulled his piece and spun on his half-brother, but the fucker was already gone. He turned, searching the venue and coming up empty. Goddamn it!

Every last member of Navarro's pack had shifted, converging on Kraelle. The burly alpha laughed, his form exploding outward. A massive polar bear roared in his place, and a handful of wolves shifted to defend him. At his side, the Bléda stood back-to-back, chanting. A green mist seeped up from the ground, and the wood planking beneath them blackened and crackled, long tendrils of rot seeping outward.

"Oh, hell no." Chanté sprinted out in front of Grim, holding her skirts in one hand and throwing weird witch gang signs with the other. The air rippled around the triad, then imploded in a soundless sonic boom. The trio staggered, bleeding from their ears and noses. One of them fell to his knees and the other two turned, hands aglow, to deal with the threat.

No longer buoyed by the witches, Kraelle shrank back, snarling at the slavering pack. They surrounded him in a large circle, interspersed with the sleek bodies of Hellspawn's hounds. Smaller groups had isolated the wolves that'd come with Kraelle and the guttural cries and growls of dogs fighting filled the air.

To one side of the main circle stood a shaggy gray timber wolf and a beast of a Cane Corso. Black as night and pitted with scars, the big dog's muzzle twitched up over its lip, head cocked toward the wolf like it was listening, eyes intent on the bear.

—fight, going to fight—

Yeah, I got that.

—wanna fight, too—

What? Who do you want to—

A blast knocked Grim off his feet, chunks of chairs and dance floor splintering down around him. He coughed, blinking the stinging grit from his eyes and clambered to his feet. A low fog swirled over the ground, knee-high, and gray particulate shimmered in the air. Grim blinked, pressing a hand to his head and trying to get his bearings.

Half the dance floor and the tent closest to the driveway had been blown apart, flames flickering through thick black smoke and debris. A loud *whomp* and a flash went off—a dog screamed. Grim covered his face at the abrupt flare of searing heat carrying the sweet rot of propane and singed fur with it.

He pinched his eyes closed, trying to blink away the spots. *Kit. Where the fuck is Kit?*

KIT STOPPED dead in her tracks at Chanté's hundred-yard Manolo dash. Her bestie passed Grim and did some kind of kick-ass witchery messing with whatever the triad of Bléda had going on. One of them was down but not out, and the other two turned on her.

"Oh, hell no." Kit turned to a prospect from Mayhem crouched behind a table. Idiot was staring slack-jawed while everything was going to hell in a handbasket. She shoved Reaper's head at him. "Hold this."

She didn't give him the chance to argue, bending down to hack at her skirts with the knife, then cursed and shifted the bulk of it away.

[EYE ROLL]

—Duh—

Oh my God, excuse frickin' me for that not being my go-to.

She took off around the circle of baying canines baiting a frickin' polar bear. Grim was somewhere on the other side of it, but she'd lost track of him in the chaos. Dogs pig-piled onto wolves, taking them down and ripping into the soft meat of their bellies, the tang of offal spiking the air. Kit slipped on something and fell against a patio heater, the thing teetering.

—Girl, you better not just be standing there, run!—

Right, run. She ducked her head and took off again. Those other two witches were closing in on Chanté, trying to pin her in between them. What could she do...

The third witch crouched down behind an urn of flowers

muttering an incantation, a ball of force growing between his palms.

—Well, that can't be good.—

No. It can't, but maybe if I break his concentration? She picked up a heavy cut-crystal water glass from a table and chucked it at him.

It totally missed the witch and soared into the space between his hands.

Energy refracted from the crystal facets, exploding outward in a blinding ball of force. Kit was thrown back, skidding across the ground. She came to a stop beneath a table, wheezing and sucking air. A warm wetness spread down the side of her gown.

Shit, not good, not good…

—Idiot. Give me the body, Kit!—

She didn't argue. Kat took over and whatever was wrong with her side repaired itself in the shift.

—Can we not do that again?— Kat sniffed at a jagged piece of wood, dripping crimson, then lapped at her side.

Oh my God. That was really bad, wasn't it?

—Ya think? What possessed you to chuck a glass into the damned spell?—

I didn't! I was aiming for his head!

—You know, at some point, it might be a good idea to gain some skills that do not involve using a credit card,— Kat muttered, nosing out from under the tablecloth. *—Holy hell. Well, ain't no doubt about it. The queen of Mayhem has arrived.—*

A huge chunk of the dance floor had been reduced to a smoking, splintered pit, and the westernmost tent was on the ground in flames.

Beyond it, the two witches had backed Chanté up to the woods, and the wights were waiting.

HANDS GRIPPED GRIM'S LAPELS, and he jerked back, still seeing spots.

"Dude, chill! We need to get you out of the middle of this." Brick's voice came from a very long way away and Grim fingered an ear, stumbling in the direction he was being led.

"What the fuck happened?"

"Somebody said one of the Bléda bit it, but it looks like the other two are still alive and well, and got Chanté between a rock and a hard place."

Grim shook his head, trying to clear it and glanced toward the woods. Fuck. That didn't look good. Assholes had her backed up within a couple feet of the trees and more than one wight was eagerly—

A streak of golden fur cut across the expanse and one of the witches went down hard, its neck twisted at an unnatural angle. A spray of blood and viscera went up, and Kat spun, stalking low toward the last of them.

[LUST LUST LUST]

"Holy fuck, is that Kat?" Brick laughed. "Girl is tearin' it the fuck up tonight. Better get used to being a house husband, there, Grimmers. Looks like she's the one who's gonna be doing the heavy lifting."

—WANT. let me out, let me out, let me out!—

Not a Goddamned chance. "Fuck you," Grim muttered, fingering an ear again and eyeing the destruction. Shit had sent him reeling. "You sure this wasn't Rockwell?"

"Nah, he's stuck in town. His bursitis is actin' up, and he couldn't get on his bike. He's gonna be pissed he missed this shit."

A bear roared and Grim turned. Kraelle and Navarro were going at it one-on-one beneath the far tent, slashing at each other. Kraelle was a decent brawler but was slow as fuck and relied too heavily on his size. Navarro's speed was already tipping the scales. Shit was not gonna end well for the bear.

The circle was reforming around them, shifters coming back to two legs. Some asshole flicked on the stereo inside and Skynyrd blared out into the night. Nervous laughter filled the air and it started to sound like a party again.

"Not taking bets?" Grim asked the enforcer.

"I don't bet on shit that's certain, and that bear ain't leaving the property alive."

Grim grunted, glancing past Brick to watch Chanté and Kat finish off the last witch. He went up like a human torch, and Kit came back to two legs to fist bump her bestie.

Grim's mouth went dry. Damn, she was fierce. He snagged a beer off a passing edward's tray, the idiot still following his directive from the vamp. The crew was scattered around, Mayhem, Hellspawn, and Navarro's pack all witnessing the challenge. It was more than just snuffing the murderous prick. Aside from living, the victor would take control of the other's territory.

Grim snorted. Navarro could fucking have it.

And the odds looked pretty good he was gonna take it. Kraelle had stacked the deck against himself, publicly issuing that challenge to all three of them without setting terms. Even if he put Navarro down, he'd have to face Lars and then Grim consecutively. Not that Grim was particularly worried about that happening. Navarro slipped behind the bear and tore at his hamstring. Kraelle roared again, stumbling.

Grim sipped his beer, searching the crowd for Shiv and unsurprised he couldn't find him, positive the prick had fucked off through the gray. Too bad Shamir hadn't. Asshole strolled over with a bag of popcorn.

"Where's the family?" Grim asked when the witch king got close.

"Oh, you know women." Shamir fluttered a dismissive hand. "Always getting a headache when things get interesting. As soon as your blushing bride stepped out, my darling wife started haranguing me about the suitability of the event for children, blah, blah, blah."

He shoved a handful of popcorn into his mouth, chewing loudly. "And now, mark my words," he said around it, "next week it will be all 'you never take me anywhere.' " He rolled his eyes and then they lit up. He snagged a keg cup from another passing edward's tray. "But, now that she's not here, I suspect she won't mind if I have a beer or seven." Shamir laughed. "Just kidding. She will mind. I don't care."

"Dad. Now, I know you not drinkin'," Chanté said, coming over and giving him a hug.

"Oh good." Shamir took a big sip. "You're a much better judge of these things than I am."

"Whassup, killa?" Brick asked as Kit joined them, snuggling under Grim's arm.

"Dude." He pulled her close and kissed the top of her head.

Kit snickered. "Not a lot, just—"

A shrill scream cut through the air, everyone but Navarro and Kraelle looking at the sky. Grim and Brick exchanged a look. Fuck.

"Dude, fifty bucks that's the fucking nest Mouse texted," Brick said.

"Thought you didn't bet on sure things," Grim grumbled. He pushed Kit toward the clubhouse. "You need to get inside. Everyone needs to get inside, now!" he yelled, his voice ringing with the dual resonance of an alpha command.

"A most astute decision," the Darkling said, appearing at Grim's elbow. "I'm afraid this may get...messy."

CHAPTER TWELVE

WHATEVER THE HELL that was screamed again and more answered it. "What? No, I'm not going anywhere until you tell me what's going on," Kit said. Everyone from Mayhem was hurrying inside the clubhouse, along with more than a few members of Hellspawn and Navarro's pack. Place was going to be standing room only.

Lars trotted over, shifting back to two legs and Kit averted her eyes. No way was she ever gonna get used to so many naked men running around.

—Speak for yourself.—

"We got incoming?" Lars asked, scratching his balls.

—Yeah, okay I take that back.—

Thank you.

"Unfortunately"—Mr. Asorav frowned, his gaze sweeping the sky—"it appears that a rather large nest of dwerdyn has been summoned."

Kit swallowed, sweat spiking her scalp. "Dwerdyn? As in bloodthirsty demonic winged imps?"

"Yes. Several hundred of them, if I had to guess. Aryanna typically handpicks which flock she sends out on jobs, but given she's—"

"Dead." Shamir said around another mouthful of popcorn. "What? She is."

Mr. Asorav stared at him. "Yes. As am I, and every other vampire in existence. I'm so pleased you've noticed."

Shamir toasted him with his keg cup.

"I was going to say, she's *preoccupied* with the witch queen, and her pets have been neglected of late. I'll wager they've all flown the coop."

"Yeah, how much you lookin' to lay down?" Brick asked.

Mr. Asorav didn't give any indication he'd heard him. "However, they can't enter a building without being invited. If we can get everyone inside and away from the windows, we should be all right. They will attempt to beguile their prey into granting them entry." A scream came from the opposite direction of the last ones.

—*Great, they're surrounding us.*—

"That's gonna be a problem," Lars said, jerking his chin at Navarro and Kraelle. The crowd had diminished, but there was still a circle of wolves around the two. "Once the challenge is accepted, there's only one way that's ending and it needs to be witnessed."

"What a quaint tradition," Shamir said, still chomping on popcorn. "Chanté, darling, why don't you throw up a bubble and shield them so they're not interrupted?"

Her eyes narrowed at him, and she flicked an errant lock of hair from her forehead. "Don't think I don't know what you're doing."

Shamir grinned. "Do you?"

"What's he doing?" Kit asked.

"Assay," Chanté muttered, shaking her head. "It's a witch thing. Damn. I walked right into that one. Fine, but the council can go fuck themselves."

Shamir grabbed another beer. "Oh, I wholeheartedly agree, and can't wait to watch you tell them to in real time." He cupped his hand around his mouth and stage whispered, "It's going to be epic."

Chanté shook her head again and started doing her witchy thing with a smug little smile.

"You need to get inside, Kit."

She looked up at Grim. "What about you?"

"I'm—"

A rapid-fire of scaled house-cat-sized bodies struck him, throwing him backward and burying him beneath a writhing mass of claws and wings. Oh God, the dwerdyn. More of the creatures dove at the rest of them, isolating their prey and attacking.

Kit screamed, backing up toward the clubhouse, slashing at them with the silver knife. Their flesh sizzled where it sliced into them and scored smoking rents through their leathery wings.

And they just keep coming. Kit grabbed one of the awful little things, ripping it away from her neck and throwing it to the ground. *Oh God, oh God...*

—Girl, you need to keep your shit together.—

Shut the fuck up, Kit snapped, stabbing another. *I am totally keeping my shit together, and will continue to keep my shit together. As long as they stay the fuck out of my hair, I'm on the high side of fucking fine.*

—Mmm hmm. And this is me, believing you. Give me the body, Katherine. For real. You feel like you're about to stroke out.—

Ugh! Yes. Fine. Take it!

Kat pushed through and came out swinging, her claws swiping the horrible little beasts from the—

A massive roar rumbled through Kat like a freight train, dropping dwerdyn from the sky and setting her back on her haunches.

—Dayum. There's my boy.— She preened, pulling her shoulders away from her ears and ending the nasty little fuckers on the ground. *—Boy Vengeance with a vengeance.—*

Does his vengeance need to be so loud? Kit bitched. *You need to talk to him about volume control.*

The fuck she did. Kat glanced over at Darke, batting the demons out of the sky by the paw-full. He shook them out of his mane with another roar, tearing out their throats, the bodies piling up in drifts.

—*The hell I will. On the off chance you're not seeing the same thing I am, that boy is on a mission and lookin' fine as hell while he—*

A shadow swept overhead, blocking out the rising moon.

The dwerdyn scattered.

Damn. That couldn't be good. Kat dropped the creature she'd snapped up mid-flight and sneezed. Gagged. An awful miasma of corruption fell over them like a veil from above. Darke growled out in the center of the smoking pit where the dance floor had been. Kat shivered, the low rumble wavering through the air like heat off hot pavement. The rest of the crew hunched down in their animal forms at the outskirts of the destruction, slinking backward toward cover.

That sneaky fucking vamp appeared in the shadows by her side. "Don't move," he murmured, black mist dripping from his body to pool at his feet and spread outward. It licked up over her, creepy and cold, concealing her in shadow. The dark pall spread, seeping around the debris and hiding the crew's furtive movements.

There was no hiding Chanté's iridescent pink bubble. There wasn't any hiding the two alphas battling it out beneath the dome, either. But, considering the way the witch king was leaning up against it with another bag of popcorn, Chanté probably didn't have a lot to worry about.

Then again, it was Shamir, and his gaze was fixed on Darke, the eye in the center of the storm.

Something told Kat he definitely needed to worry.

DARKE WATCHED THE SKY, the taste of corruption burning at the back of his throat. He growled, claws extending and retracting at the darkness licking at them.

That's Asorav, his man muttered. *He's over there with Kat.*

—feels gross. don't trust him— Darke grumbled back.

Then you're not as dumb as you look.

The shadow shot up from behind the clubhouse and banked low, back over the trees, too quick to tell what it was, other than big.

Whatever that is, it sure as fuck isn't a dwerdyn.

Darke chuffed his agreement, holding his ground, sensing another predator's gaze on him. Waiting for him to make the first move. Stupid. Good luck with that.

—You all right out there, Boy Vengeance?— Kat asked. The concern in her voice made his heart thump.

—fine— He flicked an ear and lifted a paw, grooming between his toes.

The shadow swooped behind the witch's dome, its shimmery light eaten by the thing's scaly, dull gray wings. Darke chewed on a frayed claw wondering if it would taste like bat. The dwerdyn kind of had. Neither were very good, but it was better than witch. They were terrible. Even Grapple had tasted better.

Damn. How much you wanna bet that's a full-blown fucking demon?

Darke's ears perked forward. He'd never eaten one of those before.

—Watch out!— Kat screamed.

The small hairs rose on his ruff as he sprang to the side. The creature came in low, barreling through the space Darke had just occupied, slicing a hole through Asorav's black mist. It curled and shrank on itself, then thickened again, filling in. Darke growled. Creature looked like an uglier version of Brick with wings and a tail.

And horns. Don't forget the horns...fuck. It is a Goddamned demon. I don't even know if you can kill one of those. His man swore, and Darke's fur bristled with his anxiety.

—*Already dead?*— he asked, tracking the creature through the sky.

No, but…I think they're one of those things you have to banish.

Darke glanced over at the witch king, and the idiot waved with a wide grin.

Yeah, that's kind of what I thought, Grim muttered. *So do we have a plan?*

—*bite it. tear out its guts. don't die*— Darke crouched low as the demon banked above the clubhouse and headed straight for them.

Works for me…until it doesn't…

—*heard that*—

The demon's wings flicked out, uprighting its torso as it dropped to the ground, mimicking Darke's crouch, the mist puffing up and away from the creature like it was a stone dropping into a still lake. The stench of malfeasance burned down into Darke's lungs with acrid rot. Its skin a pebbled sickly purple, it stared at him from beneath bunched brows, eyes a lurid ochre, and grinned.

Darke chuffed at it. —*s'up?*—

Oh my fucking God, you're an idiot.

The demon's grin grew, teeth black and pointed. It leaned forward, its sharp claws digging into the turf as it inched forward. Darke cocked his head, tail twitching, whiskers pinging with every slight change in the air. The demon's hourglass pupils expanded then contracted, fixating on him.

They moved as one.

The demon lunged, arms outstretched to grapple with him, and Darke jumped straight up, twisting in mid-air to land on the demon's back. His maw clamped down on the creature's neck, back legs raking over its back, tearing and shredding its wings.

The demon roared, reaching back and gripping Darke by

his scruff, ripping him up over his head and throwing him away, into the mist.

He hit hard, skidding through debris and crashing into what was left of the bower. Darke sneezed, licking his chops as he wobbled to his feet. He shook his head, a renewed sense of purpose coursing through him.

Demon was delicious.

A growl rumbled through his chest, and he roared, bulking up his form and stalking toward the creature.

The hell, dude?

—gonna kill it. kill it for Kat. better than porcupine—

Oh, Jesus fuck.

The demon snarled, one of its wings hanging and broken. It kept low, moving slowly, the black mist licking over it and making it hard to tell where the creature stopped and the darkness began.

It whipped a handful of scree at Darke, and he flinched—

THE DEMON SPRANG at Darke and Kat sat motionless, holding her breath, her heart threatening to thud out of her chest. He pivoted to the side at the last second, lashing out with his claws and tearing the trailing wing from the demon's back.

The creature spun, screaming, and the two of them collided, teeth and claws gnashing.

A subdued cheer went up, and at the back of the crowd, that asshole Brick was taking bets. Brothers had begun to venture out of the clubhouse. They stood in an arc around the perimeter of the fight, witnessing.

At some point, Chanté's thunder dome had come down, and Navarro's pack was eating what was left of Kraelle. The alpha wolf had come back to two legs and was man-spreading at one of the reception tables with a beer in one hand and the polar bear's heart in another. Gore slicked down his beard and chest, spattering his paunch as he lifted it to take another bite, watching Darke fight the demon.

And the boy was killin' it. Literally. Kat licked her chops, saliva pooling in her mouth. Darke had bulked up before he'd gone at the thing, but now, damn. He was all in, ripping the creature to pieces. The demon knew it was in trouble too. It thrashed against the big cat, frantic to escape. Darke flicked it into the air, playing with it, then slammed it onto the witch-blasted ground, a sickening *crack* echoing over the murmur of the gathered crowd. The creature went still and Darke tore into its belly and up through the demon's ribcage. He nosed into the steaming cavity then looked up, meeting Kat's eyes across the expanse.

—come. for you —

She stretched, extending it from her neck all the way to the tip of her tail and batted her lashes at him. *—For me? —*

—for you. my mate. my queen —

Oh my God! Kit laughed. *It's your winged porcupine of destiny.*

—Girl, that right there is on beyond an eight carat Cartier, — Kat purred, strutting toward her mate. She bumped her head up under his chin, rubbing along his jawline and lapping it clean.

He chuffed, bending down to rip out a piece of offal and offer it to her.

Kat took it from his jaws, the velvet mineral tang melting over her tongue. She purred her pleasure and an answering rumble started in his chest. He bent his head, retrieving another offering, then pulling it back when she went to take it.

—you are mine —

—I am yours, — she agreed, nipping at him, *—and you're mine. —*

—mmm. yes. want you —

Kat took the offering from his jaws, flipped it up in the air and swallowed it. —*Then I guess you better catch me*— she called over her shoulder as she took off running.

Darke roared, tearing after her. —*brat!*—

AFTER

"More. I want more," Kit murmured, running her fingers up the back of Grim's neck, her lips on his throat, tits pressing against his chest. Christ, he wanted more too. Couldn't get enough. Grim's lips claimed hers, devouring. He pulled her leg over his hip, dick hard as stone.

Kit's nails bit into his scalp as he rocked against her, her hips undulating in that rhythm that made him fucking nuts. A growl rumbled in his chest. He rolled over so she was on top, and she moaned as he thrust into her from below.

Someone pounded on the door.

"Jesus fucking Christ," Deuce muttered from the hall. "We got problems. Goddamn it..."

When didn't they? Right now, with his mouth full of Kit's tittie, Grim didn't much care. Her head dropped back, those thick thighs moving the rest of her up and down his cock.

"Yeah, he's fuckin' her again..." Deuce said like he was talking into his cell. "Dude, I told you, it's day four. The fucking hall outside their room is dank..."

Day four. Rationally, a very small part of Grim was aware that today was the day she'd ovulate. It also signaled the beginning of a barbed female's need; the massive uptick in their libido until they were bred. No fucking wonder Kit's pheromones were scrambling his brain.

But the rest of him, in particular the part she was riding like a Goddamned rodeo queen, didn't give a flying fuck.

Kit fell forward, panting, nails gouging his shoulders. Her pupils were blown, dark pits of lust. "Oh God, come in me, Grim. I need you to come in me…" she husked out, her voice laced with an alpha command.

He jerked up onto an elbow, hand fisting her hair. Did she even know she was doing that? It was hot as fuck and pissed him off all on one fell swoop. "Get my dick wet first," he growled, sending back a command of his own.

Incredulity flashed across her eyes, quickly swallowed by bliss as her body reacted to his command. She whimpered, grinding on him, her sodden core clenching. His thumb dropped to strum her clit, intensifying her pleasure. Kit cried out and he lost it, his balls drawing up and cock spurting ropes of thick white cum deep inside her juicy pussy.

She collapsed against his chest, panting, and he ran a hand up her glistening back, drawing a sheet up over her.

"You want something, now's the time," he yelled at the door.

It cracked open and Deuce swore. He came in adjusting his cock. "You figure out how to bottle that shit, we'd make a million, easy," he muttered, pinching at his nose. "Right, you wanted to know where shit stood. Navarro left early this morning with Lars to figure out what the fuck to do with the packs in the east. Cleared out the shifters at the front gate, but left a bunch of Hellspawn women and some of Navarro's here. Asorav can't figure out how to banish the wights, so Chanté's leaving the donut. Apparently, that makes the women feel safer here than going back to wherever they came from. I got them settled in the yurts. One of which Bones's *abuela*, sister, and cousin took over. I'm gonna tell you right now, that's fuckin' trouble waiting to happen."

Grim was pretty sure trouble was already happening.

Whatever he'd heard going down in the kitchen earlier definitely had legs. But that wasn't gonna be his problem. He kissed the top of Kit's head and smirked, running his fingers through her sweat-dampened hair. She sighed, snuggling closer, and his dick twitched, still buried between her legs. "Any sign of Stitch?" he asked.

Deuce frowned. "No. And none of Doc. Chanté said to tell you that she was able to lock the gray, so we won't be getting any more surprise visits outside of her father. Said she can't guarantee anything with him."

"He gone?"

"Yes, and thank fuck. Dude is rocked."

Grim snorted. That was an understatement. "Feds?"

"We backed the truck up and Asorav's edwards unloaded them after they hauled all the shit from the wedding out of here." Deuce bit his lip. "Dude, you gotta know—"

"Yeah, I do, and we're cool."

He scratched the back of his head. "Anyways, if the feds know something went down, they're doing a good job of playing it off. Shen got you a court date, so I guess that's progress. Have you heard anything from Cantone?"

By that, Deuce meant Triss. Grim frowned and snagged his phone from the bedside table. "Nope. Nothing from either of them."

Deuce nodded, dusting his knuckles over his palm. "I wanna go up there."

"To Ottawa?"

"Yeah. To Ottawa. I gotta get her back, Grim. I fucked up, and thinking about her up there with that—"

"You're right, you did fuck up," Kit said, propping herself up on an elbow. "And what if she doesn't want to have anything to do with you?"

Deuce's throat bobbed. "Then...then I guess I'll leave... but I gotta try. I gotta try to get her back."

Grim grunted. "Yeah, man, I get it. When you leaving?"

Deuce's mouth pinched down, his expression becoming determined. "Now."

NEXT IN THE SERIES

This one's going to be a little different. Remember those missing panties waaay back in book 2? No? Well here's how that went down:

***

Wrench's Garage

DEUCE SAT at the break room table, nursing his second bottle of Imodium and listening to Grim grill the Darkling about the Spire. Vamp was creepy as hell, and the too-small coveralls he was parading around in didn't do anything to normalize the bloodsucker.

Deuce snorted. Not that Brick gave a fuck one way or another.

"Coulda fooled me," the enforcer said, his feet back on the table. "Your foxy lady seemed pretty resigned to bending over for the witch queen before she dropped us off."

Jesus Christ, the man had a death wish bringing up the vamp queen's fucked-up features. Deuce's stomach burbled. That burrito he'd just eaten probably hadn't been the best idea either, but it's not like there were a ton of options. Olestra in those fucking chips Brick was inhaling would have Deuce pissing out his ass in under a minute flat. He upended the bottle, killing the last of the grey-green liquid. His IBS was raging with all the shit going down.

Pun not intended, but applicable as fuck.

He whipped the empty bottle into the garbage, glancing past Grim and the mangled doorframe, out into the garage at Triss.

—She's our mate.—

Doesn't matter, we're not doing that to her.

—We're not Crash.—

His inner cat was right. They weren't his fucking father, which is why there was no way in hell they were mating Triss. She deserved someone whose diapers didn't need changing along with their kids'...but goddamn, they wanted to.

She was so fucking beautiful. Not like "empty runway model" beautiful, more like a "diabolical pixie on crack" beautiful. Her white-gold curly-q pigtails bounced as she whispered animatedly with Kit, the two of them definitely up to something. Deuce ran a hand over his mouth, stubble rasping. Trying his damnedest not to eye-fuck the petite blonde.

Yeah. Epic fail.

Damn it. She was too young.

—Twenty-one is not too young.—

Fucking cat. He never said boo about anything, but this he couldn't leave alone. *Then thirty-three's too old. Drop it.*

Deuce turned his attention back to the conversation at hand, ignoring his other half's grumbling.

"May I borrow your phone again, Sergeant Arroyo?" the vamp asked.

Shit. Brick's jaw got tight, and Deuce's hand drifted toward his piece. Grim's was doing the same. Brick was mercurial at best when it came to his service. Sooner or later, Asorav bringing it up wasn't gonna end well.

"It's Brick," the enforcer bit out, glaring at the vamp.

Asorav inclined his head like he didn't give a fuck, but would humor him. "May I, Sergeant Brick?"

Yeah, prick was humoring him. Deuce's fingers brushed the butt of his gun, stomach churning. His eyes flicked to movement in the garage. Triss was taking Kit into the bathroom. What the hell were they gonna do in there? He blinked away the possibilities. Christ, he watched too much porn.

"Knock yourself out," Brick said to the vamp, sliding his phone over.

Asorav reached for it, and the rumble of motorcycles approaching cut through the room. Deuce tore out of his chair, gun in hand and Brick at his side. They needed to get the girls somewhere secure…

Behind them, Grim stumbled.

"Havin' issues there, Grimmers?" Brick quipped.

"You tell me," their alpha growled. "My cat says Kit wants me, both her and Triss are naked in the shower, and we got incoming."

"What?!" Deuce yelped, attention snapping to the bathroom door, his cock a hell of a lot harder than it should be —but Jesus fuck…what if… He adjusted himself and wet his lips, crouching next to Grim. "Like, soaping each other up, girl's locker room kind of showering?"

"Dude, that shit doesn't actually happen," Brick snorted.

"Does in every porno I've ever seen."

"Got a thing for cheerleaders, huh?"

—Just the one—

Drop it. Deuce scowled at the enforcer. "Fuck off…but seriously, Grim, ask your—"

A scream echoed from the bathroom.

Shit, that was Triss… They all leaped to their feet. At the opposite end of the garage, the bay door groaned, slowly rolled upward.

"Fuck!" Grim yelled, taking off running. "I got the girls, you two figure this shit out!"

A topless, panty-clad Triss flew out of the bathroom past him. "Holy fuck, holy fuck, holy fuck!"

Deuce's jaw dropped, gun dangling from his hand, eyes glued to her tits.

Holy fuck was right. The perfect handfuls bounced as she

ran, tipped with the palest little pink nipples… Would they move like that when she was—

"Damn," Brick murmured, shifting his crotch.

"Don't fucking look at her!" Deuce jammed his piece in his waistband and ripped off his shirt just as Triss jumped at him. Her arms wrapped around his neck, legs at his waist, her creamy white skin sliding over his—

Metal squealed, the bay door high enough to see three bikes had pulled up to the garage.

"Whatev. Get her the fuck out of here, I got this," the enforcer said, racking his gun.

Deuce ducked into the tool crib and swore. Shit didn't have a goddamned door—

Triss's breath was fast and hot on his neck, bare tits pressed to his chest. Her hand moved up his nape to tangle in his hair, and he bit back a moan, her nipples pearling against his flushed skin. The scent of her arousal teased his nose, and his cock went rock hard.

He dipped his head to breathe her in and her lips found his. So fucking soft. They opened for him, his tongue dipping inside. She tasted like bubble gum and sin. His hands squeezed her tight little ass, rubbing her core over his dick, spreading her cheeks—

"They're our's," Brick yelled.

Deuce relaxed. Must be the rest of the crew. Good, it was about time something went fucking right. Triss's tongue tangled with his and she moaned.

Wait. Fuck. He was kissing Triss.

Nope. No. Noooo.

He dropped her onto a workbench, and ran an arm over his mouth, shoving his shirt at her. "Put that on," he growled, backing away and making a concerted effort not to touch his throbbing dick. Her scent—Christ, everything about her—lit him the fuck up.

"Yes, Daddy."

His mouth went dry, hating how fucking turned on that got him. He scrubbed at his face. "You gotta stop calling me that."

She smiled brilliantly at his glare. "Not unless you make me…" she said all singsong, one knee bent, the other lax, her bare foot dangling as she squirmed into his shirt.

Goddamn. She looked good in his clothes. So fucking pretty… Deuce's throat bobbed, eyes riveted by those sweet little nipples—goddamn, they were begging to be in his mouth—his grimy grey T covered them and fell to pool around her slim hips… His gaze landed on the crotch of her thin white panties, gone sheer. He bit his lip. Jesus fuck, they were soaked through…

Her scent grew thicker, the muscles in her thighs clenching.

Deuce's eyes shot up to hers and she grinned all coy. Fuck, she'd caught him. He ran a hand over his face again—

The bay door clunked open.

Head in the game, asshole. He holstered his piece and put his back to her, scanning the crib. Fuck, there wasn't another way to sneak out of here…

"You motherfucker! You're fucking dead!"

Wrench. Shit, he was gonna—

A gun went off in the garage.

Fuck.

Brick's manic laughter followed, and a scuffle.

"Guess Wrench missed again." Triss hopped off the bench and jammed something into Deuce's hand as she skipped past him. What the hell—

Her panties.

He stood there staring them, cock throbbing.

She's too young…

—It's a pair of panties, not her pussy.—

No, but they'd been right up against it. Fuck. They'd been right up against it. Deuce glanced at the door, then lifted them to his nose, inhaling like the fucking perv he was, then fighting the urge to suck off every trace of sweet honey she'd left. He bit back a groan, his dick kicking, and pre-cum coating his thigh.

Goddamn, he needed to pound one out—

"The fuck are you wearing and where hell are your clothes?" Stitch yelled out in the garage.

Deuce's stomach dropped. Shit. Her dad was gonna think—

That he'd fucking kissed her. Felt her up and sniffed her panties.

No…it wasn't…he'd carried her to safety, then she'd kissed him, but he'd ended it.

There wasn't any talking his way out of the panty sniffing…but what were the chances Stitch was gonna pick up on that? Deuce shoved them into his pocket, willing his cock to stand the rest of the way down as he left the tool crib.

Getting around Mouse and Wrench throwing punches definitely helped. A few feet away, a gun was on the floor between them and Brick. Deuce picked it up, shaking his head at the enforcer. Asshole was gripping a gory hole in his shoulder and laughing like a lunatic.

"You owe me fifty," Deuce called back to Mouse, trying to ignore his stomach burbling with anxiety. Christ, with his fucking guilt. He'd sniffed Triss's fucking panties…

"Little busy," the tech nerd grunted, landing a right cross. Wrench went down on one knee and Mouse tackled him. "Where the fuck's that needle!"

"I got it here," Triss said, running out from the break room with a hypodermic.

Deuce turned to help hold the irate mechanic down, and Stitch was in his face, the older man's nostrils flaring as he inhaled. "You son of a bitch. I fucking told you—"

"Nothing happened!" Triss huffed. "God, Kit got stuck

mid-shift and I panicked. If Deuce hadn't given me his shirt I'd be naked!"

"Bullshit! I can smell pussy on him—"

"Like that's anything new?" Doc snarked from behind him. "Leave the boy alone."

"Plan on it, soon as I beat the fuck out of him."

"Dad! Stop it! Nothing happened!"

Wrench kicked out, and Triss fell back into a tool cart. Deuce's mouth went dry, his T riding up and flashing her bare ass. The sergeant-at-arms growled, getting in his face again—

"The fuck?!" Grim yelled, his voice ringing with an alpha command.

Everyone in the room froze for half a heartbeat, then Triss sprang forward, jabbing Wrench with her hypodermic. He went limp, and Mouse climbed off him, groaning.

"Fight was Wrench's fault," the tech nerd sniffled, wiping a sleeve across his face. "Fucker took one look at Brick and pulled his piece." He jabbed a finger at Deuce. "And you owe *me* fifty bucks, shithead!"

Triss moved to triage Brick. Beneath the ragged, blood-stained hole in his shirt, he'd already scabbed up. She sat back on her heels, eyeing the enforcer cackling before she smacked him. "Asshole. You're lucky we're healing so fast now. That would've killed you."

"Fucker..." Wrench slurred, trying to sit up.

"Worth it." Brick wiped his eyes. "Ah hah ha...did you see his face when I didn't go down?"

Triss stood, rolling her eyes, and turned to Grim. "Is Kit...?"

"She needs time," Grim swallowed, looking like he'd just killed someone's puppy.

"Way I hear tell, we ain't got much t'go around," Stitch growled, gripping the butt of his gun, and glaring at Deuce.

He tried to ignore the sweat beading on his brow. Shit.

"Um, Mouse, why don't you help me get Wrench into the break room?" Triss asked, scowling at Brick when he stood. "Not you."

"Psh." The enforcer got up and leaned against the busted doorway. "Like I'd miss this."

"There is no 'this,' " Grim growled. "Triss and Kit were in the bathroom cleaning up. She got stuck shifting, and Triss ran out, half-dressed. Deuce gave her his shirt to cover up. End of story, right?"

Yeah, aside from that kiss, feeling her up, and the fucking panties. Deuce's Adam's apple bobbed before he nodded, eyes on the floor.

"Don't fucking smell like nothin' with what the two of 'em were putting out. Motherfucker's too Goddamned old to be—"

"It's twelve years," Doc snapped. "You've done worse, fucking mollys half your age."

"Triss ain't a molly. She's my Goddamned daughter!" he roared.

"And Nikki's MK's," she spat back, "but that didn't stop you from stickin' your dick—"

"Jesus Fucking Christ, woman! This ain't about—"

Shit, if Doc was gonna run interference, Deuce'd sure as hell take the pass. He slunk away into the break room, Brick on his heels.

Triss had gotten Wrench to the table and put a dozen prescription bottles in front of him to sort. Looked like he'd done it by height, but by his frown, they weren't gonna stay like that.

Brick snagged a bag of chips and flopped down into a chair like he hadn't just almost bled out. "Hungry Deucey, or have you already eaten?" The asshole grinned, waggling his eyebrows in Triss's direction.

"Fuck you," Deuce muttered, pulling out another chair.

Triss glanced at him askance, looking pleased as fucking

punch as she unwrapped a slick of gum and slowly slid it into her mouth, tongue working it into a bubble…

No. Nope. She's too fucking young…

—Twelve years isn't forty-seven. We're not our parents—

It's two digits too many.

—She's our mate—

I don't care.

Wrench started realigning bottles again.

"Dude, just pick one—alphabetical or by height," Deuce groaned, burying his head in the nest of his arms as Grim came into the room.

"You say that like it's easy," the mechanic slurred.

Brick snorted around his mouthful of chips. "Yeah, Deucey, you're not taking the font size into account."

Wrench froze, his eyes wide.

"I think you broke him," Triss said, snapping her gum and bringing Deuce's attention back to her tongue and the panties burning a hole in his pocket.

"Hey, man, everything good?" Mouse asked Grim.

"Fuck no. You guys up to speed?" They grunted back at him. "Doc's sister's got a place to hole up, but she wants to meet at the cemetery off 4 first. No idea how this place is stocked, but it's supposed to be defensible. Pack whatever shit around here you think we can use. We're leaving in ten."

"Ten?" Wrench's head bobbled, and Triss turned to Grim.

"I might have given him a little bit too much," she said not quite pinching her fingers together. "But trust me, it's better this way."

Wrench gave her a thumbs up and tried to wink.

Deuce snorted. Man was feeling no pain.

Triss eyed her med kit. "I might dose myself if we're meeting Auntie Roe. You know that's super stupid, right? She hates you."

"I'm aware," Grim muttered. "But we're still doing it."

Deuce and Brick exchanged glances. Shit had to be serious

if Grim was signing himself up for that. They stood, going to strip the garage for supplies.

Stitch and Doc were still arguing. Deuce made it a point to keep out of the older man's line of sight, heading back to the crib to snag the tanks of acetylene he'd seen.

Triss slunk in behind him.

"Someone's been up to no good…" she purred.

Fuck my life.

Deuce hefted up a tank, his knuckles white, and it wasn't from the weight. "Triss, we can't—look, you gotta—"

"Did they smell good, Daddy?" Her crystalline eyes gazed up at him, guileless.

Christ, she was so goddamned innocent, but so fucking not. He wet his lips, trapped by those baby blues, answering before he registered what he was saying. "Yeah."

"You taste them?"

His throat bobbed. "Not yet."

Her fingers swept over his pecs, down his abs to dip behind his waistband and tug. "Can I taste you when you do?"

—Fuck, yes!—

Deuce's knees went weak, and he steadied himself against the wall, clearing his throat. *She's too young.*

—No, we're not getting any younger.—

Exactly, which is why it's no. But god*damn*, he wanted to. "Stitch is gonna kill me if he catches you in here."

She rolled her eyes. "Not here, silly. Later."

"Triss, we can't—"

"La la la! I can't hear you!" She snagged the tank from him and staggered out of the tool crib with it.

Fuck. He should help her, he should… Deuce slid down the wall and hung his head between his knees. He should fucking leave. Go nomad… find a fucking cougar to shack up with…

"Deucey, you lazy fuck—" Brick stomped into the crib and

pulled up short. "Aww. Looks like you're havin' some big feelings there, little buddy. You need to talk to Uncle Brick?"

"Fuck off," Deuce snorted, pushing up to stand.

The enforcer leaned against the door jamb and crossed his arms. "You sure? My therapist said talking things through helps. You know, better out than in, just like a fart."

"The stench you produce after chili night disputes that theory." Deuce grabbed another tank of acetylene. "And you don't have a therapist."

"No, but if I did, she'd be smokin' hot. I'd fuck her over the arm of her leather couch, then jizz between her big-ass tits spilling out of the tight button down—"

"That's oddly specific," Deuce interrupted, putting a blowtorch by the tank. "Now who's watching too much porn?"

"Psh. Ain't no such thing. Shit's hot. It's the glasses that fucking get me."

"You got a nerd fetish?"

The enforcer shrugged, poking around Wrench's toolboxes. He tossed a hacksaw onto the pile of crap they were accumulating. "I ain't into labels."

"Think most therapists are old dudes in sweater vests."

"Nah, that's psychiatrists. Therapists definitely come with tits—Well, fuck me dead, Wrenchy-boy's been holding out on us…"

"Huh? Why? What'd you find?" Deuce asked, peeking over the enforcer's shoulder.

Brick lugged out crate from under the workbench filled with bottles.

"That motherfucker. He said we'd finished the last of the 'shine."

"Probably saving it for his kid's bar mitzvah or some shit."

"What? Wrench doesn't have kids, and he's an Episcopalian—"

"Stop distracting me with facts," the enforcer said, hefting up the crate.

Deuce shook his head, snagging the tank and a torch before following Brick. Man wasn't wrong. About Wrench holding back Clay's moonshine at least. He'd probably done it when Grim disappeared after his father's memorial ride. Didn't seem right finishing it off without him.

Sucked that they were breaking it out for another shitty occasion though.

"Well," Deuce sighed. "Guess we're gettin' plastered to celebrate being run out of Mayhem."

"Psh, fuck that." Brick shoved the case into the back of the boat they'd been riding around in. "We're takin' Mayhem with us, and those SV assholes can suck it. I planned on throwing back a few in anticipation of your pending nuptials and/or funeral. Even fucking odds there. Pops and Mouse are positive Stitch is gonna put a bullet in you before you get the balls to seal the deal and fuck Triss, but I got faith in you buddy," he said, slapping Deuce on the shoulder. "My money and Grim's is on you getting your dick wet and then that pussy whipping you to the altar before he can shoot you."

"You started a fucking pool?"

The enforcer shrugged. "Fuck yeah… and Stitch is right, you do stink like snatch. Shit, I'm doublin' down…"

"I'm not gonna fuck her!"

"The lady doth protest too much, methinks," Brick said in a high falsetto, backing away toward his bike with a shit-eating grin.

Deuce gritted his teeth and got in the fucking cage, slamming the passenger side door of the town car. Goddamn, he wished he'd left his bike at the garage instead of the clubhouse. Who knew if he'd ever see his ride again—

The automatic locks clicked shut, and Deuce did a double take at the rest of the car's occupants.

Or rather, the lack of them.

Just Stitch driving and Wrench snoring in the back seat, out cold.

Fuck my life.

The sergeant-at-arms chuckled, pulling out of the garage after the sport car and bikes, to bring up the rear.

"How 'bout we finish that chat of ours?"

Wasn't a question. Deuce's stomach burbled, positive that no matter what the odds Brick was giving were, they weren't in his favor.

BOOKS BY AK NEVERMORE

THE DAE DIARIES - URBAN FANTASY WITH SPICE

- *One Night in Bliss — FREE TO READ*
- *Flame & Shadow*
- *Air & Darkness*
- *Playing with Fire — FREE TO READ (October 2024)*

THE PRICE OF TALENT - SPICY DYSTOPIAN SCI FI ROMANCE

- *Breeder — FREE TO READ*
- *Breaker*
- *Destroyer — FREE TO READ*
- *Binder*
- *Conspirator — FREE TO READ (October 2024)*
- *Split*
- *Overlord — (January 2024)*
- *Exile — (March 2025)*

THE MAW OF MAYHEM - PARANORMAL MC EROTICA

- *Bites of Mayhem — FREE TO READ*
- *The Maw of Mayhem — FREE TO READ*
- *Grimdarke*
- *Darker*
- *Kit-Kat*
- *Katherine*
- *Deuce — (Forthcoming)*

ABOUT THE AUTHOR

AK Nevermore writes science fiction and urban fantasy. She enjoys operating heavy machinery, freebases coffee, and gives up sarcasm for Lent every year.

A Jane-of-all-trades, she's a certified chef, restores antiques, and dabbles in beekeeping when she's not reading voraciously or running down the dream in her beat-up camo Chucks.

Unable to ignore the voices in her head, and unwilling to become medicated, she writes full time. Her books explore dark worlds, perversely irreverent and profound, and always entertaining.

Want more Nevermore?
Sign up for her newsletter and never miss a release!

aknevermore.com

Cover design by BookMojo

Paperback ISBN: 978-1-964466-07-1

Digital BIN: 011272-03669

www.ingramcontent.com/pod-product-compliance
Lightning Source LLC
Chambersburg PA
CBHW032248310726
48973CB00008B/2337